Nop's Trials

ALSO BY DONALD MC CAIG

The Butte Polka
Stalking Blind
Last Poems

Nop's Trials

DONALD McCAIG

CROWN PUBLISHERS, INC.

New York

Published by Crown Publishers, Inc., One Park Avenue, New York, New York 10016 and simultaneously in Canada by General Publishing Company Limited

Manufactured in the United States of America
Library of Congress Cataloging in Publication Data
McCaig, Donald.
  Nop's trials.
  1. Dogs—Fiction. I. Title.
PS3563.A2555N6 1984   813'.54
83-18980
ISBN 0-517-55189-6
10 9 8 7 6 5 4 3 2 1
First Edition

For my mother—
who always fed the strays

PART 1

The first thing I look for in a young dog is honesty. It is something in the way they look at you. If it is there, it can be seen immediately. An honest dog will never let you down when you are in difficulties.

DAVID MCTIER

A Dog's Work

Early Christmas morning, like every other winter morning, Lewis Burkholder and Nop went out to feed the livestock. The Stink Dog came to the door with Nop and, as usual, Lewis said, "Stink, get back," and shut her up in the kitchen. Nop did all the stockdog work on the farm though eight hundred woolies and seventy cows are really too much for one young dog.

Lewis's boots crunched the frozen dirt. Although it was plenty cold, in this part of Virginia snow doesn't stick until January.

The Big Dipper careened brilliantly overhead. Lewis chafed his leather mittens together and hunched deeper into his jacket. He was a rangy, brown-haired man who farmed his family land along the Shenandoah River.

On account of the holiday, Lewis will feed special this morning. Instead of the fine, fluffy orchard grass, he'll feed the thick-stemmed, furiously green alfalfa, normally reserved for she-woolies with nursing lambs and he-woolies before they're turned out to breed.

The tractor's headlights throw fans of light on the frosted weeds beside the lane.

Nop scrambles onto the back of the hay wagon, among the aromatic bales, shivering in the chill and straining for the first glimpse of woolies. In the east the sky is deep dark blue and the stars are fewer and brighter.

They chug past the cornfields, past cow droppings like frozen black rocks among the stubble.

Tractor smoke smells bad, like burning things that have been too long dead. Nop can smell nothing but bad smoke.

When Lewis stops to open a gate, Nop climbs up on the very tiptop of the bales, balancing himself for a look-see.

Nop spots a few woolies, young ewes under Cinnamon Nose. Nop can hear their bells. One ewe stamps a warning, another bleats to a pal.

Nop skids down the hay bales and runs on ahead.

"Nop! That'll do, Nop!"

Ah, how Nop hates that command. His instincts surging in him, instincts to run among woolies, to order, to gather woolies and bring them to his master.

"Nop!"

Nop returns to Lewis's feet, drawn surely as by wire.

The field is twenty acres, sloping gradually upward to the scrub locust trees along the fence line.

Clumps of woolies. The end of the field looks like a moonscape—these scattered boulders are white sheep. More bleats. The woolies know the tractor sound.

Lewis pulls beside the long row of feeders and when he dismounts, Nop is down too, belly flat on the frozen earth. One eye cocked at his master. One eye cocked at the woolies. Oh, it's hard to lie still when your body's all aquiver!

The slats of the feed bunks glisten silver.

"Nop, Nop. Way to me!"

And Nop's heart hurls blood into his arteries and his muscles flow and he is floating above the winter-killed grass, skittering like a stone on ice. As commanded, he runs out to the right side of the sheep. Balance: to come in near enough so the woolie sentries will see him but not near enough to panic them.

He races out, out, for a quarter of a mile, feeling the rush in his blood and the soaring in his lungs, running until he's well past the flock before he turns inward, running flat behind them now.

More bleats. The sheep hurry to each other for comfort, for safety in numbers.

Nop pauses and comes on toward the sheep at a walk.

Before Nop began his run, Cinnamon Nose's woolies were scattered, going about their separate enterprises. Now they were gathered tightly: a solid mass—one animal, one mind, faced away from the dog at their heels.

At a trial, with a smaller group of sheep, Nop would drive directly, pursuing them like a nemesis, like an unwanted, embarrassing relative. With a large flock like Cinnamon Nose's, Nop casts from one side to another, rousting one flank of the retreating flock and then the other.

It was too dark for Lewis to see Nop. Behind the flock even the white tip of his tail and his ruff were quite invisible.

Nop had become his instinct. His moves were smooth, automatic and greatly satisfying in his bones.

Nop was a black-and-white Border Collie with tufts of brown at his ears. His habitual motion was low slung as a film star's sportscar and quite as fluid. Anyone who hunts with bird dogs would remark the similarity between his approach and a hunting dog's point. Anyone who's ever seen a red fox slipping up behind an unsuspecting young groundhog has seen Nop's delicacy.

Nop moved sheep by careful and specific intimidation; his sharp snout close to the ground, his eyes flaring and fixed, his forward motion implacable.

Sometimes, at play, a Border Collie pup will eye a human as Nop eyes his sheep. It's odd and unpleasant.

Nop's eyes were like searchlights with vague shapes behind the glare—shapes who might be armed.

He ghosted across the rear of the flock and the flock trotted briskly forward. Some of them pulled out in front, forgetful of the dog at their heels, hungry for the hay in the bunks, the warm excitement of heads together feeding side by side. Cinnamon Nose did a little jump in the air from sheer joy and a couple pals did the same. These were the young ewes born last January, bred late and fed heavy because they hadn't finished all their growing and were carrying lambs of their own.

The hay wagon pulled forward.

"Nop, Nop. Come by!"

Though Nop was at the far corner of the flock and going away, the call threw him into the tightest turn he could contrive. In three lengths of his body he was around and digging in, full-tilt, because the woolies were far in front of him and Lewis wanted him around the left flank of the sheep.

From the hay wagon Lewis saw past the sheep to the flicker of white that was Nop's ruff and called, "Nop, Nop!" just to encourage him.

Nop was running hard and fast, breathing in new life, breathing out the life he had no more use for. He passed the left shoulder of the flock and came around the head.

Twenty yards in front of him the tractor was stopped beside the feed bunks. Nop passed the first sheep in front of the tractor's front wheels.

"Stand!"

When Nop swung past, the woolies turned inward, forming a bulb shape. The dog braked in Cinnamon Nose's face and eyed her rushing flock.

Cinnamon Nose thought: _Woolies need to feed. Feed in usual place. Woolies hungry. Dog. Dog teeth. Dog threat. Oh. Food beyond the dog's teeth, behind the light in his eyes._

The woolies in the rear climbed onto the leaders' backs —hungry woolies press hard to reach feed, sometimes right over the man with the feed bucket.

The woolies stopped hard against Nop's warning eyes.

Lewis stood easy beside the bunk, cutting twine from a hay bale. He wound the twine around his hand and stuffed it in his jacket pocket.

Nop paraded before the flock, full of menace.

Cinnamon Nose took a step and lowered her head to butt. She pawed the ground. Nop slipped toward her, drawn to her resistance. He held. She held. Lewis arranged the hay in the bunk and turned his back to shelter his pipe.

7

The flare of a wooden match shone in the eyes of a hundred sheep piled up against the dog's will.

Cinnamon Nose backed and turned her head away. One woolie bleated. Another shook herself like a sponge re-arranging itself.

"Nop, that'll do." Spoken quietly and Nop returned to his master for a pat and an ear pull before scrambling back on the hay wagon.

At each feeding station Nop gathered a flock and held them until Lewis finished his inspection and let them feed.

Once, on the outrun, Nop cut in too close and Lewis whistled "Get back" and Nop veered wider.

Once, he missed a few ewes hidden behind a low rise of ground and Lewis whistled a correction.

Like all dogs, Nop's tail was the semaphore of his feel-ings: his fear, his welcome and his smile. Like all Border Collies it signified his work habits too. Once all the sheep were fed, his tail curled, happy and foolish, over his rump. Though he'd run ten miles this morning and reacted with the intensity of a quarterback calling Superbowl plays, he had extra energy and bounced from tussock to tussock, snuffling for the mice who sheltered there, finding no mouse but finding plenty of good mouse reek. When the tractor turned toward the hill pasture where the cattle grazed, right away Nop's tail dropped into the working position: low, following the line of the buttocks, almost concealed by the legs except for the uptilt at the tip. (In Scotland, breeders sometimes refuse to certify a working dog if he works with his tail held high. A high tail indi-cates a frivolous disposition.)

The cows usually ate silage augered directly into troughs from the silo, but this was a holiday and today they were to have alfalfa too.

The cows were Chianina-Charolais crosses, great slab-sided things the color of a fawn's belly. They put on weight faster than the black cows Lewis used to run. These crossbreds were much rougher than the black cows. Though Lewis had sold the cow who hurt the Stink Dog, there were plenty more where she came from.

The cows trotted toward them before Lewis had the gate fastened.

"Nop, you stay." And Nop lay his head down on a hay bale and watched the huge silly things lumbering and bawling toward them. A growl came to Nop's throat but he swallowed it. The stockdog must not growl and snap at the livestock like a house pet.

Their udders swung from side to side as they came on. Several stretched out their necks to moo. Lewis broke bales and scattered them on both sides of the wagon, re-mounted his tractor seat and drove forward to repeat the process. A cow's digestive system can't stand a sudden change of diet. Lewis fed out fifteen bales for the entire herd. Accustomed to ensilage, a full ration of alfalfa would start the cows scouring and by tomorrow morning the pasture would stink. The hay was a holiday treat. No more than that.

Nop lay at the edge of the empty wagon bed, hoping.

A few cows came near to investigate but lost interest after they saw the dog. Nop watched the cows eating, tossing the hay in the air. Lewis counted. Counted again.

The first-calf heifers were bred to calve while the weather was still good enough to get to them and help if necessary.

"One gone, Nop," Lewis advised. "Let's see if we can find her."

Like all cows she'd hidden her newborn—safe from whatever ancestral predators sought young calves. She was alone at the edge of the woods feigning disinterest. Lewis called Nop to his heels as he circled the cow. When he was directly between her and her calf, the cow lowered her head and snorted.

"Nop," Lewis spoke softly and Nop froze, on guard. He was trembling on his hocks, eager as a sprinter at the starting line.

The cow snorted again with less conviction. Softly, Lewis moved back into the woods, ten, twenty feet.

"Little bull calf, Nop," he called. Nop's ears were pricked like a bat's. Disturbed by Lewis's examination of her newborn, the heifer mooed unhappily. Lewis returned to the tractor toolbox for the banding device, a small bottle of iodine spray and several thick green rubber bands, just big enough to go over your little finger. In another twenty-four hours it'd be real work for him and Nop to catch this calf, but right now it was birth-weary and one man could kneel on its chest and hold it. Lewis worked each testicle down into the scrotum. He sprayed the sac with iodine and the calf bawled against the sudden cold.

Mama bawled back.

"Steady, Nop," Lewis said.

Nop was precisely balanced between his own urge to hurl himself at the heifer and his master's command.

Though he'd seen the Stink Dog hurt by an animal just like this one, he wasn't afraid.

"It was the excitement that betrayed me, Nop," the Stink Dog had explained when she came back from the veterinarians with the steel pins in her hips. "If I'd been rightly settled, it wouldn't have happened."

Lewis cast a glance back where Nop held the heifer. The Stink Dog's ribs and both hips had been shattered. Lewis's cracked ribs had hurt him all summer and made weary work of the haymaking. He slipped the bander over the bull calf's scrotum and released the band. He double banded it. It's the least painful way to make a steer. The calf bellowed. Mama charged.

Nop looked into the cow's eyes and it was like the eyes of a snow-covered mountain. Mama was a mass of wrath, coming on, picking up speed.

From the tip of his flat tail to the tip of his nose, Nop was a projectile, poised.

Her dim sense had deserted her and the cow's eyes were mad and opaque. She lost sight of the dog until the dog cocked itself: a small move. It got her attention. She dug in her forefeet, forgetting her urge to protect her young, forgetting her rage, forgetting everything except this silent weapon directly in her path.

The cow thought: *wolf/thing/glowing eyes.*

She filled Nop's vision and peripheral vision. A clump of frozen dirt dislodged by her hooves slid through the air over his back. Particles of dirt and cow dung and dead grass rained down on the dog, on his drooling transfixed face and his lolling tongue. Nop did not blink.

Brought up short, the cow recoiled two, three steps, like she meant to try the matter again.

"Nop, Nop." Ah! Lewis was near! Nop felt his presence and drew from his closeness and strength. Nop's eyes glowed hot.

The heifer tossed her head. At once, she became quite unconcerned. No concern of hers what old two-legs was doing in the woods. She lowered her head and found a patch of dead grass and pulled at it like it was the best feed a cow ever ate.

A clatter when Lewis dropped the bander in the toolbox. Nop broke his gaze. The calf was up on its feet, stretching. It hadn't been hurt bad, just alarmed. Ma grunted and hurried wide around the dog, man, tractor and wagon. She licked her worry off her calf.

"Good boy, Nop." Lewis's pat was heartfelt and Nop released. Nop had some foul-tasting stuff on his tongue. He wondered where it had come from.

Briskly, Nop trotted along beside the tractor and, while Lewis put the machine away, Nop galloped up on an unsuspecting barn cat and set her spitting and scurrying up a tree. Nop's tail was as gallant and silly as a plume.

Food smells at the kitchen door. He and the Stink Dog touched noses.

"Did thou work woolies?" she asked.

"Oh, I worked them well! Worked cows and woolies. Oh, I am a fine stockdog."

He retired to his rug beside the woodbox and started cleaning himself, happily.

His master, Lewis Burkholder, mixed vitamins and

heartworm pills into his dogfood. The Stink Dog didn't get medication because Lewis didn't intend for her to travel again.

The Stink Dog weighed fifty-odd pounds; Nop, wet, forty. Her coat was short and dense. His was long and silky. Like him, she was a black-and-white dog. Her muzzle was white splotched on one side, black on the other and she seemed the clown. His ears were pricked, hers folded over. Nop's two eyes were as soft brown as one of hers. Stink's left eye was moonstone blue. Before the accident, when Lewis trialed Stink, he'd joke about her different eyes—said it meant she had two fathers. Now she spent most of her day lying behind the stove and he never joked about her.

Lewis set the bowl down more roughly than necessary and said, "I'd like to thank whoever didn't leave me a cup of coffee."

"Well," Beverly said, "I suppose that'll be my fault. It'll just take a minute for the coffee water to boil if you'll take instant."

Beverly Obenschain had been Mrs. Lewis Burkholder for thirty years, but she still looked every inch an Obenschain: her black hair, the way the skin pulled in tight on her cheeks, her eyes blue as faded denim.

As a girl, Beverly had been pert. She'd bloomed as a woman and threatened to get hippy and busty unless she watched herself with the chocolate cakes and coconut pies (with real coconut shredded on top, the way Lewis liked them).

Lewis and Beverly had eloped. Just up and ran away

13

together across the state line into West Virginia where they found a J.P. and got married and lived for a full week as man and wife at the Petersburg Motor Court before Beverly called on the phone to let everybody know where they were.

Beverly took the instant coffee out of the cupboard and set it on the table as evidence of her intentions.

Lewis grunted, meaning, "Don't do me any favors," and peeled the jacket off his shoulders.

"Say, can't you smell that turkey?" Beverly asked.

Lewis's daughter, Penelope, sat at the very end of the kitchen table. Her brand-new husband, Mark Hilyer, sat beside her. There never had been any Hilyers in this part of the country.

Penelope (Penny) Burkholder Hilyer burped.

Both Penny and Mark had full cups of percolated coffee before them.

"Here," Penny said. "You can take mine."

"I don't use sugar in mine," her father said.

"It doesn't have sugar in it," she said. "I don't ever use sugar anymore." She pushed the cup toward him, somewhat uncomfortably on account of her stomach.

"It's cold," Lewis said, folding the cup in his hands. But he drank it anyway.

Lewis (Lewiston) Burkholder had never wanted to be anything but a farmer. A livestock farmer—he never liked the driving-tractor part of farming. Lewis was about ten years shy of Social Security payments, if there was any money left when it came his turn. He made too much money anyway, almost eighteen thousand dollars last year. As a young man, he'd shown sheep and cattle at livestock exhibitions in Chicago and San Francisco, California. Lewis was the three times reelected chief of the White Post Volunteer Fire Department, treasurer of the state Border Collie association, and he worked six days a week, fifty-one weeks a year except for the vacation he and Beverly took at Virginia Beach each year. Not a paid vacation. He had to pay a neighbor to look in on his stock. Maybe this year his new son-in-law would do it. On second thought it didn't seem likely.

That worthy wore an off-white shirt with pink flowers along the yoke and little pearl buttons on the cuff. Faded jeans, scuffed pointy brown boots. Only lacking the damn cowboy hat.

Lewis had never met any other Hilyers. None of them had seen fit to come to Penny and Mark's wedding.

Penny asked, "How was Nop?"

Lewiston Burkholder had a real soft spot for his daughter, the apple of his eye. He replied briefly, "Nop was fine. Held one of those heifers off me while I banded a calf. Nice calf."

Before she left home to go to ag school out in Ohio, Penny had worked dogs right alongside her daddy. Some days she just couldn't do anything wrong. That was, let's see, three years ago, when she was just sixteen, before she met up with Mark Hilyer and got married and pregnant, not in that order either. Oh, she'd been a _real_ dog handler, Penny had.

At his name, Nop looked up from where he lay beside the Stink Dog.

The Stink Dog said, "Nop, thou must be wary of cows with new young."

Beverly set a plate before Lewis. Sausage, three eggs and biscuits. The plate was one of the blue-enamel plates they sell at the Farmer's Co-op in New Market.

The Home Comfort stove was the first thing Lewis and Beverly had bought when they came back from their wedding trip and it had taken every bit of the three hundred dollars they'd saved up between them. Oh, it had been thin pickings then. Lewis's parents helped all they could, but the Obenschains never kicked in a nickel. They gave plenty of advice and felt they'd done their part.

Lewis and Beverly had lived in the tenant house on this very farm; the house was torn down now and had been falling down then. No kitchen table, chairs wired together from attic junk and their big new stove gleaming and gleaming like a bank vault. They hadn't had anything but each other and had been happy. Sometimes Lewis wished he and Beverly could relive those days.

Beverly took his cold coffee and replaced it with hot instant. She already had the percolator going.

Mark cleared his throat. "Fellow came by from the Buckhorn Hunt Club. Dark-haired fellow named Ashby or Asher, something like that. . . . Says you know him."

Lewis grunted. The Buckhorn Hunt Club drove deer through his woods on Doe Day every year. Lewis's land wasn't posted, but most hunters asked permission since the road to the wood lot passed right by the two-story frame house where the four humans lived with two dogs. The dogs were more comfortable with the arrangement than the humans. The Stink Dog wished someone was working her again. As she reminded Nop, "The master was crushed and we both felt bright pain. Now he works and I do not. Why is that, Nop?"

Nop licked her silky cheeks in lieu of an answer he couldn't provide. "Do not worry," he said. "Thou art a good dog."

She always lay with one hip high because of the discomfort caused by the pins.

"Fellow, Ashby, or whoever, said he knew you. He's put his jeep over the bank—you know that red bank by that camp of theirs. I guess they were pretty drunk."

"Ashby? Fat fellow, short black hair, little mustache?"

"That's him."

Lewis grunted again. The food was sending warmth through him. His ribs, which always ached in the cold weather, seemed to creep back into place once he warmed up. He sopped up egg with biscuit.

His only daughter said excuse me and hurried through the dining room into the bathroom where she was sick. Lewis Burkholder set down his biscuit because he wasn't hungry anymore.

The Stink Dog wasn't hungry because she lay around all day, round and sleek as a torpedo.

Nop was ravenous, but the air was charged and no dog likes to eat in the presence of danger unless he must.

Trouble in the air—Nop could smell it. The young man was the trouble—Nop knew that too—knew it from the way the young man sat on the very edge of his chair and his place at the far end of the table.

Mark Hilyer had slightly too long, slightly too glossy brown hair and his mustache was more intention than fact. He probably didn't weigh a hundred fifty pounds and he hardly ever ate anything. Nop had no dislike for Mark but never went to him from choice when he could go to Lewis or Penny.

"That fellow, Ashby, wanted me to come up with the tractor and drag him out. It's worth fifty dollars."

Lewis pushed his plate away. "No," he said.

The younger man pursed his lips. "You gonna be needing it?" he asked.

"It's Christmas Day. A Holy Day."

Mark filled his cheeks with wind. His face was pale.

Nop began to bark. He rushed into the front parlor and put his forefeet on the window sill, wagging his tail, nose to the glass, barking.

"Hush, Nop," Lewis said. "There's no one out there." He unbent very slightly. "Did anybody hear someone pull in?"

Brightly, his wife went to the window. "He's just barking, Lewis. Are you done eating, then?"

Mark Hilyer lighted a cigarette. The flame trembled slightly and they all noted the tremble, even the dogs.

Nop returned, wagging. The Stink Dog stood beside Lewis's leg and growled at Nop when he came too close.

"Stink," Lewis warned. "You can stop that foolishness."

And he rose from the table without making the explanation that weighed down his tongue like a sack of rocks. A tractor can never pull a vehicle back onto the road once

18

it's below the road surface. You need a wrecker for work like that. Any jeep that went over that red bank needed a wrecker from Mike's Wrecker in Spotswood, no doubt about it. There are things a tractor just can't do. Not even Lewis's spanking new John Deere.

Mark was already getting into his jacket. A leather jacket cut just like a Levi's jacket and just as worn as the rest of his cowboy gear. "It can't be done," Lewis said. "A tractor can't lift a car. It can pull in a straight line, that's all. Ashby needs a wrecker."

"Never know until you try," his son-in-law said, brightly.

Penny came out of the bathroom, face scrubbed and her cheeks flushed. "You goin' out?" Penny asked.

"Yeah."

She looked her question. Nop went to his bed and lay down. Soon the danger would go out of the air, he could smell that.

Stiffly, Mark Hilyer looked out the window. "Yeah. I thought I'd go down to Crossroads Exxon. Think I'll go down and help Teddy Rexrode on his car."

"I've tried it," Lewis said.

"What?"

"You said, 'You never know unless you've tried.' I've tried to jerk a car up a bank with a tractor. It can't."

Mark said, "Seems like there isn't anything you haven't tried, is there?"

"Not much!" His own outburst surprised Lewis.

Nop lay low and bristled.

"Yeah. Well, I'll be back in plenty of time for supper."

"Mark," Penny said. "That's your best shirt."

A faint smile. "I guess it is."

When the door shut behind Mark, Nop went to his bowl and ate hungrily, bolting his food down with an occasional anxious look over his shoulder. He didn't like people standing near while he ate.

Mark's VW starter whirred, growled and whirred again before it hiccupped and caught. Time and time again Lewis had heard the boy warn Penny, "That old motor's coming around for the second time and it needs a good warmup," but today he shot away while the motor was still running ragged.

No helping it. Lewis cracked the oven door and said, "My, that bird sure does smell fine."

Penny scraped her chair back and stalked out of the kitchen. Lewis kept his face toward the stove so he wouldn't see her go. She slammed the bedroom door.

Lewis sighed. "I wish I knew what gets into me."

"Darned if I don't wonder myself. The way you treat that boy you'd think he was a criminal instead of your daughter's chosen husband."

"She didn't have very much choice," Lewis said, dryly.

"Lewis Burkholder, where have you been? I know of four girls from right around here who went ahead and got rid of their baby instead of having it. Penny could have done that and you tell me who'd be the wiser? She had her choice, Lewis, and it seems to me that Mark had a choice too. He didn't have to marry her, you know!"

Lewis bit his tongue. Any man would be a fool not to want to marry Penny. Why, she was so pretty and so quick and it wasn't just the dogs she was good with—any kind of livestock. If some old cow or sheep was down, wasn't anybody better to have nearby than Penny Burkholder. Lewis had it in his mind to say those things but saw, from the set of her mouth, that Beverly had other things on her mind. Beverly could be sweet as syrup, but once you went too far with her there was no turning back. Lewis tried, "What time your family coming over?"

"I told you already. Three o'clock—same as last year and every year. Lewis, what have you got against that boy?"

"Oh hell. Hell, Beverly, I don't know. I wish he had some kind of job. This farm can't support two families."

Beverly rarely spoke up when Lewis said Hell or Damn, and he almost never used any stronger language than that. But, with Beverly, there was no turning back. "I always thought a man who stooped to profanity lacked the ability to express himself."

"There's two families on a place that was only meant to support one."

"One more mouth to feed, Lewis." Beverly held up one finger. "We always fed Penny, and Mark makes one more, and since when couldn't we feed family in trouble? When Aunt Alice was so sick we took her in, didn't we? We didn't have any trouble finding food for her plate and we managed to bury her decent too."

"That boy plain aggravates me! Always wantin' to do this thing or that thing and no more sense than . . . than . . . no more sense than a fool! Pullin' a car up the red bank with a tractor!" Lewis snorted.

"He just wanted to earn some money, Lewis. He's been

huntin' work just everywhere. Friday he went all the way down to Dayton to make an application at the poultry plant. They said they always laid off after the holidays."

"There's always work for willing hands."

Stink crept to sanctuary behind the living-room couch. Nop scratched at the door. When the top dogs are quarreling, it's time for the underdogs to make themselves scarce.

Beverly had her hands on her hips. "When you hear of some work, you be sure to tell Mark. He was hopin' to find some work towing a car."

"I told you and I told him. It can't be done. Not in a million years."

"Lewis, will you let that dog out before he peels the paint off the door?"

Nop was released to freedom and the open air. All his oppressions lifted right off him. He was a young dog in the pride of his strength. Like a brusk watchman, he roamed the farmyard, checking scent: mice, barn cats, the Stink Dog, the lingering oily smell of a polecat who'd passed through three days ago, moles beside the gatepost, the hot smell of winter birds.

Nop voided himself in the corner he always used for that purpose and trotted off, ignoring his scat. He marked some of the trees and bushes that served as billboards:

NOTICE! INTRUDERS MAY EXPECT TO ENCOUNTER A STUD DOG ON THESE PREMISES!

Beverly and Lewis tired of saying awkward things to each other. Lewis switched the radio on. Christmas carols.

Lewis felt ashamed. He felt tired. He wished things were different. He wished it was lambing time when a man could get too busy to think.

He plugged in the Christmas tree and it glowed its cold glow. Beverly never was one to hang an icicle straight. He straightened several.

Beverly followed him into the living room. "The tree's right pretty."

"I cut it down in the Junction Bottom, you know, near that big dead elm where we had the picnics. Remember, Penny used to call that elm the ghost tree. Most of the limbs are off it now. The trunk's still standing. . . ."

"Sometimes I wish Penny was still a little girl."

Lewis met his wife's eyes and they were brimming with concern and he wanted to say something, do something, that'd make everything all right. He didn't have it in him. Lewis Burkholder smiled, patted his wife's arm and turned away.

Though Lewis had made it through two years at Virginia Polytechnic before the draft took him for Korea, he never acquired a taste for reading. When Penny was born, it was Beverly who bought the encyclopedia (Grolier's 14th Edition) that still graced the lower shelves of the corner cupboard. Beverly subscribed to the _Reader's Digest_ ("Improve Your Word Power") and _Woman's Home Companion_ ("Six Ways to Beautify a Kitchen with Green Plants").

Beverly had read articles about "The Midlife Crisis" and "Male Menopause" but wasn't convinced that these interesting problems were her husband's. Lewis Burkholder wasn't quite like the men those articles talked about. Lewis wasn't quite like anybody.

Beverly slipped the sweet-potato casserole into the oven at 350. Soon the Hicklins and Obenschains would arrive. Lewis was still fiddling in the front room. He got so restless in the winter months!

Beverly dated Lewis's trouble from the day the cow hurt him and the dog. Before the accident Lewis and Beverly had been muddling along, just like they always had— maybe a little testier than usual, but basically on an even keel. Lewis was impatient for Penny to finish ag school, and any time he got the excuse of a dog trial in Ohio, he'd stop and visit her. When the trials were too infrequent, he'd hitch up the gooseneck trailer and hang around the Friday market until somebody needed a livestock hauler going west.

(Penny never introduced him to Mark. She never introduced Lewis to any of her boyfriends.)

One day in July—it was a hot day in July—the cow hurt Lewis and the Stink Dog. The vet bill was almost a thousand dollars. Selling the cow brought three hundred of it. Lewis could have got more for the cow if he'd sold her as a brood cow, but he sold her by the pound for slaughter.

The vet saved Stink's life but said she'd never be the same.

Beverly thought Lewis was never the same either. Oh, he still had his young dog, Nop, but Lewis had had something special with that Stink Dog, something real special.

And next thing they knew, Penny came home without finishing the fall term to announce that she and this Mark Hilyer were going to get married.

Couldn't they wait?

No way.

Lewis didn't hide his distress. The wedding was a quick affair at the county courthouse and Lewis didn't know Mark well enough to ask him why his folks hadn't showed up.

Beverly had put her hopes on Christmas, praying that the Big Holiday would help pull her family together.

Last night they put up the tree and decorated it, just like they'd always done on Christmas Eve. Penny didn't feel well. Lewis went to bed early. Mark went to see about Penny and never returned, and Beverly finished the tree herself, humming "God Rest Ye Merry Gentlemen," slightly off key.

The Hicklins, Joyce and Eugene, were the first guests to arrive. Joyce was Beverly's first cousin. Eugene worked in the NAPA Auto Parts and Joyce was a nurse's aide. They'd been separated once but got back together a year ago and everybody had their fingers crossed. During the separation, Joyce had taken up with another man, a lab technician from where she worked, but since then, he'd quit and left the county.

Joyce Hicklin wore her hair in a blond beehive and her long eyes, outlined with green eye shadow, were her best feature. Eugene was comfortable as a saggy armchair. He had a comfortable belly and his thighs rubbed together when he walked. He was disappointed Mark was out and started to say how he might mosey on down to the Cross-roads Exxon, but a hard glance from his wife nipped that idea in the bud.

Gene had brought his new coon dog along. Dixie Rebel Yell sniffed the corners eagerly until she caught sight of the Stink Dog. Dixie squatted and wet.

"Omigod! Stop that!" Gene's blow rolled the puppy over. Stink, who'd been prepared to offer the formal growl that establishes dominance on these occasions, got excited by the blow and snarled deep in her throat and the puppy yelped, half in surprise, half in fear. Nop hurled himself at the back door trying to get inside where, obviously, a dog was in trouble.

Joyce hurried for a paper towel, Lewis quieted Stink with a word and the puppy sheltered herself behind Penny's legs.

"Don't worry yourself," Beverly said. "It won't be the first time my floor was wet by a dog. Is that Mama and Papa out there? I believe it is."

Nop barked furiously when the Obenschain's Chevy pulled up. He barked because he felt left out of things.

The Obenschains were one generation away from Old Order Mennonites and their plain black car was considered somewhat radical by their neighbors (and coreligionists) who farmed with the most modern equipment but drove horses and buggies to the store and church. Carl Obenschain was a slight, nervy sort of man. His wife, Emma, had the unlined, sweet, assured face of someone whose life is lucky, ordered and close to the earth.

Beverly poured Gallo Burgundy for her husband and Joyce. Penny said she'd wait, thanks. Eugene went into the refrigerator for a brew and the Obenschains weren't having any, "No thanks."

Every year Lewis felt obliged to make a remark about the last supper: "If wine was good enough for Christ," he said, "why isn't it acceptable to the Christians?"

The Obenschains had never forgiven him.

He'd never forgiven them.

Carl Obenschain was talking about the livestock market. He'd heard feeder lambs brought forty-eight cents. Awful. Awful. What was going to happen when the spring lambs hit the market?

Like an old wagon track, Carl Obenschain had two deep ruts, and once you skidded into either of them, it was the dickens to get out. Farming and the weather. Carl Obenschain remembered every year's weather back to when he was a boy, and Carl was the thin side of seventy. If today was a dry day, he remembered when it had been dryer. If today was cold, Carl remembered the winter when the bulb fell out of the thermometer. He could recall, perfectly, that June twenty-first hailstorm in 1947 that beat the new oats flat.

Emma Obenschain leaned forward in her chair. "When did you say you're due, dear? We'll have to plan the baby shower."

Penny always blushed when she lied.

Beverly asked could she pour more wine?

Lewis gave her a look. They never had more than one glass before dinner. Lewis checked his watch.

"Come on, everybody," Beverly said, "where's that old Christmas cheer?"

"I'll never turn down a beer," Gene said and heaved his bulk off the couch. "Don't bother to serve me. I can help myself."

Beverly waited, with the wine bottle in her hand, and Penny felt sorry for her and took a glass, though alcohol —any kind of alcohol—gave her the gas.

"I hope that bird isn't overcooked," Lewis said.

"It's cooling."

"If he don't get back soon, we'll have to start without him."

Penny asked about the black-and-tan puppy's breeding.

Lewis said, "I don't like these new digital watches. I like the kind where you can see the hands."

Nop wasn't much older than a puppy himself. When he was let back into the house, it was love at first sight. He made the ritual growl but his plume tail was fluttering "hello" as he performed the introduction ceremony. She wriggled. He dropped into the invitation-to-play.

She giggled. "I'll bite thy ear, black-and-white dog!"

"Thou shan't."

She did.

The two of them rolled around on the floor nipping and biting. Beverly shook her head. It seemed a long time since they'd had a pup in the house. Such foolishness!

Mark's VW pulled up. Everybody made conversation that nobody was listening to.

Mark made his false, cheerful apology and went to the bathroom to wash up.

Penny offered to carry dishes to the table.

"Penny," Emma said, "you'll have to be careful not to strain yourself!"

"I'm not crippled," Penny snapped. She said she was sorry. Everybody said it was all right. Emma remembered how testy she'd been when she was carrying Beverly. The first time she'd felt Beverly kick was at a social, down by the Winthrop's farm. Mrs. Winthrop's gone now, poor thing.

When Mark returned, Lewis asked, "Did you get what's-his-name's car fixed?"

"The coil's shot. We'll have to wait until Wednesday to get a new one."

Gene said Mark should stop by the NAPA Auto Parts while he was behind the counter. He gave Mark the wink.

Mark hadn't changed his shirt and Lewis opened his mouth to comment but closed it instead. When Mark and Penny had arrived at the farmhouse door, they only had two little suitcases between them and Lewis figured Mark didn't own any other dress clothing. It was too bad the cuffs of his cowboy shirt were smudged with motor oil.

Never mind. It was Christmas.

Beverly and her mother kept up the chatter while they ate. It always amazed Lewis how much the Obenschains could say to each other without ever actually saying anything.

He and Gene Hicklin talked dogs. Hicklin hadn't started hunting Dixie yet because she was too young.

"Uh-huh."

"But I'll tell you, she has the instincts. Before she was

two months she was putting cats up the tree, and she'd stay right at the bottom and cry."

"I love that sound," Lewis said. "Pass me more of that corn casserole."

As he ate, Lewis Burkholder relaxed. Man shouldn't do anything when he's tensed up and unhappy, but the world had never learned to wait on his moods. The dinner was real good though the turkey was a little drier than he usually liked it. He had a double helping of dressing with gravy. He watched his wife eating, talking to her mother, and felt a sweet unusual satisfaction. He breathed a prayer: thanks that his wife and daughter were healthy. He prayed they should stay that way. Though it wasn't his custom, he helped clear the dishes away once they were done.

They opened gifts. Nothing expensive. Plenty of baby things for Penny.

Penny had bought a new collar for Nop; hand made, hand riveted, of pale yellow leather. "To Mom and Dad from Penny and Mark. Much Love!" That's what she'd written on the card.

"Mark picked it out," Penny said.

"Well, I'll just put it on right now," Lewis said and got the needlenose pliers and transferred Nop's tags: his county license and the name tag.

Though the collar was quite handsome, Nop preferred the old one which smelled like a proper collar.

Mark opened the plain envelope. Five twenty-dollar bills.

Lewis said, "From me and Beverly. Merry Christmas."

Mark held the bills like they were strange, maybe counterfeit. When you must eat humble pie, you must eat it—every bit. "Thank you," he said.

Lewis smiled. If everybody just kept trying, things would work out, wouldn't they? He said, "Maybe, after a bit, we could take the tractor over to the Buckhorn Hunt Club. I've got that old logging chain in the toolshed. If that jeep isn't too heavy, we could chain it to the front-end loader and jerk it out that way. I've never done that before, but I can't see why it wouldn't work."

"Mike's wrecker got it. I passed them coming in."

"Oh."

Penny said, "Could we put these darn dogs out of here? They're giving me a headache."

The Stink Dog slipped back to her refuge behind the couch. Mark opened the kitchen door for Nop and Dixie.

The outside smelled wild and free. Indoors was too close, close as a closet filled with musty histories.

Dixie wasn't interested in prowling the farmyard. She wriggled on through the side gate and Nop jumped the rail fence where he always jumped it.

He'd show her. The master kept his rams in a lot behind the barn. "Follow," Nop said, and galloped off, his hindquarters flouncing.

Dixie took a deep sniff, lowered her nose and snuffled along in his track.

The yard was enclosed by a five-foot board fence but Nop launched himself over in a single leap and landed hard and fast enough to startle the rams who'd been picking through remnants of the morning hay.

They fled from him.

Neatly, Nop made an outrun on the side Dixie could see, creating an almost perfect gather. Down he went into his crouch and he brought the rams toward Dixie, like she was Lewis.

Dixie backed away from the fence. She barked. "Black-and-White, why dost thou pursue thy master's woolies? It is not dog's work to move woolies. Dogs hunt. Hunting is dog's work and scenting delicious scent." She flushed the fence line snuffling furiously though the ground held no fresh scent of consequence.

Nop was so surprised he lost control of his woolies. "Not work woolies?"

"The hunting of animals makes a good dog. The hunting and the giving tongue." And the diminutive black-and-tan proved her point by sitting down and loosing a plaintive howl.

Nop stopped dead.

The terrified rams stampeded past him.

"Leave them be," Dixie counseled. "Come with me and we shall hunt wild things."

Nop's tongue hung out, puzzled. He took two steps forward, stopped, took another two steps. She flaunted herself at him shamelessly.

Nop followed.

Usually Nop stuck pretty close to the farmyard but Dixie Rebel Yell had no such scruples. Snuffling along, she tracked through the cross pattern of scents, going always for the fresher, more aromatic trace.

Scent is no more than the oil from the pads of animal feet and that was the trace Dixie now pursued, through the barnyard, up onto the hill where a wide band of trees separated the farm from the state road.

Though the groundhogs had all retired to their dens for the winter and there were no raccoons in this stretch, there was deer scent, astringent and musky in the fallen leaves bordering Lewis's pasture. This late in the year the only green grass was Lewis's rye and the deer bedded in the woods next to their food.

Nop hurried around, heading his new pal. He dropped down into the crouch and, wagging his tail, invited Dixie to a romp.

"Black-and-white dog, thou block my path. Thou interrupt dog's work."

Nop looked pure puzzlement as she snuffled right around him. He dropped his own nose for a sniff. Like her, he could smell the deer but unlike her attached no significance to the scent.

Up ahead a squirrel thrashed loudly through the deep leaves. Dixie bolted. When the squirrel whipped up a tree trunk, Dixie put her little paws on the trunk and barked and howled.

Ten feet over their heads, the annoyed squirrel chattered and scolded.

Dixie howled. Nop sniffed, circled the tree and lifted his leg.

The squirrel had important business to get on with. There were uncollected hickory nuts in this grove and his winter cache wasn't quite full. Though he had buried so many nuts he couldn't remember all of them, his instinct to gather was strong. With a final irritated complaint he rushed along a branch until the branch narrowed, and he dropped onto another tree, his new perch bending like a bow.

Now this was more like it! Like all Border Collies, Nop had bird dog far back in his ancestry and he chased this flying creature through the woods, leaping at the springing branches.

Surely the squirrel must miss a jump! Surely he must fall into the dogs' open mouths. Over the road a great black walnut and a squat red oak scarcely touch—just brush—at their furthest extremities. Surely now his branch will bend and drop him to the hard dirt road and the excited dogs.

The truck was light blue, robin's egg blue, though that wasn't the color's official name. The Ford Motor Company called that particular shade of blue Andalusian Blue. Andalusian Blue was reserved for Ford T Birds, LTDs and certain custom truck packages.

Big Foot had the optional trim package, the optional chrome wheels, an antenna for AM and another for CB and a black roll bar behind the cab. BIG FOOT was stenciled on the hood.

It was fat-tired and high enough off the ground you could push a tricycle clean underneath it.

"Goddamn," Lester Gumm said. "Now that's a real black-and-tan."

"Take my beer," his half brother said. "Don't you spill it now."

Big Foot coasted, clutch in. Dixie sniffed through the leaves beside the road.

"You're gonna hit that dog, Grady."

"No I ain't. Goddamn, get a look at that little bitch. Lester?"

"Uh-huh."

"When I come beside her I want you to open your door and get her in here. Set your beer on the floor. Lester, be quick about it."

With a spring squeak, Big Foot stopped. *Click, click.* The latch unlatched. "Come on over here, doggy. Come on. Nice doggy."

Dixie didn't hesitate a minute. She wagged her way right up to the door of the truck, and when Lester Gumm lifted her in, she licked his hand in gratitude.

"Okay. Let's roll." Lester Gumm hissed his words.

"Hold your water. Ain't that Lewis Burkholder's dog?"

"How the hell would I know Lewis's dog?"

"Oh, yeah. That's him all right. I seen Lewis with him. Lester, that's a three-hundred-dollar dog. Merry Christmas."

"He's just another stockdog," Lester whined. "The black-and-tan's worth some money, but that other dog's common!"

"Come here, son. Come here." Grady Gumm knew the way of dogs and whistled a low whistle. "Hold that black-and-tan. Hold her where he can see her."

Nop slunk down. His tail was curled under his buttocks and the tip of it touched his belly. One false motion would set him to running.

But Grady had dog sense and patience. Nop inched forward. Grady stayed still, giving him no excuse to bolt.

Nop was trained to obey. His daddy and granddaddy had been trained to obey.

"Come over here, Old Son. Nobody's gonna hurt you."

Oh, Nop didn't want to come and even the sight of Dixie wiggling and wagging didn't convince him, but man had called him and leashed him with his words and Nop dragged himself along the road until, quick as a wink, Grady Gumm had two fingers under his new collar.

"Three hundred dollars!" Grady crowed. "Hot damn!"

All Dogs Are Formal.
Some Dogs Are Mad.

❦

Grady Gumm's eyes were the exact color of pond water in the light of the full moon: silver, opaque. His lackluster brown hair was combed off his forehead in a pompadour more usual in the 1950s. Once he made his mind up, Grady Gumm never changed it. His hands were never still.

His half brother, Lester, asked, "What we gonna do with a stockdog?"

"Just you never mind."

Nop lay on the floorboards just where he lay in his master's truck. His dark brown eyes were terribly worried. Not so with Dixie, who clambered up Lester's pant leg, grunting determined little grunts.

Lester batted at her. She yelped.

"Stop foolin' with her."

"No dog's gonna muddy my trousers," Lester said. "Damn, you see where she splotched me?" He smacked Dixie again and the pup howled.

There isn't much room on the floorboards of a pickup truck—not even when that pickup is a three-quarter-ton with the stretch frame—and there's no room at all for panic. Nop breathed deep. He told himself this journey was his master's will, just like all the other rides he'd taken. "Lie still," he counseled the younger dog.

Lester said, "Hush, down there. I won't tolerate whinin' in a dog." He set his boot on Nop's fluffy tail and pressed to punctuate his point. Nop jerked his hindquarters until the thrashing made Lester turn him loose.

Lester Gumm had been confined in the state penitentiary for three years. The last two years had been on the road gang and that wasn't so bad, at least you got to work out of doors. The first year had been bad. Breaking and entering the VFW Post after hours Saturday night when he was out of cigarettes and beer. It wasn't hard to break in and Lester hadn't been hard to catch.

Prisons are designed to create fear: fear in the heart of the would-be first offender and fear in the hardened criminal. The design works with some. Lester was certainly afraid. Though Grady and he had probably stolen fifty, a hundred dogs, Lester was afraid. He was afraid right now and he knew he'd be afraid next time. He was more afraid of Grady.

Grady had never been convicted though he'd been tried twice: assault and grand theft auto. Both times, the complaining party withdrew his complaint. Grady never smirked at the sheriff or the judge. "Them fellows just made an honest mistake," he'd explain. "Could happen to anybody."

Grady never bucked the Law. He slipped around Law

or lay doggo when Law swept on by like a spotlight at night.

Grady spied a ruffed grouse crossing the road and braked. Lester bagged the plump bird with a single shot and tossed it in back under a feedbag.

Lester running on about the black-and-tan: "This here's a *real* dog. I'll bet we can get some *real* money for her too. You heard about Nelson Purvis up to McDowell? You know what he give for that Walker hound of his? Two thousand dollars—that's what he give. 'Course, that was a tried dog and this ain't but a pup, but Grady, you ever see such a pup?"

Dixie slurped his hand. When she tried to crawl into his lap, he swatted her one. Nop pressed himself flat against the floor.

Lester knew every high-priced coon dog in the county. He cited them.

"Most of them dogs had papers, Lester," Grady observed.

"Well it don't make no difference to a raccoon whether a hound has papers or not," Lester insisted. "Hell," he laughed, "you can't read no registration papers by a coon hunter's light."

Grady Gumm was quite bright and sometimes he just hated his life. This time, he swallowed his temper but it left a sour taste in his stomach, like heartburn.

At the head of Sally Gap, a sign said END STATE MAIN-TENANCE, but the road wandered on, indifferent to the requirements of the state, around sharp rocks (the state would have graded) hugging the stream bed.

Four families lived in the Gap and they were all more or less kin and though some hated the others' guts, they closed ranks against outsiders and their mouths against the law.

Grady flipped his beer can on the pile of tins and busted washing machines that mounded up outside the kitchen window of Lester's shack and threatened to slide downhill into Sally Branch. Twenty years ago, when Grady was making potlikker downstream from here, he might have said something about that mound but it didn't bother him now. That mound turned a lot of folks back right at the entry of the hollow and saved him the trouble.

Half-ton trucks sagged beside the creek, a backhoe (ex-Highway Department yellow) leaned against the clay bank, its tracks frozen stiff as concrete.

In the spring, with wildflowers pushing through the ruptured machines, the hollow was rather lovely—like Mayan ruins gradually being folded back into the earth mother's lush arms.

In winter, the hollow stank of woodsmoke and slurry mud slid down the clay bank onto the road.

Grady eased along in low-low. These ruts could snap a leaf spring clean in two.

Grady's house was a Ten-Wide mobile home with an addition built on back. The addition was fairly well insulated. Grady's three youngest slept in the Ten-Wide because they had better circulation than Grady or his wife.

The Ten-Wide was pale green. The addition wasn't painted any color. Somebody had the radio on inside, and Hank Williams, Jr., sang, "I got a shotgun and a four-wheel drive and a country boy can survive."

Grady's dogs set up a clamoring. Eight dogs bayed welcome and alarm. One gray bitch lay inside a chain-link yard, chin in the dust, indifferent.

Nop was struggling to get where he could see what kind of dog pack was hollering and Lester was batting at him and Dixie slithered across the floorboard trying to get somewhere bombproof and she got a paw under the accelerator pedal and Grady had to kill the engine though he felt like stamping down, once, hard, like he would with a bug.

"Shut your mouth!" he hollered and his dogs fell quiet. Despite Lester, Nop was at the window and his teeth were bared in a snarl and his tail was tucked and if Lester hadn't a good grip on his collar, Nop was coming out the window where he would see what was what.

Bear dogs was what. Some of Grady Gumm's dogs were purebred foxhounds, some were coonhounds and a couple carried the thick ruff and distinctive markings of Norwegian elkhounds. Some of them hunted coon. All of them hunted bear, just harried at the bear and snapped at him until Mr. Bruin was confused, turned around and stopped dead in his tracks. Then Grady would walk up and put a bullet right through the side of Mr. Bruin's head where it wouldn't ruin the pelt which brought three hundred, sometimes three hundred fifty dollars.

The gray bitch stood up. She stretched. Hounds have long jaws and she had a long jaw for a hound. It would have suited an alligator better, rows and rows of teeth and they were all yellow, sharp, perfect.

When she spotted Nop, she growled her welcome. "Thou scat," she said. "Thou piece of turd, thou mouse-head, thou sack of dead kittens bobbing in the creek." She yawned. Nop's mouth dropped.

Sourball—for that's how she was named—was undisputed top dog of Grady Gumm's pack. A four-year-old bitch, she'd been in on some rough bear hunts and never once turned tail. Sometimes, she'd go without eating for two or three days at a time, just lie on her chair chewing her toenails, neglecting the slops when the other dogs ate. Her eyes were yellow and deep.

"Come here, thou scat," she whispered. "Thee and me, why, we'll have fun."

"You are the female," Nop said.

"I am chief of the bear pack," she said. "I am a good chief. I hunt the black bear. Tell me black-and-white dog, do thou hunt?"

"I work woolies." Even as he spoke Nop saw her sneer broaden.

"Hey," Lester said, "listen to him growl. I believe this gent wants to tangle with Sourball. Ain't that a laugh."

"Lester, will you reach down here and get this dog out from my feet?"

And Lester did and two dogs struggled for purchase on the uncertain terrain of his knees and lap.

Grady climbed out of Big Foot and stretched. Somebody had strung a piece of plastic baling twine across the window of the Ten-Wide. The single plastic word NOEL dangled from the twine. Grady thought about the John Denver song. The one where Denver says his old farm seems like a long-lost friend.

Sections of hollow gum tree served his dogs as doghouses. Slap a couple boards across for a roof and it stayed more-or-less dry. Sourball had the big enclosure to herself. Six by twelve feet of chain link, with a good gate in the middle. It had often served as pit for dogfights.

Sourball paced. She didn't look at Grady. She never did. He'd had to take a stick to her a couple times, but she knew enough to mind.

Sourball had fought a couple money fights and won them though she wasn't really a match for a good pit bull. Sourball was an elkhound.

Grady thought he could probably sell Nop as a sparring partner. Depended if the stockdog showed spunk. No use in a fighting dog that'll just roll over and die.

"Lester, you bring those dogs over here."

Grady looped a short lead of brace wire through Nop's collar and paraded him back and forth before the gate. Lester hunkered down with his fingers through Dixie's collar. Grady yanked at the chain link and shook it and said, "Brr, brr. Huh, huh, huh," to excite the elkhound.

Sourball's lips drew back, her eyes smoked and she froze, trembling, as the black-and-white dog was paraded past, just beyond her reach.

Dixie was whimpering in terror. This wasn't puppy stuff. If Lester hadn't held her collar she would have run away fast as she could.

"Black-and-white: thou scat, thou cat's anus, thou scrap of guts the vultures reject!"

"Bear dog, thy life is a bore, tied up far from freedom and thou art a bore too, with thy rage and no real work to do."

Grady shook the fence until Sourball rushed at it, clicking her teeth just shy of the heavy steel wire.

Grady's blood was up and he wore a grin stretched across his jaw.

Dixie whimpered.

Lester said, "If that stockdog's worth three hundred bucks, Grady, how come you're fixing to feed him to Sourball?"

Grady's hand on the latch. Dixie wriggled over to him and squatted and submissively peed.

Grady looked at the wet spot on the toe of his boot. "Well, ain't you the one," he said, softly. When he opened the gate, instead of Nop, he threw Dixie into the pen.

Dixie yelped.

A normal dog won't hurt a puppy. It's one of the commandments of dogdom. Sourball wasn't normal and, to give her some credit, the fight was over before she knew who she was fighting.

Something alive flew at her and before Dixie could submit, Sourball had her by the neck and flung her out, sideways, her long puppy legs like a pendulum. Broke her neck.

Dixie Rebel Yell felt no pain; only surprise. Her eyes flared and faded, her tongue flopped out of her slack jaw, her nose picked up one last whiff of air, "Ah," she whispered, "Nop . . . the beautiful scent . . ."

Nop didn't know Dixie was dead when he jerked the wire lead through Grady's hands. He heard the yelp and crashed the gate.

Like most dogs, Nop fought symbolically, to establish

dominance. Like a few dogs, Sourball fought to kill. She weighed eighty pounds, he weighed forty. From his everyday work, he had condition, speed and endurance. She had strength and fighting skill.

Nop nipped and she slashed. She flayed his ear to the skull and the wet blood flew. She fastened her teeth in his ruff and jerked him over. He came back, low and snarling, perfectly balanced and scored her flank as she turned to meet him.

Nop fought as a counterpuncher, provoking her into a move and punishing her for making it.

In the open, where Nop had plenty of room to maneuver, the outcome might have been different. Inside that close cage, it was just a matter of time until the heavier dog crushed him against the fence.

She cut him. She bled him. She ripped his leg open so the white tibia bone showed through a flesh tear. Nop fought low on his hocks where, three-legged, nipping, he couldn't be upset.

When Dixie was tossed into the ring, Lester was stunned. Mentally, he'd already spent her price on his car payment. She wouldn't bring anything now, the dust settling on her beautiful slack body.

Systematically, Sourball was killing the stockdog. Maybe Grady was fooling about the three hundred but the stockdog was worth at least twenty as a sparring partner. He'd last three or four fights before the pit bulls killed him.

Every time Lester looked at the dead puppy his heart was sick. "Sourball's gonna kill that dog too," he said.

Grady Gumm was entranced. Though the smaller dog was losing, sure enough, he was all game, coming back at her slashing and drawing blood.

"Thou dead thing," Sourball snarled. "Thou creature smashed on the road."

The blood pounded behind Nop's eyes. His leg didn't hurt him but it destroyed his balance. When Sourball lunged, he dropped down and raked her chest. The shock flipped him on his side, but he flailed back to his feet before the heavier dog could seize her advantage.

He was about to die. It didn't occur to him to quit. He snarled his deathsong.

A tremendous jerk on the lead pulled Nop off his feet and a kick crashed into Sourball's neck. Lester lifted Nop clean off the ground before hurling him out of the pen. He jerked the gate closed as Sourball crashed into the chain link, howling her disappointment. The black-and-white dog was hers. Legitimate prey!

Lester said, "We already lost a week's pay when you threw that hound in there. If this one's worth a nickel, I mean to have my share." Little Lester was puffed up with fury, so mad he walked funny.

Grady Gumm had to laugh. "All right," he said. "Take it easy, Lester." Grady shivered. It was always like that once the fighting was over. He always felt cold.

Nop lay on his side in the dust, bleeding and gasping for breath.

Grady said, "Clip that chain around his neck. Give me his collar."

And Grady took wire pliers and cut Nop's identification

tags and tossed them into the woods. He tossed the collar to Lester. "That blue tick hound of yours needs a collar," he said. "This one's good leather."

They fastened Nop to a hollow gum. Though Nop desperately needed water, Grady'd already watered his dogs that morning.

The yellow collar Lester held was worth all of ten dollars. He didn't trust himself to speak. Lester nodded tersely and stalked away.

Grady inspected Sourball. He poured a mixture of pine tar and kerosene into her wounds.

When Grady kicked Nop in the ribs, he raised his head, his eyes cold. Grady poured the remedy onto the stockdog's hurt leg. Grady was distracted. Grady was upset. Grady Gumm had a hard, unpleasant task before him.

Grady Gumm put it off until next day but, finally, he had to come to it. He had to write a letter.

To get the spelling right he had to let his children read the letter. Directly, everybody in Sally Gap heard about Grady's unusual letter and what it said.

Grady's wife took the letter into the post office at Ottobine where the postmaster ticked his teeth with a pencil while he looked up the zip code in the big book under the counter.

Grady's letter went into the Charlottesville bag where it was sorted into another bag, a larger canvas bag, that was trucked out to the Charlottesville airport and wrestled into the belly of a Piedmont Airlines turboprop. It snowed during the flight and snow clung to the bags on the luggage cart at the Cincinnati airport.

The post office van carried it downtown where another sorting routed it into the bag labeled WESTERN SUBURBS.

First thing next morning that bag traveled to Monte Verde Heights. The mailboxes were far apart in the expensive suburb and it took the mailman a good while to make his route. It was nearly five before the envelope found a mailbox. It lay inside the quiet gray aluminum box with circulars from Brooks Brothers, Neiman Marcus, Gumps (of San Francisco), telephone and gas bills, an angry notice from Englehardt's Menswear and appeals from Father Flanagan's Boys' Town, the Indian Mission in South Dakota (free gift enclosed) and Disabled American Veterans.

Nobody bothered with the mail. The next afternoon, again just about five, the harried mailman slipped in more circulars (Post-Christmas Sale! Big Reductions!) and an envelope from Paine Webber. The Paine Webber envelope was printed inside so you couldn't tell from holding it up to the light whether it contained a check.

The next day (Friday) was New Year's Eve and the mail was later and scantier than before and the mailman cursed as he stuffed more circulars and bills into the overstuffed box.

Three A.M. The sportscar stopped just beyond reach and the woman had to open her door to get to the mailbox. "Hey," she said. "How often you empty this thing?"

The driver of the De Lorean mumbled an answer.

She said, "You hold this in your lap while I get the rest. There's a ton of junk in here."

"Don't take all night."

The car bucked down the drive and grazed a couple garbage cans just outside the attached garage.

The girl asked, "How'm I supposed to get out of this thing? You got me wedged in here, Charlie."

"Doug."

"Back up so I can get out. I'm not gonna crawl over the transmission."

The De Lorean hiccupped in reverse.

"What's that barking? I hope you don't keep guard dogs. Those guard dogs give me the shivers."

Doug bellowed, *"Shut up!"* The barking stopped.

The girl laid the mail on the kitchen counter. After they had drinks, they did some kissing and went into the bedroom.

Once their lovemaking stopped, the house was quiet— just the sounds of servomechanisms doing their duty: the freezer, the thermostat, the electric clock burred.

Five-thirty A.M. Doug Whitenaur padded back into the kitchen wearing blue bikini shorts. He leaned against the counter, laid his head in his hands, moaned. He washed six Excedrins down with a warm Coca-Cola, belched.

MISTER DOUG WHITENAUR
1412 Blandings Road
Monte Verde Heights, Ohio 45204

The penciled envelope caught his attention. His dogs must have heard him padding around because they started barking again. He opened the back door long enough to holler and they shut up which was fortunate because his shout was throbbing behind his temples. He wasn't in any shape to get out and teach them a lesson. The Coke sloshed in his gut. He didn't want to be sick.

"Doug? Doug? What you doin', honey?"

Doug made a face. He owned one of those slightly perfect male faces that good childhood nutrition and an excellent orthodontist can provide. At present, his good looks were smudged.

"I'll be there in a sec," he said.

"What? Dougie!"

He didn't have more to say. He held the envelope under the stove light and tore it open.

MISTER DOUG. I DONE LIKE WE TALKED ABOUT WITH MR. LEWIS BURKHOLDER'S SHEEP DOG. LEWIS WON'T TRIAL THAT DOG NO MORE. SEND THE THREE HUNDRED DOLLARS YOU PROMISED TO STAR ROUTE B, BOX 18, OTTOBINE, VIRGINIA. SINCERELY YOURS, GRADY GUMM.

Doug said, "Ohh," and pressed the heels of his hands into his aching eyes. Grady Gumm? Grady Gumm?

It had been in some dive. Some country beer joint in northern Virginia. Doug had stopped there after Lewis Burkholder beat him at the Innisfree Stockdog Trial. That trial. He'd lost his temper that time. Dog wouldn't do anything right. Just ran around and around the pen making Doug look like an idiot. When the Innisfree trial was done, Doug needed a drink, but it was a redneck joint: beer only. No tequila, no rum tonics, just beer.

Grady Gumm was the guy with the Elvis Presley hairdo. Rat-faced guy. Grady Gumm. Ugly name for an ugly man. Grady never bought his share of the beers, either. Doug Whitenaur remembered that fact too.

Doug Whitenaur pushed Grady Gumm's penciled letter under the light. Gumm had printed it with child's block printing. Had Doug really given that creepy hillbilly his home address? God he'd been drunk. Next morning he woke up in a motel, not remembering how he got there, just grateful he hadn't wrecked the trailer with his ten-thousand-dollar dog.

Ten thousand dollars for a Bit O' Nothing. His expensive imported dog, "Bit O' Scot—Bit O' Nothing." That's what Doug had said. And Grady Gumm had bared his tobacco-stained teeth in a friendly smile.

Doug Whitenaur had leaned over close enough to smell Gumm: bitter sweat, beer, woodsmoke. Grady Gumm kept one hand clutched around his beer like it'd fly away if he let go.

Grady Gumm was a dog man too, or so he bragged. "I don't fool with stockdogs, myself. I've hunted coons and fox and bear. Got down in the fighting pit with dogs."

Drunk, Doug Whitenaur weaved on the bar stool. "It'd be worth something to me if that dog of Burkholder's never trialed again."

And so sweetly, Grady Gumm had smiled. And wetly shone his brown teeth. "Three hundred dollars?"

And a chill ran down Doug Whitenaur's spine from top to bottom. "Yes."

Had he really said that? Really? What was Burkholder's dog called? Nip? Nap? A young dog with brown feathers behind his ears.

"Doug honey? Come back to bed. Dougie?"

So. This morning was the first morning in a brand-new year and headache as usual. But Lewis Burkholder wouldn't have a dog to run on the trial circuit this year. Gee, what a sad thing to happen.

Doug Whitenaur grinned with his mouth and pained eyes. He took this as a sign—a good omen. He crumpled Grady Gumm's painstaking epistle and tossed it in the garbage where it belonged.

THREE

Country Fears,
Country Pleasures

"Take a couple those dry extinguishers inside," Lewis said. "The big ones. Our pump is froze up."

The big red-and-yellow light on top of the fire truck: *flick, flick, flick.* Two White Post VFD trucks, and Luray VFD had sent its brush truck. Most of the firemen leaned against the trucks swapping lies. Heck, it was only a chimney fire.

The fire shot out of the preacher's house, whooshing like one of those firework cones, noisy, hot as hell but, so long as the chimney was sound, not particularly dangerous and no reason at all for three fire trucks.

Luray's chief ambled over, blowing on his cold hands. "You think you boys can handle it now?" he asked.

"I expect. I don't know why the fool called two departments. It makes a lot of driving for you fellows coming all the way out here."

"That's true. But there wasn't too much doing at nine o'clock on a Thursday night, except watch the thermometer drop. How cold you reckon it is?"

"It was five below when I left home. Cold enough to freeze our pump solid."

"You can't drain yours? We always drain ours in this sort of weather. It takes a mite longer to catch the prime when you get to the fire scene, but a slow priming pump's better than a pump won't do nothin' at all."

"Our pump's got a little draincock underneath."

"Oh, oh. Somebody forgot?"

"That's right." To his firemen: "Get that roof ladder up there. Just wrestle it over the porch. I don't want nobody climbing up that roof without the ladder in place."

"Well, Lewis. I guess we'll be gettin' on home."

"Yeah. Thanks."

"You-all ever find that dog of yours? I seen one of your posters outside the Kroger in town. Five-hundred-dollar reward. That's a fair price to give for a dog. 'Course, I know how it goes. Man gets attached to an animal . . ."

"Dog's worth a sight more'n that to me," Lewis said. "Nobody's seen him. Nor the coon dog that he was running with."

"Two dogs together can get in a mess of trouble, where one dog wouldn't."

"I've heard that. Nop always stayed close to home."

"Well, Lewis, if I hear anything I'll surely let you know."

" 'Preciate it."

Late on a subzero night, twenty men had gathered for the fire call. About half were volunteer firefighters. The other were neighbors who happened along. Most of them clustered in the front yard, gossiping. A chimney fire usually wasn't dangerous though it could scare the pants right off you when it was your house. Many of these old houses had burned oil for years and then reconverted to wood stoves. People had gotten out of the habit of worrying about their chimneys and these new airtight stoves put so much creosote up the flue you had to clean it out every month or six weeks.

The house was tidy but the porch woodwork could have done with a coat of paint. This was the Full Gospel preacher. The Methodists and Presbyterians gave their preachers enough to keep up the parsonage but Lewis guessed the Full Gospels didn't have so much money.

Jack Wade was the preacher. Several years ago Wade had lost an eye. Usually he wore glasses with one clear lens and one opaque one. Now he had a piece of cotton stuffed in the empty socket.

"I believe we'll put her out directly, Mr. Wade," Lewis said. "We got a ladder on the roof and we'll drop some chains down her and clean all the gunk out and starve the fire. You mind if I go on upstairs and check the chimney?"

The preacher was flutter-handed. "Now, you go on right ahead. I'm sorry the house is such a mess. My goodness, I was just sitting down to eat when I heard that roar from the chimney, like to scare the life out of me. You go on upstairs, just help yourself. I'm sorry the house is such a mess."

Lewis and Mike Pearson, assistant chief, climbed the stairs, feeling the chimney wall for hot spots. In some houses, the chimney mortar is old or rotten and the fire gets out and into the floor joists or walls. Lewis felt the warmth from the chimney fire but there wasn't any place he couldn't keep his hand.

"Wade says they rebuilt this chimney four years ago. Tiled her, bottom to top."

"That's fine, but I've known the chimney tile to crack, if it gets hot enough."

"I wouldn't want to put out a fire in this house," the assistant chief said.

"Our number-two truck will pump."

"Yeah. The other one isn't worth nothing."

On the roof Mark Hilyer dropped a chain down the clogged, flaming chimney and a cry came from the bowels of the house as the soot and ash billowed out around the thimble of the stovepipe, coating the entire downstairs with soot.

It's a peculiar fact about firefighting. You can save a man's house but if you track up his kitchen doing it, he won't thank you.

Lewis could feel the vibration as the chain clunked around knocking the hardened lumps off the chimney walls. Lewis climbed into the attic and touched the chimney bricks at the floor and where it passed through the roof flashing. It was warm but not real hot. The mortar looked smooth, new, professional. Should be okay.

Mark Hilyer poured dry chemical down the chimney and it puffed, choked, and the roaring stopped.

In the kitchen, Lewis accepted the preacher's complaints about the fine dust that covered every surface, every knife, spoon, pot and pan; refused the coffee (tea?) ("If I got something clean enough to boil water") and stepped outside into cold that took his breath away. It must be bitter on the roof peak where his son-in-law was trying to collapse the roof ladder. It was funny how the fire department was such a family affair. The Goodwins—father, brother and sons—had had it until Lewis got elected and Mike Pearson and his brother would take it over when he quit.

Pearson had heard of a dog killed on Route 340 up by Boyce.

"That was a brown dog. Belonged to a man name of Roberts. Lives in the green house across from the motel there. Dog just loved to roam. Well, his roaming days are done."

Lewis and Mark had plastered posters all over the county. A Xerox of Nop's photograph, description and Lewis's phone number. Five hundred dollars for information leading to the recovery of.

Eugene Hicklin had put out a few posters for Dixie and an ad in the Lost and Found. Eugene offered a reward for his pup's return but never did say how much it would be.

Lewis Burkholder and Mark had visited most of the gas stations, grocery stores and taverns for thirty miles around. They'd bothered the sheriff, the state police, the dog wardens, even the game wardens. Nobody had seen a thing.

Lewis turned to Mike Pearson. "I was just sitting down to my dinner when this call sounded. This fire is knocked down now. You take the second unit. Mark and I'll put the pumper back."

Mark and Lewis rode together. They stopped at the Crossroads Exxon and woke up the owner to gas up because they always put it away with a full tank. One nice thing about the chimney fires: they never used water and didn't have to refill the pumper's five-hundred-gallon tank which was a nasty cold business, drafting from a narrow beach on the edge of the river.

The heater worked well. Lewis drove slow. The old pumper was pretty heavy and there was no sense pushing it going home from a fire.

"Mark, I want you to go to the firehouse tomorrow, first thing in the morning, and use a butane torch on the draincock. I believe you was the one who forgot to drain it, last time you put this pumper away."

After a bit, Mark lit a cigarette. He'd quit tailor-made cigarettes and rolled all his smokes from a can of Bugler Tobacco. He always had a dozen ready-rolled smokes with him in a crush-proof Winston box. Lewis didn't like them because they looked like marijuana cigarettes but he couldn't say anything. 'Course Mark could have quit smoking altogether . . .

"Sorry," Mark said. "Nobody told me about the drain."

Mark had gone out on three chimney fires, one barn fire, one auto wreck and one brush fire but hadn't had any of the state training. Lewis was figuring on getting the state instructors out for a refresher course in the spring. Winter was too rough to hold a fire school.

"Just make sure it's working in the morning."

"I told Jim Campbell I'd come over and help him load cattle in the morning. I don't get paid for this." Mark's choppy wave indicated the truck, their turnout gear. "Jim Campbell promised me twenty dollars. You been lucky in your life, Lewis, if you never made a mistake. I have made several and they don't surprise me like they once did. Sure, I'll thaw the pump, after I load cattle."

"You know," Lewis said, "I surely wish your family had seen fit to come out to Penny's wedding. It may be her only wedding, you know, and I would have liked to meet your kin."

"My father, he ran out on us. Long time ago. There's only me, my mother and Scottie."

"My," Lewis said acidly, "it sure is interesting to learn a little something about the people my baby girl married into."

Mark blew air through his teeth. After a while he told Lewis a story Lewis had already heard. Somebody had seen a stockdog in Sally Gap.

"There must be three hundred different stockdogs in this county. There's Aussies and English shepherds and lassie collies and working collies. I can't run down every one of them. You know what I think? I think Nop's gone. I think some farmer down the road caught him and that coonhound in his sheep and shot them and left them where they lay. That's what I think happened."

"You've always said Nop wouldn't wander off."

"What else could have happened? He's been gone three weeks now. By now, I would have heard something."

They parked the pumper in the firehouse and hung their helmets and turnout gear in the big lockers on the side of the truck. Some volunteers carried their personal turnout gear (coat, boots and fire pants) in their own vehicle, but Lewis left his gear with the truck.

They didn't fool around, but it was 11:30 before they got home and Lewis was so tired he'd lost his appetite. The lasagna was in the oven, on low heat. Most times, Lewis liked lasagna but this looked mighty unappealing.

Penny and her mother were at the kitchen table with cold cups of coffee. Beverly had her magazine. Penny was doing some baby knitting though she didn't have the knack.

"How was it?" Beverly asked.

"Nothing at all. Every time that fire call goes off, I'm afraid it's gonna be somebody's house—a nasty fire, but it's most always just brush or a chimney fire. I suppose I ought to be grateful."

Penny said, "I'm glad you two can go out together."

Lewis grunted.

Penny said, "I mean, it's kind of nice, in this rotten weather to have some company."

Mark put down his fork. "I think I'm gonna take me a glass of milk to the bedroom."

"Something wrong with the food?" Lewis asked.

"Naw. I just don't have any appetite. Come on, Penny, let's hit the hay."

Penny had a look in her eye. She took her husband's hand. Lewis sure hoped they knew enough to stop having sex before the baby came. Lewis surely hoped Beverly had told them to stop. He looked down at his plate. Ugly lasagna, ugly green beans, ugly coleslaw.

"Good night," Beverly said.

The Stink Dog limped over and laid her head on Lewis's foot, which annoyed more than pleased him. You ain't

Nop, he thought but didn't say. Stink went back to her corner and flopped down with a sigh.

"Lewis, you're just picking at your food. Come to bed. I'll rub your back for you."

Lewis tried on a smile but it was shoddy material. "Sure," he said.

By lamplight he watched his wife of thirty years as she readied herself for bed. A funny thing about women—how they thought they got less desirable as they grew older. Beverly had become inexpressibly more dear. Lewis didn't know what he would do without her.

The bed dipped under her weight. Though there was none to overhear, she spoke softly, "You heard nothing about the dog?"

"Not a darn thing."

"I hoped someone at the fire might have some news. Oh, Lewis, I'm so sorry." She lay her hand on his chest and rubbed in a slow circular motion. "You know, maybe we should get another pup. It might be fun to have a pup in the house."

"I just don't have the heart for it, Beverly. Nop wasn't a runaway. He never went farther than the barnyard unless I took him. Every morning, when I feed . . . God, it's so much harder to work without him. He'd get out there, just doin' his work and I'd stop what I was doing just to watch him. He was so full of himself, so beautiful . . ."

"Hush, now," she said. "Hush, now, Lewis," and she pressed him to her breast like he was a weary child.

Nop had been Lewis's farm dog. Though he was young for it, he'd been Lewis's trial dog too. Last fall, at the Blue Ridge Trial, Nop finished second. At the Hop Bottom Trial, he ran first. They weren't the biggest trials—nothing to compare with the Stockdog Superbowl or Dothan, Alabama or the Kentucky Bluegrass, but to run a dog in the open class before his second birthday was unusual and invited comparison with Nop's legendary forebearer, Wiston Cap, the great Scottish sire who won the Supreme Championship, defeating the finest dogs in all Britain before his second year.

In September, at the Innisfree Trials in eastern Maryland, that comparison was made. Many who saw Nop run at Innisfree said, afterward, they'd never seen anything like it.

The trial was held in a long cow pasture, bordered on one side by standing corn and on the other by a board fence. The pasture rose steeply and Lewis wouldn't have wanted to be on it with tractor and mower.

The grass was short and dark green. The day was overcast and muggy.

Though Innisfree wasn't a real important trial, it was conveniently timed to catch handlers on their way home from the Tennessee Open and attracted a pretty good crowd.

Ralph Pulfer was here with his famous Shep dog and his brother, Lewis Pulfer, had the red bitch, Dell, and a young dog, Liz. John Bauserman had brought his Nell dog and Rory, his five-year-old male. Bruce Fogt of Ohio was here with Hope, the bitch who'd won the Bluegrass two years ago and Jack Knox of Wisconsin had brought Craig and Jed.

They came in campers and vans and station wagons with metal screens to separate the dog compartment from the humans. Some towed their dogs on special trailers: flatbeds with dog cages bolted to the wooden platform.

Some handlers were stock farmers, some were vets. Richard Karrasch was a feed specialist. Tom Conn was a carpenter. One was a machinist, another a dentist, several were retired. They brought their wives and their kids or they came alone to sit in lawn chairs beside their campers with the cooler at their side. Many had come a thousand miles to see good dogs run.

Eighty spectators and perhaps as many dogs. Border Collies: large and small, white ones, red ones, blue merles (mottled with a bluish cast) as well as the more common black dog with white ruff and stockings. Some were thirty pounds; some big males, sixty. A few puppies were for sale.

The dogs lay in airline crates and stainless-steel kennels. Some were chained, others stayed underneath their masters' trucks in the shade. They didn't bark or run around, and quarrels between them were rare and brief.

The first stockdog trial was held in Wales a hundred years ago. Trials haven't changed much.

The designers of the trial course intended it to replicate work every stockdog does on the home farm. The trial is more difficult than daily work—bringing a few strange sheep through trial obstacles is much tougher than moving a larger flock about.

A stockdog trial is an attempt to coordinate the brains and instincts of three animals: man, sheep and dog. The sheep are often uncooperative and are not helpless. The dog is severely penalized for biting and must move them by threat and bluff. A young ewe, running downhill, can outdistance a dog for several hundred yards. Since the ewe outweighs the stockdog by two or three to one, in any collision, it's the dog who's bowled over.

The course presents two sorts of obstacles: panels and the pen. Panels, which represent open gateways, are sections of board fence with a gap between them. The pen is a six-by-eight box.

Every dog starts his run with a hundred ten points. Deductions are taken for every tiny mistake. It's a sport that rewards the conservative and the tried-and-true. The standard is precision, brilliance and calm. Anything less costs points.

The trial course is shaped like a crucifix, stood on its head. At the head stand the handler and his dog. At the foot, far up hill, sheep are released; three, four or five of them.

"Hsst." The stockdog, operating solo, makes his out-run. He may run left or right but must not cross over once he starts. The perfect outrun is pear-shaped. The dog hooks behind the sheep without alarming them. He pauses.

Outrun faults include requiring a redirection command, stopping short, stopping long, swinging so wide the dog loses eye contact with his sheep or so near he alarms them.

The lift is the instant the sheep notice the dog. The lift

is a moment, a clash of wills, no more. If done skillfully, the sheep drift off downhill. A clumsy lift scatters them or panics them.

Coming on too hard is a fault. Freezing is a fault. Allowing the sheep to seek a path that isn't directly toward the handler, that's a fault.

At the finals of international trials the stem of the crucifix is eight hundred yards long and the sheep are barely visible from the handler's position. In this country most outruns are shorter, a mere three hundred yards or so.

The dog fetches his sheep directly through the fetch panel to his handler's feet. Any variation from a straight line is a fault. Any hesitation is a fault.

The fetch panel is slightly above the point where the stem of the crucifix meets the cross arm. The drive panel and crossdrive panel are at opposite tips of the cross arm.

The dog takes his sheep around his handler's feet and through the drive panel. A faultless drive is straight from the handler's feet through the exact center of the drive panel and a neat sharp turn onto the crossdrive.

The crossdrive traverses the course and passes through the crossdrive panel at the far tip. Faults include weaving, wavering, overhaste, balking.

The dog haunts his sheep across the field, slipping from side to side, always seeking fresh balance points and, if he's very good and his handler is able to anticipate each sheep move, the line will be straight.

The dog turns his sheep once more and brings them to the pen where the handler will have opened the gate. The sheep never want to go into the pen. They can see the pen's a trap. They aren't stupid. It is a test of the dog's power, pushing them one step at a time into that pen. Delays are faults. Pen circling is a serious fault; allowing the sheep to escape is a fault. Failure to pen will cost all the pen points.

After the handler and dog complete their pen, they release the sheep into the shedding ring, generally a thirty-foot grass circle marked with chalk or mowed short. One or more sheep are ribboned and the dog must shed these from the flock and hold them until the judges announce that the separation is good. "That's a shed."

From the handler's first "Hsst" to the judge's "Shed complete" can take ten, twelve or fifteen minutes depending on the trial and the number of dogs entered.

The stockdog trial is a grueling test. For the dog it's like playing a chess game while broken-field running top-speed downhill. Dogs rid themselves of body wastes through their tongues and the pads of their feet. Dogs have died on the trial course, collapsing when their body wastes simply overwhelmed them.

Before the first dog runs, the judge meets with the handlers to explain his biases. "I'll want a good outrun. Every redirection will cost you half a point, two points if the dog doesn't take the command. The dog has to do his outrun without your help."

Lewis listened with half an ear. Ethel Harwood asked him how many dogs he was running. "Just the Nop dog, Ethel. My young dog."

"Didn't he take a first at the Hop Bottom Trials?"

"He beat out some pretty good dogs there. Doug Whi-

tenaur had one of his imported dogs and Nop beat him."
Lewis laughed, not very pleasantly.

"What's Nop's breeding?"

"Jack Knox's Craig dog is the sire. Craig's here today.
Stout-looking, prick-eared dog. Craig's fast but he's
hyper. The dam's a little bitch named Maid. Maid never
won anything but she's got good blood. She's got plenty
of Gilchrist Spot in her and Craig's a Wiston Cap son.
Nop's real responsive but hasn't got much confidence yet.
On his good days he can't be beat. Bad days, tough ewes
will run him right out of the field. I'll use him with the
cows this winter and ewes with first lambs. That'll put
some power in him. He's turning out better than he
ought. I bought him because he was handy when my Stink
Dog got hurt."

Ethel Harwood wore tight (too tight for her hips) whipcord pants cut for riding. Her boots were alligator hide
and her belt buckle pictured a gold barrel racer on a silver
background. The horse's eyes were red rubies and the
legend was the championship Ethel had won fifteen years
ago when she was still the baby side of forty. She had a
sunbeaten face and her black eyes didn't miss much. For
as long as Lewis could remember, she'd been a quarter-
horse dealer, selling colts, brood mares, racers, ropers and
a few pleasure horses too. The only animal she loved as
much as a quarterhorse was an honest stockdog.

"I was awful sorry to hear about Stink," she said.
"Awful sorry. That bitch had the smoothest action I ever
saw. And speed, goodness, she had some speed on her."

Lewis looked at his boot toes.

"Can you breed her?"

"Way she's busted up? You'd never get her pups except by caesarian. I don't know if she'd even breed."

"It was a cow with a new calf?"

"If you don't mind, Ethel, I'd just as soon not talk about it. See, Tom Conn's gonna make the first run. Let's see what we can learn about this course."

Lewis's eyes were fixed on the distant sheep. Ethel Harwood bit her lip and moved away. An old friend of Lewis's, she knew his moodiness.

The sheep were Suffolk-Dorset crosses, yearlings and two-year-olds. The sheep had been worked by dogs before and were of average difficulty, neither as docile as the Barbados Blackbellies some trials favored nor as wild as the Texas sheep imported for the Kentucky Bluegrass.

Lewis, who'd drawn a late slot, watched the first runs intently. From below, the course looked to be left-handed, but those dogs who took the left flank were winded by the time they reached their sheep. Though the hill seemed perfectly smooth, Lewis noted several dips where, briefly, dog and sheep were out of sight of the handler.

The sheep jumped down that hill, stiff-legged and bouncing.

They'd come fast, all right, and it'd be the devil to turn them.

Ethel was beside her van, a six-window blue Dodge with Texas plates.

"I'm sorry," Lewis said. "Is that ice tea you got in that jug?"

"Help yourself. You don't have to talk about the Stink

Dog, Lewis. Last time I lost a good dog I couldn't hold anything in my stomach for a week."

"Naw." Stubbornly Lewis shook his head. "It wasn't that, though that was part of it. It was just so crazy. You know, most times I get into trouble, I can see it coming. Like that time I was fixing the guttering and came off the barn roof. I knew I shouldn't be up there at the time. But this thing with Stink. It was . . . it was like a meteor came out of the air and hit me. I couldn't have been more surprised. This is good tea, Ethel. Look at that red dog go. That's Pulfer's Dell, isn't it? Isn't she a pretty thing?"

Lewis didn't really expect an answer and Ethel didn't provide one. She watched the Dell dog make a perfect fetch, directed by Lewis Pulfer's whistled commands.

"A cow with a new calf, I would have been careful. You know how cows get sometimes. They forget who's been feeding them all winter and suddenly it's like you're some kind of wolf after their young one. But this wasn't a new calf. Calf was a hundred eighty days old. I had the calf and twenty others penned up beside my loading chute because I was weaning them. That afternoon I meant to take them down to my river field. Oh, they'd bawl and complain, you know, but after a couple days they'd settle down and forget about their mama. You never been to my place, Ethel. There's the loading chute right beside my equipment shed and the lot with the mama cows is all bare earth because my daddy used to use it as a hog lot. There's some old fenceposts standing in the lot but no wire or boards on them." Lewis sighed. "Oh, that Stink Dog. She could run. She could run like the wind. You saw her at the Bluegrass this spring. Wasn't any dog there could touch her."

"Once she lifted her sheep, she had 'em," Ethel agreed.

"I was doin' some fool thing. Walking across that lot toward the equipment shed with my head in the clouds. I don't know what I meant to do—grease the rake or adjust the haybin—I don't know. One minute I was walking along and the next thing, by God, I was flat on my back and my mouth was full of dirt and all the wind knocked plumb out of me. I was starin' at this dirty brown patch of hair pushin' against my chest like that cow meant to drive me right into the ground. Just the top of her head, that's all I could see. It hurt bad, Ethel. I wound up and slugged that cow. Hit her in the side of the head hard as I could, one hand, then the other, but a cow's skull is all bone and I hurt my hand more'n I hurt her. She just naturally kept on pressin' on me and I didn't know it was possible, but I swear I heard my ribs snap. It was so surprising. I'd got between that crazy cow and her calf and she meant to murder me. My vision was going out so I didn't see why she pulled her head off my chest. She gave a noise, like a grunt, and something hot and wet fell on my face. I figured it was some of her snot, but later I found it was her blood that fell on me. With her head off me, I was cryin' for help, but Beverly was in the kitchen and she said she never heard nothing except the Stink Dog bark. I wasn't awful far from that loading chute and I pushed myself back with my legs and grubbed around for a corral post because if I could pull under the loading chute, she couldn't get me. The loading chute is two-inch oak and she couldn't touch me there, no matter how she tried. She had her head lowered and was coming for me again. I never saw Stink hit her that first time, when the cow lifted up off me, but I saw Stink hit that cow the second time. Stink flew through the air like she meant to kill and gripped her nose, just clamped down hard as she could. I wasn't thinkin' much—I was backin' for the cover of that loading chute. Cow jerked her head. Old Stink hung on like a stick-tight. Cow wasn't going to shake her this time. I got myself under the loading chute, just kind of curled up in there, and I wasn't any more use to the Stink Dog than if I was a baby.

"When that cow jerked her head, Stink just hung on like crack-the-whip. The cow went up to one of those useless fenceposts and smacked Stink against it. Stink made an awful noise but wouldn't turn loose. The cow was frantic, bawling and bucking, and mashed Stink against the post again. Stink never said nothing but she didn't let go this time either. The third time that cow slung my dog against that post, the dust flew. Stink just slid down the post, black-and-white fur covered with red blood. The cow was backing up. She couldn't back fast enough.

"Beverly had heard the squalling and it was her who put the cows out of there. I couldn't walk except all doubled over, so it was Beverly who put me and Stink in the truck and took us to town. Me, I had busted ribs and some bruises and I gimped around the farm for a month or so, but I been hurt worse before. Later on I went into that lot. That post had been set in the packed dirt of that old hog lot like cement. That cow had shook it so bad I could lift the post right out of the ground. Both Stink's hips were broke. Vet said I should put her down."

Lewis took a breath and when he spoke again, his voice went back to that time, last July, standing in the vet's office with Stink unconscious on the cold steel table.

"I said, 'This dog has won the championship of the Kentucky Bluegrass Open Sheep Dog Trials. This Stink Dog here is a true champion. I want you to fix her best you can.' So he operated on her. Her hips—I saw 'em— they looked like they'd been shredded. He fastened them back together with steel pins, three in one hip and five separate pins in the other. After she came out of the anesthetic we drove home. She rode on my jacket for extra padding. Me and Beverly—every time Stink had to go outside, we'd carry her and hold her until her business was done. She can get around herself now, but there's an awful hitch in her stride. She'll never run in a trial again."

Because she didn't want to intrude, Ethel busied herself pouring ice tea though her cup was already half full. "That run at the Bluegrass. The way Stink brought those sheep into the pen. She was a beautiful dog, Lewis. Most handlers go through their whole life and never have one dog as good as her."

Tom Conn came over and rescued them from their intimacy. Tom wasn't pleased by his run: he'd lost his sheep at the pen. He'd admired Lewis's new Nop dog. "I watched Nop run at Hop Bottom but never saw him close up."

Nop was perfectly willing to be admired. He wagged.

He snuffled Tom's trousers and Ethel's hand. He grinned. He yawned happily.

"You see those brown patches behind his ears. One of Bill Dillard's dogs has coloring like that."

"Well, Nop's not much to look at," Lewis said.

"Doug Whitenaur was sure mad you beat him at Hop Bottom," Tom Conn said. "He was fit to be tied."

Lewis grinned. "My pleasure," he said, "beating Doug Whitenaur's expensive imported dogs."

"Doug isn't a bad handler. He's a good handler."

"He's got a heavy hand."

Tom was careful. "I've seen him beat a dog. He never says nothing about it, just takes the dog out back and beats it. That isn't my way, but Doug's won some big trials."

Ethel Harwood said, "He beat a dog to death once."

"Were you there? Did you see it?"

"No. I heard it from people who did. It was at the Texas Open, five years ago and . . ."

"Well," Tom said, "I heard that but I never saw it either. Wasn't that about the time his daddy died? Did you know Doug's daddy?"

Ethel laughed. "Old Tyler Whitenaur? You bet I knew him. Wasn't a better dog handler or kinder man on the circuit. Him and Arthur Allen were really the first ones to bring Border Collies into this country. They set up the first big trials. Did you ever read Tyler's book, *Forty Years in the Doghouse*? It's a funny book."

Lewis could just see the tail end of Doug Whitenaur's silver sportscar tucked behind somebody's camper-bodied pickup. "I wonder what dog he'll run."

Ethel Harwood was surprised. "You haven't heard about his new dog? Imported him from Jock Gilchrist. A two-year-old bitch, Bit O' Scot. Jock was hoping to run her in the International this year, so you know Whitenaur paid a pretty penny."

"I'm surprised Gilchrist would sell."

"I heard Doug made it worth his while. Ten thousand."

Lewis emitted a soundless whistle. Tom Conn shook his head. Tom said he'd see them later, that Ralph Pulfer was running Shep and he didn't want to miss Ralph's run.

Ethel Harwood said, "You don't care for Doug, do you, Lewis?"

"Oh, Doug's all right. So long as you don't mind him looking down at you because he's rich and you're not. And if you don't mind him never passing the time of day or admiring your dog, he's okay. If you don't care that he's got a heavy hand. Ethel, I never once saw him go out after a trial and have a friendly beer. Not once. As soon as the trophies are handed out, he hits the road. And where in God's name does he find those women?"

Ethel Harwood laughed. Usually Whitenaur came to the trials alone. The girls he did bring were never the same one twice but were cut out with the same cookie cutter. They were never dressed for the weather. If it was a Texas trial they didn't have a hat. If the trial was in Indiana, they didn't have socks thick enough to keep their feet warm throughout the chilly afternoon. They always started by gushing enthusiasm for "The marvelous dogs. Aren't they simply spec-tac-u-lar!" Always they ended the day in the sportscar where the weather was climate controlled and they could listen to the tapes or the radio. "There's Doug now," Ethel said.

Doug Whitenaur shot them a glance like he knew they'd been talking about him. He was a blue-eyed blond in his late twenties. His beaver felt Stetson was glossy as a hundred-dollar bill. He walked with thumbs hooked in his belt.

Ethel Harwood said, "Oh, oh."

His walk was offensive. His stare was offensive. In his own sweet time he said, "That's the dog that won Hop Bottom?"

"That's Nop. He's not two years old yet but he makes a nice run."

Doug Whitenaur was young and good looking. He thought he knew what money could buy. "What kind of a name is that?" His eyes surveyed the young dog like maybe his answer was written in Nop's coat or the brown patches behind his ears. Nop withdrew a step.

"You know Jack Knox and that Scottish accent of his. He had a dog I liked and Jack would call to it, 'Come by, Nop. Get up, Nop.' Of course the dog wasn't N-O-P at all. The dog was N-A-P, only it sounded like N-O-P on account of Jack's accent. I had Nop half trained before I learned my mistake." Lewis laughed. Ethel smiled. Doug Whitenaur spared Lewis a smile normally reserved for the feeble-minded.

So Lewis asked, "You runnin' the same dog Nop beat before?" Just so Whitenaur would lose that smile.

"Sold him."

"I hear you don't keep so many dogs as your daddy did."

"I don't keep any dogs you can beat." Whitenaur's new smile was nastier than the smile Lewis just ruined. Doug Whitenaur showed them his back.

"Whew." That was Ethel.

"Doug's quite a character." Lewis's facial muscles might have been graven bronze.

"He's not too fond of you."

"That cuts both ways. You know, Ethel, there's plenty good dog handlers. Some of the best are out on the course today. I'd rather win than lose, but we all came out to watch the pretty dogs run. It's supposed to be fun. It's no fun between me and Doug Whitenaur. Ten years I've known him. I knew him when he was still runnin' his daddy's dogs and I knew him when he started sellin' his dogs off. I don't guess he keeps but one or two now. I don't care who beats me, so long as it isn't Whitenaur. I know that's harsh and I don't ever talk to Beverly about it because she's a Christian and . . ."

"Thanks, Lewis."

And Lewis, who'd been about to tell Ethel Harwood a thing or two more about Doug Whitenaur, apologized instead and they stopped talking to watch the dogs run because there was no sense letting Whitenaur spoil the day.

"I believe I'll go get a hotdog," Lewis said. "Can I bring you anything?"

"Not just now." Ethel was intent on the course where a confused young Border Collie had lost all control of his sheep. The sheep were broken up (two and one) and the handler's whistles were frantic: "Nell, Nell. Look back, Nell. Look back!"

Munching on his hotdog, Lewis made the rounds, talking dogs with the handlers he knew, saying hello to a few new faces. He heard about good dogs and good runs. He heard about dogs killed by cars or in freak accidents. Some of the handlers had flown to Scotland to watch the Internationals where Johnny Templeton's Glen had beat out some real good dogs for the title. One day, Lewis promised himself, he'd get over for that. He'd love to watch those Scottish dogs run.

A young couple introduced themselves and their new puppy who promptly jumped up on Lewis. The couple wanted to know how to train their dog, when would he start working sheep, would he be ruined for sheep if they started him on ducks; if Lewis would be willing to train their pup, how much would he charge?

"That's not my kind of work," Lewis said. "I only keep a dog or two for the farm. I'm not in the business."

Well, how much would they expect to pay to have a dog trained?

Lewis didn't know. He'd always trained his own dogs. "Excuse me," he said. "I want to see this dog, Bit O' Scot, run."

Bit O' Scot was a small bitch, black with blue merle breast and the very tip of her tail was merle too.

Whitenaur came out, impatient, too impatient; and Lewis couldn't help it, he grinned when Whitenaur ignored the dog's obvious preference for the right-flank outrun and set her up to run next to the fence.

The bitch almost made up for it, streaking uphill, slowing and then throwing herself out farther; all without a redirection from Whitenaur. He whistled her down, abruptly, and she skidded to a stop and the sheep were alerted to her presence and the lift wasn't quite as smooth as it might have been before that single peremptory command.

The sheep were coming on too fast and if Bit hadn't taken each of Whitenaur's whistled commands flawlessly, they would have been uncontrollable. Left, right, she dodged, dropped, got up again. Whitenaur was doing plenty of whistling. She lost points coming around the handler into the drive because she couldn't get around fast enough on the balance point. Lost a few more points at the drive panel because all three sheep went through at a dead run.

The crossdrive was adequate and she hit her crossdrive panel, but she was still coming on too fast as her sheep headed for the pen.

The most common fault of a novice handler is at the pen where he'll let the sheep circle the pen with the dog chasing them. Since the dog's on the outside track, he can never catch his sheep to head them, and every time the sheep circle the pen, the handler loses another three points, one per sheep. The handler has to quit, relax, drive the sheep out and begin penning again, but it's hard to remember that with the sheep circling and the dog circling too, panting so hard you can hear it fifty yards away. When the first sheep broke at the pen, Bit O' Scot lost one point. When Doug Whitenaur panicked and hollered at his dog, she backed off and two more sheep bolted, starting the chase every handler dreads. And as the points dwindled away, the panting dog raced around the pen putting all her heart in it while her master screamed commands, "Come by! Way to me! Get back, I told you, get back! I'm talking to you. I'm talking to you."

Some handlers turned away because there are those too delicate to watch another man playing the fool.

"Time!"

Whitenaur dragged his dog off the course. He was white with rage. Lewis didn't see Whitenaur drag the terrified animal into the woods at the back of the course.

Everybody heard the dog's howls. Lewis closed his ears and his mind. Twenty-five dogs had run. He was number twenty-eight. He unhooked Nop and took him for a walk, away from the others.

Nop strolled with his customary jauntiness. The trial was a big deal to his master but to Nop it was just another piece of work.

His master's voice in his ear, talking, keeping him easy, lending him some of Lewis's good humor and strength.

Nop's tail was plumed as he trotted through the empty pasture sniffing the sniffs, enjoying the looseness in his own body, enjoying his life.

The autumn sun was lower in the sky when Lewis and Nop took their place in the handler's circle. It was chilly and Lewis wished he had a coat. His mouth was dry. Every trial his mouth was dry. Just him, his dog, three sheep. It was simple.

"See sheep? Nop, Nop, see sheep? Steady now. Come over here on the right, Nop. You just stay outside that tall corn." With Nop quivering at his knee, Lewis took a half step to the rear because Nop would run shallower set up that way. "Away to me!" And Nop was off, skirting the corn. He chanced a quick sideways look to see the sheep growing in his vision. He came up behind a touch too quick and, for a second, nearly lost his concentration but Lewis's sharp whistle, "Steady!" pushed him on to the balance point. That was all Nop needed—the simple reminder that he and Lewis were in this thing together.

He stalked those sheep like he had come up the hill *for them*. They faded away before him. They were heavy to the right, so he stayed on that side pressing them back to the line, straight through the fetch panel, around Lewis's heels. Nop made it look easy. Straight again through the drive panel.

Nop flicked from side to side. A black-and-white dog harrying black-faced sheep across dark green grass on a muggy day in Maryland.

Lewis stayed dead still at the pen, gate wide open, whispering commands: "Walk up. Stand. Come by. Walk up." The sheep went into the pen like they had absolutely nothing better to do on such a fine afternoon.

The audience was dead quiet. Nobody was gossiping now. Lewis checked his watch. He had a minute and a half to make his shed. He positioned Nop back, far back, and reopened the gate. Three sheep dashed out, single file, and the ribboned sheep was last. Lewis took a short step forward, leaned his torso, and if that ribboned sheep paused or did not, Nop came through. Blasting through a gap so tiny no human had seen it. The two lead sheep bolted from the ring. The ribboned sheep froze in her tracks and Nop stopped, standing in her vision. She backed until her butt pressed against the pen she'd just quit.

"Lewis, that's a shed," the judge said. And went on to say, "That's a pretty good shed," and the crowd was laughing and clapping their hands and one handler (a Texan, no doubt) was hooting from sheer joy.

Lewis rubbed his eyes with the heel of his hand. Must have got some dirt in them to make them water like that.

Everybody had their hands out trying to shake his. Nop jumped into the cattle-watering tank, submerging and cooling his parts, lapping at the waves he made.

Ethel Harwood said, "Lewis, I don't believe I've seen a better dog than Nop, here or in Scotland. I'll give you five thousand dollars for him, if you'd like to sell."

But Lewis couldn't have been any richer. He shook his head.

While the winners were accepting their awards (gold belt buckle for Lewis, silver buckle for second, silver tray for third) Whitenaur was revving his engine. *Vroom. Vroom.* He roared away like the devil was chasing him.

Lewis paid it no mind. He wasn't annoyed by the noise or flattered by the congratulations. Everything was a haze. In his mind's eye, he was reliving it: Nop blasting through that tiny, tiny gap. The most beautiful animal alive.

FOUR

For the Kennel Dog, the Nights Are Long

Sourball snarled, "Thou art scat." Nop yawned. Sourball was pacing her cage, same as always, and Nop lifted one eye to watch the elkhound's back and forth. The chain around Nop's neck had pulled cars before and was still stout enough for the job if it was called for. Some of Grady's coon dogs wore rope leads but Nop would have chewed through a rope in a second. Because of the weight Nop didn't do much pacing. He lay outside his hollow gum doghouse whenever the weather was good and often when it wasn't. Unlike the coonhounds and the foxhounds, he never barked when the Gumms drove into the yard.

Most of the coonhounds were okay. Some of the males might have tangled with Nop and sometimes they growled insults, but they were all sissies compared to Sourball.

Sometimes when Grady Gumm was drunk, or badly out of sorts, he'd put one of the dogs in with Sourball for thirty seconds, no more, no less. It was long enough. Sourball's attack was so sudden and so contrary to ritual that, besides Dixie, she'd twice killed dogs put in with her before Grady could snatch them back.

Grady Gumm didn't fight Nop again. Having nearly killed him, Grady got it in his head that Nop was more valuable than he'd thought. If Whitenaur was willing to spend three hundred dollars to keep him away from the trials course, maybe somebody else would pay too. Grady Gumm waited for the money Whitenaur had promised.

Nop's leg healed, though the scar was wide, ugly and permanent. With the low nutritional level of the dogfood (the cheapest dry dogfood in hundred-pound bags and deer offal) it was a miracle the leg healed as well as it did. Nop had only a slight limp now and that might have cured with a little exercise. Nop never got any exercise.

Grady took the coon dogs out and the bear dogs too. One memorable night the hollow was emptied entirely except for Nop at the end of his chain and the moonbeams walking through the deserted shacks, the quiet road, the hollow gum houses. When the dogs returned and piled out of Grady's pickup, they were very excited, reliving the chase, the scents they'd followed, the bear they'd hounded into Grady Gumm's bullet. They smelled of blood. Their excitement was infectious. Nop almost felt he'd been on the trail himself.

It fell to zero, below zero. Sometimes it snowed and Nop lay inside the hollow gum, smelling the stink, the scent of all the dogs that had been confined there before him.

He dropped his scat in the same place every day, behind

his house. Grady Gumm never bothered to scoop the offal away but the smell wasn't bad because of the cold.

Nop lay, breathing through the hair of his curled tail, silent, watching the moon roll across the ice-cold skies. He lay awake most of the night. No bird that found Gumm's trees or rested in the scraggly bushes was beneath his notice. Sometimes he fixed on Sourball's crazed pacing, hypnotized by the other dog's compulsive rhythm.

Nop's winter coat was patchy and dull. His slashed ear never would be erect again. It hung on the side of his head like a prizefighter's mistake.

When Grady Gumm didn't hear from Whitenaur, he wrote another letter, angrier than the first. No reply. Grady'd seen Burkholder's posters all over the county and Lester was pestering him to sell the dog back. Lester said they could claim they just found Nop wandering down the road.

Grady put out a few feelers, just had Lester drop some hints at the White Post Mercantile and then at Galloway's place out on Route 340. Word was, for five hundred and no questions, a certain missing stockdog might turn up found, not mentioning any names, mind you.

But before the message could reach its intended, the sheriff intercepted it and before the sun went down behind the Blue Ridge, Lester was answering a whole lot of awkward questions at Sheriff Lohr's office, about what dog and where and the sheriff scared the life right out of him, but Lester wasn't one of the "talking scared"—he was one of the "dead-silent scared" and clammed up.

If he tried to collect the reward, old Grady was going

to answer some questions he might not enjoy. Lewis Burkholder had so pestered Sheriff Lohr about his dog that the sheriff jumped in too hard, too fast and the fish were scared away.

Every day Nop ate every single scrap of food he was given and every day he was hungry. His eyes were too bright. The snow melted into icy mud and clung in balls to his belly fur. He knew to a millimeter the reach of his chain and lay in the same places every day. When it thawed, water stood inside the hollow gum tree and when it froze, Nop slept outside. The chain rubbed galls on his neck.

Occasionally Grady Gumm would come out and kick Nop. That kick was by far the most interesting event in his life.

Grady was worried about the sheriff. The lawman picked up Lester again and allowed as how he'd forget one of the DWI's (driving while intoxicated) on Lester's driving record if he happened to remember where he'd heard about Lewis Burkholder's stockdog.

Grady Gumm cursed Doug Whitenaur. "I been a lot of bad things," Grady said, "but, by God, I never once in my life broke my bounden freely given word."

He had to get Nop off the place. No telling when that damn sheriff might take a notion to come up to Sally Gap for a look-see.

Grady phoned a man he knew. Man raised pit bulls. The man came out and looked Nop over, checked his teeth, listened to his breathing, inspected his scars. He shook his head. "I don't care how much spunk he's got," he said, "my pit bulls will kill him too quick. Tell you what I'll do. I'll give you ten dollars now or twenty if you feed him until April when I start training. I'm breeding now. Once I start training, my dogs'll kill a bitch in season rather than breed her. How's that for instinct!"

Nop eyed the pit bull trainer with open curiosity. The man might become his master. Nop wagged his tail.

The pit bull handler was disgusted. "I'll give you twenty for that elkhound bitch of yours, right now," he said.

Sourball cursed in the dog tongue and the handler smiled. "Twenty dollars. She'll last four or five fights. I like her ways."

Nop had been dismissed. He crawled back into his log.

Several times that winter, parties gathered at Grady's house to go deer hunting. The deer season was long past, but it was more fun hunting when the woods weren't cluttered up with others.

Most of these hunters lived out of county—one or two as far away as Alexandria. They held jobs in tire stores and garages, in small factories, and one worked at the poultry plant where Mark Hilyer had applied. They came out to get away from their lives: to shoot, cuss and drink.

T.T. Raines was drunk the first time he saw Nop and sick hungover the second time, which is how Nop acquired a new master.

T.T. had been a fair bull rider ten years ago and five years ago had made a barely good rodeo clown. He never made a success at that line of work. He'd never made a success at anything, but he sure did love to rodeo.

"How you makin' it, T.T.?"

"Still foolin' 'em." That was always T.T.'s answer.

He wasn't a bad man. He was just forgetful.

T.T. was some kind of distant kin to Grady Gumm. They traced a connection through the West Virginia Raineses.

In between rodeos, T.T.'d come up to Grady's place and drink some beer and brag on all the big-time rodeo men who were his nodding acquaintances. Whenever he got drunk he'd pull out his Rodeo Association card from his dog-eared brown wallet and lay it down for everyone's admiration like it was maybe a license to practice law or medicine.

He was a good sort, bought more Old Milwaukee than he drank and was unfailingly polite to Grady Gumm's wife and kids (who retired to the Ten-Wide and shut the door whenever the hunters drove in).

T.T. never cared for bear hunting. Out west, where they had grizzlies, he could see bear hunting. But in these hills a big bear didn't weigh three hundred pounds and, hell, it wasn't fair or anything like an even contest—that was T.T.'s opinion.

When the boys went out that night, they left old T.T. alone in the same house with Grady Gumm's wife and kids and T.T.'s mason jar of oily slick popskull liquor. Though T.T. was godawful lonesome once the boys were gone and nothing for company except Father Willie Nelson singing on the tape player, he would have died before he knocked on the door to the Ten-Wide to visit with Grady's wife. He didn't really like being in the same house though the door between the two sections was sure stout and locked too. A man oughtn't to find himself in a situation like this: it might be misinterpreted. He took another sip of whiskey. Every flat surface had its share of round beer cans. He dumped them in the garbage bag and hauled the bag to the porch. Willie sang about "do-right women and do-right men."

T.T. went around the corner.

Nop was all alone in the yard. T.T. grunted, zipped himself up and approached the dog. Nop got to his feet. That was all. He didn't slink away, he didn't wag a welcome, he just eyed old T.T. like he would a sheep. Steady, unafraid.

T.T. waved a hand in front of Nop's muzzle, trying to break the gaze, "Whoa, Son. No need to get nasty with me. You are a Border Collie, ain't you? You look just like the dog Buster Wilson trailed around in Mexico. Dog was a trick dog, he was. Made Buster a good piece of change. His name was Spot. What's your name?"

Nop wagged a hello.

When T.T. hunkered down to pet the dog, he had to set one palm flat on the ground for balance. "Hell, Son. Old earth just wants to pull me down. One day it'll manage it, sure enough. You just sniff at my hand all you want to. You and me are gonna be friends."

T.T. sat out in the moonlight rumpling Nop's fur. Nop was a young dog and it had been long since anyone touched him except in anger and Nop wriggled and twisted his pleasure. T.T. lowered the level in the bottle. If T.T. was passed out when Grady Gumm came home, he wouldn't have to fear Grady's jealous suspicions.

T.T. took another piss. Companionably, Nop lifted his leg. Nop smiled and was very charming.

When, finally, T.T. Raines stumbled back inside, Nop felt great loss. An emptiness where his heart had been. He sat on his haunches and cried out his disappointment and his loneliness to the round white eye of the moon.

Next morning, T.T. barely made the door before he was sick and he had to clamp down hard or he would have fouled his pants too.

The bear hunters hadn't found bear last night, but a couple gutted deer lay frozen and stiff in the bed of Grady's pickup. They looked more alive than T.T.

T.T. wobbled down to Sally Branch and scooped up ice-cold water which chilled but failed to clean the whiskey grease on his forehead and cheeks. "Oh mama," he said, "why do I do me like I do?"

A thin wisp of smoke from the Ten-Wide's chimney where Mrs. Gumm was making breakfast for the kids. T.T. smelled the fatback frying and it smelled not good.

The rodeo would be in Roanoke. It was four hours down the interstate to Roanoke. T.T. had a pint of bonded whiskey in the glove compartment of his Impala. It was half empty though he couldn't remember when . . . It helped some. Damn sun. Damn sun, anyway!

Something was very wrong with the man who'd befriended him last night and he smelled terrible, but Nop wagged his tail.

" 'Lo, Doggy," one hand raised in an awkward wave.

"Say, T.T. You like that dog?"

"Mornin', Grady. Yeah, that's a fine stockdog."

"Smart as a whip. Man could teach that dog to do anything."

"Uh-huh."

"Something wrong, T.T.? You look poorly this mornin'. You see those deer we got? I dropped that doe from two hundred yards, one shot right through the lungs."

"Uh-huh."

"So. You was waitin' around here last night all by your lonesome. I don't suppose my wife came out, did she?"

"Naw. Never heard a sound from that Ten-Wide. Not all night, Grady. Not a peep." The acid was rolling around in T.T.'s gut.

"Yeah." Grady didn't look like he believed him. He walked over to Nop, same as he always did for a kick. Nop stood up and eyed Grady, same as always but this time no kick. "I got no stock, you know. No cows, or sheep either. What do I need with a stockdog? I think I'm gonna take this one out to the ravine this afternoon and put him down. He ain't no use to me." He unclipped the chain from the hollow gum tree and gave it a jerk. Carefully, on tiptoes, Nop walked toward Grady. "Hell, he don't even like me. He likes you though, T.T. You can have him for twenty dollars. You'd've spent that much if you'd spent last night in a motel."

"Would have had a bed too," T.T. grumbled. Nop walked right up to him and looked him right in the eye and it was T.T. who turned away. "Ain't got but thirty dollars," he said. "And I'll need half that for gas."

Grady grinned at him. Unshaven, splotchy with booze

and bad sleep, Grady Gumm looked like the devil.
"Well," he said, "I'd plumb hate to see you stuck beside
the road, T.T. You give me fifteen and the stockdog's
yours."

T.T. nodded his head, very slightly. Large moves hurt
him.

"I don't want to give you the chain because I'm short
on stout dog chains but I got some baler twine that'll hold
him."

And so, in not too long, Nop found himself on the
floorboards of T. T. Raines's Impala as it bumped its way
out of Sally Gap. With his chin on the transmission hump
and his nose full of the odor of this new master, Nop was
real happy. Perhaps this man would take him to woolies.
What could be better? Nop yawned his happiness and
watched T.T.'s feet on the accelerator and brake.

Out of the hollow, the jouncing stopped and the tires
whirred on hardtop again. Politely, Nop remained on the
floor, though he much preferred the seat where he could
look out the window. The rumble of the drivetrain, the
hum of the tires.

Politely, he didn't mention his hunger, though yesterday's feeding had been particularly meager and no feeding
this morning. Nop closed his eyes.

T.T. drove, squinting against the pale winter sun. He
almost had a headache. He almost had a bellyache. He was
almost detached from the planet. He didn't like his smell.
He vowed he'd get to a Laundromat in Roanoke, first
thing. He wished he was healthy as a dog.

He kept his eyes on the road, taking the same back roads

he always took to the interstate. Farmers feeding cows and sheep. Farmers towing manure spreaders behind their tractors. Several waved and T.T. waved back.

He patted the seat. "Come on, Son," he said. "You climb on up here. God knows I can use the company."

Neatly, Nop curled his tail around himself before looking out the window.

He knew this place. This road. Knew woolies. Knew home. The hair stood up on the back of his neck, his ruff fluffed out like a peacock's, his tail stiffened and he jammed his snout against the window glass.

Nop's nose confirmed what his eyes had told him and when he passed the entrance to the Burkholder farm, Nop went crazy. Wagging, barking, jumping from front window to rear window, howling his heart. He pawed at the glass. He yipped.

Down at the Burkholder barn, Penny said, "I don't want to go into this ewe yet. Let's give her ten more minutes."

"It's been an hour since she dropped her second waterbag," her mother advised.

Wincing, Penny got off her knees and brushed at the straw that clung to her coveralls. The ewe in the pen grunted her labor but nothing showed at her straining, pulsating vagina.

"I don't know, Penny."

"Just a little longer. I hate to pull lambs when the ewe's still strong and trying."

Burkholder's barn was corridors and lambing pens: short wooden structures where ewes could take care of their newborn until they were strong enough to face the bitter weather outside. Lights in conical shades glowed overhead. Heat lamps bathed pens where weak lambs gathered, roasting in the warm pink light like bathers on the Riviera.

Beverly Burkholder said, "Listen. Is that a dog barking?"

Penny cocked an ear. "I believe it is. Sounds like it's coming from the road. Nop?"

"I don't see how it can be. Some dog in a car, most likely. It's quit now."

"Well, I sure wish it was Nop." Penny rubbed her sore knee. "Maybe Dad can take it when those big old ewes smash him against the feed bunks, but I swear I can't. My knees are so sore now I could scream. I need some kind of dog to keep them off me. If he won't buy a trained dog, I'll start working Stink again."

Beverly tried to duck trouble. "Lewis will feed tonight. He should be back from the sheriff anytime now. Listen, there's that barking again. . . ."

"I can barely hear it. It's gone down the road. . . ." She paused as the ewe groaned, strained and produced a perfect pair of lamb's feet. "Well," Penny said, "will you look at that. That's the girl." Penny was smiling.

Half a mile down the road, T. T. Raines pulled off on the shoulder. His arm hurt from beating the dog. Fool dog had run around the inside of the car like a crazy thing, barking, scratching at the windows and clawing the door upholstery. Bad as he felt from his hangover, T.T. had landed some pretty stout blows. Dog hadn't bit him but he lay on the floorboards now, panting and drooling, eyes hot with anger.

"What the hell you mean going on like that? What got into you? I don't need no crazy dog. I thought you and me was pals."

Nop bared his teeth silently.

"Well, we'll see about that! We'll just see about that!" And if he hadn't been so queasy, T.T. would have gone for the dog's throat right then and there because he'd never had him a cross dog in his life and didn't mean to start. But the way that dog was looking at him—well, it'd be a real fight and T.T. wasn't looking for a fight. "You just wait until we get to Roanoke," he said.

Still eying the dog, T.T. jerked the steering wheel and pulled out right in front of a green three-quarter-ton Ford with a couple men in it. Another quick jerk to miss it. T.T. raised one hand—half wave, half apology, but Lewis Burkholder didn't wave back.

FIVE

A Dog's Work Is
His Love and His Pride

An hour south, T.T. pulled off the interstate and followed the signs to a Hardee's Restaurant. T.T. identified with Hardee's advertising. Hardee's used stock-car drivers in its advertising and T.T. identified with stock-car drivers. He was glad to get out of the car and, tell the truth, if he hadn't paid fifteen dollars for that dog, he would have left the door yawning open while he went in for his sandwich. T.T. was sick of the dog. Sick of the dog's eyes.

He ordered french fries (small), a burger (char-broiled) and a Coke (regular). He did drink the Coke and choked down a couple french fries. He went back for a cup of coffee. Since he wasn't a hard-hearted man, he wiped the gunk off his burger and dropped the patty back in its plastic container.

The sun was weak as yesterday's dreams. Cold enough to see his breath. Hell of a time to be out of work. T.T. slipped through the door, leaving no room for Nop to bolt by. He broke the greasy patty into chunks and tossed them on the floorboards right in front of the dog's nose.

Nop just glared like the meat had no more appeal than hunks of stone.

T.T. worried what he'd find in Roanoke. Except for the top riders and ropers, nobody ever made much money rodeoing and that was in *good* times. When the boot pinched, men like T.T. were always first to feel it. T.T. had always done something around the rodeo. Something. He'd been advance man, concessionaire, sold tickets and worked the cleanup. For a while there, he'd sold life and vehicle insurance, but the cowboys collected too often and T.T.'s insurance company quit writing policies.

Sometimes T.T. scouted calves for the calf roping; sometimes he looked after the bucking bulls. Sometimes he took care of a rider's string when the rider had to go home for a wedding or a funeral. Anything would do. T.T. was the first to admit it: he wasn't particular.

The rodeo was at the Roanoke Civic Center and the setup crew was bolting together the prefab chutes and panels when T.T. walked through the big arena, waving his how-de-dos. His headache was gone and his bellyache —well he'd had worse bellyaches in his day. He set his Stetson at a jaunty angle and hustled upstairs to the management offices like a young man.

Like always, a bunch of cowboys standing around. "Howdy, T.T. How's she hangin'?"

"T.T., whatever happened to that little redheaded gal you had trailin' you in Waco? Man, she was some piece."

T.T. stood as tall as his full height and nodded to some and stuck out his hand. Hell, ol' T.T. knew *everybody*. Things were gonna be just fine.

Good Ol' Red Paulson, rodeo manager, alone in his inner office. T.T. heeled the door shut behind him.

Good Ol' Red was working through papers on his gray steel desk. He dabbed his calculator and wrote a few figures. He folded his hands and laid them on top of his paper. "T.T."

"It's awful good to see you, Son. How's the tickets moving? Remember when I did the advance work in Austin—must have been '73—no, '74—and every ticket was sold before the first rider checked in?"

Good Ol' Red said, "Those were good times all right. How can I help you?"

"I don't suppose you got anybody handling the concessionaires?"

"Jake Thornley's doing that. Now don't tell me, at your age, you want to start hawking programs?"

"Well, I don't know . . ." T.T. laughed too heartily. "I been with the rodeo most of my life." Big laugh. "Hell, I don't know how to do no honest work."

Good Ol' Red didn't crack a smile. "Hard times . . ."

"Don't suppose you'd need somebody for the cleanup?"

Red's headshake was a no headshake.

T.T. didn't want to hike up and down the aisles with programs or peanuts or those trays of soda pop, but man has to eat. "Maybe I'll go over and see Jake. I done his job enough times. . . ."

"It's too bad you don't want to be a clown no more. The crowd never gets tired of clowns."

"I never was no good as a clown. If I wasn't almost gettin' me killed, I was almost gettin' some other poor son-of-a-bitch killed. I'll go see Jake. I'll bet he ain't got his crew yet."

"Suit yourself."

T.T. had one hand on the doorknob before he turned around, "You ever see a dog used as a cutting horse?"

"A dog? A cutting horse?"

"Yeah. You know. A trick dog. I seen Buster Wilson once down in Mexico. Dog had a saddle, little lariat hanging from the roping horn and a monkey was the cowboy. He'd go out and round up calves, just like a miniature cuttin' horse."

"Ain't no dog can do that."

Okay. Probably T. T. Raines shouldn't have bragged up Nop the way he did. He had nothing better than Grady Gumm's word that the dog could work at all. But it was easy for T.T. to imagine himself hawking soda pop, the sticky drinks slopping over his hands. Threats like that make enthusiasts of us all.

They released three roping calves and once those calves saw the big open arena, they hightailed it, slowing only when they were dead-center, equidistant from the roustabouts and forklifts that were constructing the physical rodeo.

A forklift roared. Men shoved a piece of bull-proof panel into place. "You got to picture my dog with a saddle," T.T. said. "Little red saddle like a pony saddle, only smaller. And the monkey on his back dressed up like a real little cowboy. You have to imagine that part."

T.T. knelt beside Nop and touched him like maybe some of his hopes would be transmitted right to the dog's heart and intentions.

Nop saw loose calves. He saw his work and waited for his command, trembling. After months without work, T.T.'s "Do it!" set him off perfect. He ran wide, he ran careful and made a perfect lift, working farther back on the three calves than he would have worked sheep. The calves tried to scatter but he outran the escape artists and turned them back. The calves trotted toward the two men, with Nop directly behind.

"I seen Border Collies before," Red said.

"Yeah. But you never seen no Border Collie that was a cuttin' horse, now have you? If I'm lyin', I'm dyin'. The crowd'll love it."

The calves were squeezing toward the two men, Nop swinging wide, far back on his balance point. T.T. yelled, "You quit now. Sit down. Dog, sit down."

And Nop laid down and watched the calves. Things were looking up.

They named the monkey Festus. Festus had been raised by a suburban couple who thought he was cute as the devil when he was an infant until, at two years old, he systematically destroyed their living room, entry foyer and equity. The rodeo bought him for two hundred dollars. The monkey didn't mind wearing the tiny cowboy outfit. He didn't object to the diminutive cowboy hat. To Nop, he objected. Generations of monkey memories warned him about quick animals with long teeth. Animals like Nop lived on the jungle floor and ate animals like Festus.

Festus screeched. Festus howled. He clawed at T. T. Raines's shirt when T.T. tried to set him in the saddle. T.T. felt like quitting the whole idea but, like he said, he didn't know anything but rodeo.

Nop didn't mind the saddle. So long as he was working again, Nop would have put up with almost anything.

T.T. had a harness maker cut four wide leather straps which he fed through the girth strap, two to a side. He shot the monkey with tranquilizers: three cc.s. T.T. strapped the monkey's legs to the girth strap and when Nop turned his head to snap at his rider, T.T. whacked him with his hat. "Dog, you're gonna carry this buckaroo, so you best get used to the idea."

Festus and Nighthawk—THE LITTLEST BUCKAROOS— that's how they were billed. Trainer: T. T. Raines.

From their first appearance, they were a hit. After the rough shocks of the rodeo—the hard riders, the enormous Brahma bulls, the maddened bucking horses—the dog and monkey were a welcome diversion, almost like the rodeo was mocking itself.

Nop didn't care about the cheers, didn't seem to hear them. The monkey thought they were great. Cheers woke him up and excited him despite the tranquilizers that T. T. Raines began to reduce once he thought the monkey would stay in the saddle. By Philadelphia, the monkey was wide awake and playing his part. He waved his little cowboy hat, he jabbed Nop in the sides with his heels, he slapped his rump with the hat. Nop went about his business gathering calves.

The show started at 7:00 P.M. and lasted until 11:00. Weeknights and Saturdays and between shows Nop lay in a cage out behind the horse trailers next to the monkey cage. Festus jabbered at him and tried to provoke him by throwing scraps of food and other scraps too, more offensive than food. On the road Nop traveled in the back seat in a small airline cage. Except for his time in the arena, he was rarely out of the cage and never off a chain. T.T. never forgot that crazy moment driving down the road when the dog attacked the windows trying to get out. T.T. never trusted Nop after that.

Throughout the long nights, Nop lived in his dreams. He dreamt of woolies, of the Stink Dog, of thrilling outruns on lovely foggy mornings. He dreamt about Sourball and whimpered and his legs jerked in his sleep. Nop accepted what the world had to offer. He didn't have to like it, but he wouldn't pine away.

Lewis Burkholder was less realistic than his dog. Though his reward posters (LOST DOG $500) had tattered and blown off the telephone poles, though local storekeepers had tacked more recent announcements of church socials and yard sales over Nop's photograph, Lewis wouldn't stop looking.

He and Mark were off at the sheriff's office this cold April afternoon and, once again, the two women had the farm.

Beverly Burkholder dried a dish and watched her daughter working the Stink Dog in the empty cornfield below the house. Stubble and mud. Lewis had grazed cows in the field and they'd churned it, the way they will.

The dark sky wasn't far off the earth and streamers of night were already falling around the clumsy woman and her broken dog.

Beverly shook her head. "My," she said, "oh my," and turned away because she couldn't watch anymore. Every afternoon, after her nap, Penny took that poor dog into the cornfield and turned in yearling rams. Oh my, how they tried.

Beverly wiped the sink clean. Six o'clock. Though the nights weren't so cold as they had been, Beverly kept a good fire going in the Home Comfort. She slid more sticks in the firebox and was pouring herself a cup of instant coffee (decaffeinated) when she heard Penny's footfalls on the porch. Life was beautiful on the farm in the summer and fall but it was surely hard in bad weather. Two thuds as Penny pulled off her rubber muckboots.

Penny's face was ruddy as sunburn and her hands too. "You should use some of that cream on your hands," Beverly said. "That Horseman's Dream."

Mud spatters on Penny's pants legs and, of course, the Stink Dog was mud to her belly hairs. Mud and ice balls. Beverly never was able to keep a floor clean in the wintertime. Each time Stink swung her muddy tail, she slapped the wall like a filthy mop. Oh well. "Water's hot in the kettle," Beverly said.

"Thanks, Ma." She pulled off her yellow slicker and unzipped the quilted coveralls. Under the coveralls she wore another wool shirt and a neckerchief at her neck. All those heavy clothes. Beverly couldn't wait until warm weather when they could peel some layers.

"The ram lambs are yelling to be fed," Penny said.

"I guess the men will have to feed in the dark."

Penny said, "It takes twice as long after dark. By the time they get through feeding and dinner, it's time to go to bed. Sometimes I don't hardly know the man I'm married to."

When Stink scooted under the stove, her ice balls clattered like stones. She was too weary to clean herself.

"Won't it be nice when it starts getting lighter? I swear, when the days get longer, it feels like I'm getting longer too, like my body is stretching itself."

"Oh Ma, I'm so unhappy."

So Beverly took Penny in her arms like her daughter was still a baby girl. Directly, Penny pulled away and took a paper towel and blew her nose—*honk*. "I believe I'll let Stink rest tomorrow. She's keen but her hips pain her something terrible. When she's fresh, you can see the dog that won the Bluegrass, but she gets tired and she tangles and shrinks and hurts." Penny looked at the dog under the stove. Stink thumped her tail. "I wish Dad would come out and watch us. Just one time. Dad could really help."

"You know how he is."

Grimace. She sat down heavily and took a cup of tea. "Dad and Mark are pestering Sheriff Lohr again?"

"I just don't see why the sheriff can't be around when he says he'll be. Twice they've gone up there when he was supposed to be in his office and made the trip for nothing."

"Maybe the sheriff's got other things to do. Maybe he's tired of looking for a dog that's likely been dead since Christmastime."

Beverly had a retort right on the tip of her tongue but didn't utter it. No sense everybody getting out of temper. "Sheriff Lohr had some kind of new lead. That's why Lewis went up there today. Lewis don't give up easy."

"Nop is gone. Why can't Dad realize that?"

Beverly thought Lewis was changing, that he was caught between what he'd been and what he was to become. Softly she said, "It's real important to him, Penny. I'm not sure I'd want him to quit before he'd tried everything he could."

But Penny was shaking her head, exasperated, before Beverly had finished. "I don't think you understand. Me and Mark—we're about ready to give up on Dad. I don't think we can keep on living here with Dad treating him like he does. Mark was studying ag science, Ma. He grew up in the Future Farmers. He knows things. He could be a good farmer. But Dad won't give him a chance. Yesterday, they stopped at Crossroads Exxon for a Coke. Dad wouldn't let Mark pay for it. 'You're too poor,' that's what Dad said to him. Ma, we're not that poor."

It was late when Lewis and Mark finally got in and later still when they finished feeding and crawled into bed. The next morning, quite early, they drove out again and by nine o'clock they were bumping past the sign that said END STATE MAINTENANCE at the head of Sally Gap.

"I hope Sheriff Lohr is right," Mark said.

"Uh-huh. Would you look at that pile of trash? This'd be a gold mine for the recyclers. I suppose if you pulled that trash heap away, the whole shack would fall in."

"Who lives here?"

"I don't know. One of Grady's kin. Lester maybe. I don't know many of the Gumms. Used to see them at the dances when I was a younger man but not anymore. Couple years back Grady came by, wanted to drive our river bottom during hunting season, and I let him."

"That backhoe's old enough for the Smithsonian. Damn these ruts!"

"Oh, it's a bad road all right. That's Grady's place up ahead, the mobile home with the addition on the back. Those are his dogs."

"I don't see Nop."

"Well, it was a long shot. Sheriff Lohr told us that. He said Lester Gumm had been talking about a stockdog and then denied everything. We followed up thinner leads than this one."

They pulled up scanning the pack of barking dogs. "Bear dogs, coon dogs. I don't see no Border Collies. Man who'll keep a dog in one of those hollow gum doghouses will do anything. Look at that Norwegian bitch. Now there's a cross dog if I ever seen one. No. Don't get out of the truck. It ain't good manners until somebody invites us to step down."

One of Grady's youngest came out of the addition. Smudged T-shirt and loaded diapers. The boy had a thumb in his mouth and eyed the strangers warily.

"Why don't you honk your horn?"

"Oh, Grady knows we're here. He's just deciding whether he wants to come talk to us or not. We might wait out in this yard all day."

Another young 'un squeezed through the door and stood next to the first. A little older, wearing too-short corduroy pants, no socks above his runover tennis shoes.

"Don't that boy know it's cold out here?" Mark asked.

"Roll down your window and ask him if his daddy's home."

Mark did. The kids stayed mum as statues. The older slipped back inside. Couldn't see much through the door crack except a piece of fabric, might have been the end of a coverlet or a blanket.

Grady Gumm emerged wearing an oil-stained jacket and one of those sports fisherman's caps with the extremely long bill and braided hatcord.

He looked them over, quite expressionless. He spat tobacco juice in the yard. He looked them over again.

He slapped his youngest on the butt. "Get inside now. You got stink in your drawers, boy."

Still sucking his thumb, the boy disappeared. Grady walked around the front of the truck. "Mornin', Lewis. I wasn't sure it was you behind the wheel. I never met this other fellow."

"Mornin'."

"You think it'll ever warm up? Seems to me it's been awful chilly. Winter's supposed to have quit us by now."

"Uh-huh."

"You get all your lambs yet?"

"Oh my, yes. Our lambs come in January and February. We're about ready to take a load to market."

"Uh-huh." Grady spat again.

"This here's my son-in-law, Mark Hilyer."

Grady nodded. "Hilyer. That's not a name I'm familiar with."

"Mark's from Ohio. Where'd you say?"

"Columbus. That's where I was born."

"Right good farms out in Ohio." Grady could be polite as long as anyone.

"Grady, I been meanin' to ask you about a dog."

Grady's broad grin. "Well hell, Lewis. You know me. Ain't nothin' I'd rather do than talk dogs. Now I got me a real fine Walker coonhound I been wantin' to sell. That bitch over there, second to last doghouse. That's her. I'd keep her but I already got one litter off her and I'm gonna keep a couple pups."

"No," Lewis said, "my coon-hunting days are done. That's a sport for young men, traipsing through the woods all night."

Grady ran his hands through his hair. He picked at the chrome strip on the side of Lewis's pickup. "You know," he said, "I like a Ford truck. You got the F-250 three-quarter ton, same as my blue truck. 'Course you don't have the four-wheel drive."

"Grady, I don't know if you heard, but I lost me a good stockdog on Christmas day. Best young dog I ever owned. Now that dog's worth five hundred dollars to me and I wouldn't be asking too many questions were I to get it back. Black-and-white dog. Here, I got a picture of him. That's my wife, Beverly, standing by the dog. Dog answers to 'Nop.' "

Grady's smile was strained. "Five hundred dollars. Whooee, that's a powerful sum. I'll let you have the Walker coon dog for fifty."

"I don't believe I'd be interested in any coonhound," Lewis said. He got out of the truck, just like he'd been invited, and Mark followed suit.

"Man, don't you love to hear coon dogs cry," Grady said, backing a step.

"Sheriff Lohr says Lester might know something about my dog. I surely would like to get that dog back."

Grady puffed up his chest and cheeks. His hands clenched at his sides. "If it's Lester you want, maybe you better talk to Lester."

Lewis turned around. Lester'd come up pretty quiet, just like he was stalking after deer, and the rifle in his hand would have done for any deer, sure enough.

Lewis breathed in. Lewis put both hands on his hips.

Lester pasted on a smile that somewhat overlapped his lips. "Groundhogs," he said.

"Groundhogs ain't out yet," Lewis said. "End of the month you'll start seeing your groundhogs." Lewis took a deliberate step toward Lester, then another.

Like a hockey player, Mark Hilyer bumped the older man out of line. Mark got in front and stuck out his hand. "I believe that's a genuine antique gun you got there. Mind if I take a look at it?"

Relieved, Lester gave up the rifle without a murmur. "It's an old thing, sure enough. Grandpap brought it back from the Spanish War, the Teddy Roosevelt war. I been meaning to put a scope on it but ain't got around to it yet."

Mark read the barrel. US ARMY ORD. KRAG CAL. 45-70. "It's an old-timer all right. I'll bet you've killed yourself some deer with this."

"I expect I have," Lester replied modestly.

Grady went to the cage and peered at Sourball. He spat a stream of tobacco into the dog's face and Sourball attacked the wire that confined her.

Lewis had been pumping himself up to take that rifle

away from Lester, so he was white and his hands shook a little. He walked away from the dogs to the far side of his pickup and leaned against the fender.

Mark said to Lester, "You know, maybe you and me ought to talk this over. About the dog and all." Mark never looked to see how Lewis was taking it. Mark never lifted his eyes off Lester's face.

Lester's grin was odd shaped. Lester didn't have too many teeth but the ones he did have were strong and yellow.

Grady Gumm shook the wire cage; Sourball's barking got louder.

When Mark returned his rifle, Lester looked embarrassed. "Okay," he said. "Why don't we go up to my house. That way you can see all our dogs and satisfy yourself we ain't got yours. What was its name?"

"Nop. Black-and-white Border Collie."

Lester led the way up the hollow, hopping the ice-encrusted mud puddles, and Mark followed right behind. Lester skirted the great pile of garbage outside his shack. The tiny yard had room enough for his rust-spotted Datsun and the motorcycle he was trying to get ready for the summer. Lester never was any great shakes as a mechanic but never let that stop him.

"You kids get on back in the house," he hollered and two scruffy-looking young 'uns vanished.

Lester's coon dog was chained in front of a plywood doghouse.

"This is the only dog I got," Lester said. "Unless you want to look at the house dogs my wife keeps."

Mark smiled. Didn't say anything.

When he couldn't stand the silence anymore, Lester Gumm yelled for his wife to bring Trixie and Pug out of the house. He added, "Move your lazy butt, woman."

Sounds of a scuffle from inside. The walls of that shack were not much thicker than cardboard and anything said inside was audible outside just as clear.

A fat woman came to the door with two fat pug dogs clutched in her arms. "What you want these dogs for?" she asked. "These dogs are my dogs." She kissed one of the pug dogs on the ear. The dog panted.

"Now that's *all* our dogs," Lester said. "These two and my coon dog, Jim." He capped his triumph with a smirk. "What you say your dog looked like?"

Mark felt very tired. He looked away at the spindly timber that lined the slope, at the pile of garbage, at the peeling asphalt shingles on the side of the shack, at the doghouse. He didn't want to look at Lester.

"Go on, woman. Go on back inside. You can take my rifle too. I just hope the house is clean for a change, in case this man here wants to search it."

Mark didn't want to search the house. Didn't want to look for Lewis's dog anymore, any place. Since Christmas Lewis and Mark had been down most of the unpaved roads in three counties looking for Nop without luck. Beverly and Penny had handled all the lambing, lambed out better than eight hundred ewes, with no help though they had two strong men on the farm who might have lifted a hand if they hadn't been so . . . preoccupied.

And though the two had spent hours together in the cab of that truck—knew what the other took in his coffee—

knew how the other acted when tired at the end of a day
—knew how each other smelled—nothing had changed
between them. They'd got themselves stuck in the mold
of who they'd been.

Mark extracted a home-rolled cigarette from the crush-
proof box that served him as a cigarette case. The odd jobs
he'd found had kept him in tobacco and Penny's baby
shower had provided baby necessaries, but Mark didn't
know where he was going to come up with money for the
hospital when the baby came.

Respecting the appeal in Lester's eyes, Mark extracted a
second cigarette and Lester cupped his hands for the light.
"Obliged," he said. "Old Lewis Burkholder, he gets real
hot. I thought we were gonna tangle down here."

"Lewis's got a temper. I expect Grady Gumm's got a
temper too."

Lester laughed knowingly.

Mark had hoped to learn something from Lester. He'd
hoped to show Lewis a thing or two. The trees on the hill
were smoke gray. Lazily, the coon dog thumped at his
ear.

Mark felt a tingle at the base of his spine. His mouth
went dry, so he had to moisten his lips to speak and still
he sounded funny. "Jim. The dog's name is Jim, you
said."

"That's what I said."

When Mark knelt, the dog came right up to him, belly
crawling like a dog that's been often beaten. Mark tugged
the dog's floppy ears. Hunkered over the dog, Mark
turned the dog's terribly familiar broad yellow collar

111

around in his hands. Trembling, he noted the twisted rivets that had once held Nop's name tag and dog license.

He scratched the dog's ears and murmured something soothing and unbuckled the collar. His skin felt tight, the arm hairs coiled up like springs.

That quick, he dangled the collar in Lester's face. "What'd you do with Lewis's dog?"

Lester had completely forgotten the collar. His habits favored silence, but the evidence of that collar was right before his eyes, the torn rivets where Grady Gumm had used the wire cutters that cold December day. Lester stuttered. "I d–don't know nothing."

Mark might have explained how he bought the collar himself, how the little leather shop would certainly identify it, but he had enough sense to keep mum. He simply swung the collar, like the object was proof positive. "That dog was worth a lot of money," Mark said. "More money than many an automobile. Man who stole that dog will go to prison."

Lester had lipped his cigarette and now he threw it down and picked tobacco flecks off his lip.

"J-j-j-jesus," he said. "It was just a dog."

"You killed Nop then?"

"No. We never!" Lester blurted.

Mark didn't let up for a minute. Elaborately he pocketed the collar like it was all the evidence needed to convict. "When I take this collar to Lewis, he won't mess around. He'll bring it right to the sheriff. 'Course, if you was to give me Lewis's dog, I'd keep quiet."

"Grady . . . Grady'd kill me." Lester wished things would slow. If things slowed, he knew he'd do better.

"I don't care about Grady. Don't care about you. I'd guess Lewis Burkholder's dog is dead."

It was all too quick. "I never heard he was," Lester said because that was about as noncommital as he could say.

"Nop's alive?"

"I never heard otherwise."

Mark wanted to shake the truth out of Lester, but Lester had been shook before and no truth had fallen out of him. Lester achieved a certain calm, even a certain dignity. He set his lips tight. "I don't want to spend no more time on the Law than I have already, but I don't reckon I have a choice. If you're gonna give that collar to the sheriff, I hope you give me time to say good-bye to my family."

The fat woman and her two yippy dogs, Lester's scruffy kids. Mark had a moment of sympathy for Lester's life. Mark lit up another cigarette. He put the crush-proof box back in his pocket, ignoring the appeal in Lester's eyes. "Old Lewis and Old Grady. Just the same. Only room for one he-bull on their stomping ground. Shame to be goin' to jail this time of year. Couple weeks, the redbuds will be flowering and the dogwoods. I'll give you this collar if you give me a lead about Nop."

Mark took the collar from his pocket. He dangled it, like bait.

Lester stuck his right hand behind his back so he wouldn't snatch. He wanted to say something. He didn't want to get Grady in trouble. His brain slewed from side to side like a drunken pickup on a gravel road.

"There's a man in Ohio." Lester stopped, like he was counting his words, or listening for their echo.

Mark kept still, except he had the rolled-up collar

cupped in his hands and was pressing his hands together like pressure could generate something.

"This man in Ohio don't love Lewis Burkholder."

Lester's glance asked Mark if he'd said enough. Mark kept still.

"Doug Whitenaur, of Monte Verde Heights, Ohio." Lester Gumm's lips locked up. He stuck out one dirty hand for Nop's Christmas collar.

False Witness

There is no good road through West Virginia—none. The best you can do is catch bits and pieces of interstate, always under construction. Non-interstates are twisty mountain roads where you can't do better than 30 mph unless you opt for the wider highways where you can tailgate the coal haulers while battering your vehicle to scrap on the broken pavement, ducking potholes that have swallowed small cars whole.

Lewis spun the radio dial seeking the noon farm report but all he got was canned news or rock-and-roll. He didn't have an ear for any kind of music.

Lewis had a load of five-hundred-pound black-and-white calves going to Lebanon, Ohio, which was just north of Whitenaur's home. From time to time a calf would kick the side of the stock trailer—*bang*.

Lewis coughed. The road climbed into the Alleghenies and Lewis downshifted into third, coughed again. "I been wonderin'," Lewis said quietly, "why you gave that collar back to that Lester Gumm. Me, I would have kept it."

The *rurr* of the tires. Lewis went down to second for a sharp turn, upshifted again.

"Why?"

"How do you know he didn't lie to you?"

"It was a dog collar. You know how many dog collars they make every year?"

"But it was Nop's collar. You bought it from that leather worker yourself."

"Uh-huh. Would you have kept it to hold over him?"

They passed a sign for the L & J Diner, Elkton, West Virginia. "That's the best eatin' between here and Nitro," Lewis said. He upshifted, downshifted, upshifted again. "Don't reckon I would have," he said. "It's like most of the advice I give: be harder than me, be tougher. I want for you and Penny to have a good life. You're gonna have to find steady work."

"Sometimes I wondered about that."

"Wondered about what?"

"Sometimes it seemed like you would have been happier if I was to run off and Penny abort the baby."

Lewis swerved onto the shoulder. The trailer tilted when the smaller wheels hit the softer ground. Lewis pressed steadily with his brake foot and bit his lower lip and steered carefully until he was on asphalt again.

Mark's knuckles were white on the door latch, but his voice was steady. "I been thinkin', Lewis, me and Penny might just move on down the road. We been livin' off your hospitality since September now. And"—he grinned—"all good things got to come to an end."

They both stayed silent through Elkton. Neither of

them was particularly hungry and they gave the L & J diner a miss.

Fifty miles and eighty minutes deeper in the mountains, they stopped for gas. Forty gallons filled the regular tank and the saddle tank. Fifty-two dollars and change. The truck had burned a quart of oil.

"Maybe I haven't been looking far enough," Mark said. "Maybe we should come over here. I got to have work. We need money for the baby."

Near Nitro, the Gauley River was lined with chemical plants: Du Pont, Westinghouse, Allied—plenty of big names. The valley was narrow, just room for road and river and chemical stink.

The signs outside the Du Pont plant said NO HIRING TODAY. In different words the sign outside Allied Chemical said the same. You could read the signs right from the road, didn't even need to slow down.

Lewis couldn't help himself, "Looks like the land of opportunity."

The tips of Mark's ears got red. He said, "There's other places. There's work in Texas. Plenty other places."

They stopped at a traffic light. "I want you and Penny should stay with us," Lewis said.

"You got a funny way of showin' it."

Lewis rubbed his chin. Resolutely, he kept his eyes fixed on the road ahead of them.

A coal truck honked behind them. "Hold your horses," Lewis muttered as he drove through the green light. "Man like that ain't got no patience. No. I never been noted for patience either and sometimes I speak quicker than I should. Tell the truth, I didn't think a thing of you when you and Penny landed on our doorstep. I feel some different now. I was used to bein' the only man in Penny's life."

They crossed the Ohio at Charleston and picked up the interstate. Rolling west. Mark fiddled with the radio but had no better luck than Lewis.

"It's pretty country once you get out of the mountains," Lewis noted. "You done real good getting Lester Gumm to confess, the way you did. I been thinkin'. Me and Beverly, we got a few dollars put away. It isn't doin' any good sitting in the bank. We'll help pay for the baby."

It was after 10 P.M. when they pulled the calves into their new owner's barnyard. He hadn't expected them until morning and was ready to go to bed. He'd want to inject them against shipping fever before he took them off the trailer. Tomorrow. That's what he said.

"Suit yourself," Lewis said. "They're yours now. If they was my calves, I'd unload."

"Tomorrow."

Lewis said they'd unhitch the gooseneck. Tomorrow they had business in Monte Verde Heights, which was a suburb of Cincinnati. They'd be coming through again, headed north to Columbus. Mark's mother was expecting them. Could they leave the trailer?

"Sure thing. G'night."

They found a TraveLodge right outside of Lebanon. No Home Box Office or swimming pool, but they only needed a bed and shower and theirs wasn't the only battered pickup out back.

"I wouldn't want the money as a gift," Mark said. "Or

a loan, either. I can work for it. There's plenty of jobs on the farm you haven't been getting to. Three dollars an hour."

"That'll be fine."

It was awkward going to bed in the same room. Though, normally, Mark slept naked, tonight he kept his shorts on, just like Lewis.

Lewis had his hands under his head. "I'll be curious to have you meet Doug Whitenaur. He's a character."

"You figure he's got Nop?"

"I do. I figure he paid Grady and Lester to steal him. He couldn't ever trial Nop so I figure he's keeping him as breeding stock."

"I hope you're right."

" 'Course I am. How else would Lester Gumm have known Whitenaur's name. Doug Whitenaur's a *real* character." Lewis flicked off the light. He said, "Tomorrow we'll get Nop back again. I've missed that contrary dog. I'll start working him so he'll be ready for the Bluegrass. I always meant to run him in the Bluegrass this year."

Next morning was one of those bright blue days. The spring air couldn't have been nicer. At 6:30 in the morning the only place open in downtown Lebanon, Ohio, was a Donut House. The scrambled eggs and bacon came on paper plates but the coffee was good. One of the early Shaker settlements was nearby, so Lebanon is self-consciously "historical" and "antiquey" but that isn't the worst vice a town can have; the town is smug but pretty —much prettier than the sprawl outside Cincinnati which is housing developments and malls. Lewis had driven I 75 and I 71 before, but he'd never got off downtown before. He parked the truck in the first parking garage he saw. It wasn't 7:30 yet.

He queried the parking attendant who gave him a wary look, wondering what Lewis might want with the cops.

Cincinnati is pure midwestern, maybe a little better scrubbed than most. Some old parks and some new arcades too. They passed the office of the *Cincinnati Enquirer,* a newspaper Lewis had heard of.

The pedestrians were night people, cleaners and watchmen going home. A couple window cleaners washed display windows of the Stone and Whitenaur department store.

Inside the windows the mannequins held their dramatic poses under sheets. The transom over the front door said SINCE 1892 in gold leaf. The building was yellow brick— very solid—imposing.

Lewis rubbernecked unashamed, turning around and walking backward when something took his fancy. Oh, it was a great day to be alive!

He stopped before every shop window: office supplies, men's shoes, ladies' fashions. He even paused at the opaque glass window which concealed the Ohio State Liquor store. Grinned, moved on.

"You know," he said, "you know . . ."

Mark agreed, "Sure is a pretty morning."

City halls and police stations are always hard-used and the Grebe Street station was no exception. Plenty policemen coming in and out. Roll call. The police hats were two-toned like a layer cake and had a curiously nineteenth-century air.

"My name's Burkholder," Lewis introduced himself to the desk sergeant. "Lewis Burkholder from White Post, Virginia. I'm a farmer. I need a policeman to help me get my dog back."

The desk sergeant said Lewis should fill out a report if his dog was stolen. Lewis said the dog was stolen in Virginia, in December, but the dog was here in Cincinnati now with a fellow name of Doug Whitenaur. "Have his address right here. I got his name from the man who stole the dog and his address from the NASDS, that's the stock-dog registry. You see, Mr. Tyler Whitenaur, Doug's daddy, was a famous Border Collie handler."

The desk sergeant wrote Lewis's data down on a police form and put it on a pile of other police forms. He told Lewis to take a seat and wait, which he and Mark did for the better part of an hour. Uniformed men came and went. A black man stumbled through the door, a bloody handkerchief held against his head. Lewis got up to help, but the desk sergeant said they'd take care of it.

After some minutes of sitting, Mark stood and read a poster which detailed the specifics of the U.S. Equal Employment Act. He sat down again.

Detective Sergeant Steve Nelson wore his hair short, took forty-medium slacks and a forty-short jacket. He was in shirtsleeves. His hat rested in the out box of his neat, oiled wooden desk. Previously, that desk hadn't been treated right. Deep nasty scratches, brutal gouges; but it was oiled now, Nelson had done it himself. Nelson was wide cheeked, blocky in the teeth. The eyes behind his plain metal-rim glasses wouldn't flinch.

The long wait had taken some of the steam out of

Lewis. He had reason to believe (Lewis said) that Douglas Whitenaur had hired two men to steal his dog.

"What kinda dog?"

"It's a Border Collie. Nop is registered with the North American Sheep Dog Society. He's got Wiston Cap on his father's side and he's just two generations away from Gilchrist's Spot on the dam's side."

"What makes you think he didn't wander off?"

"Nop never strayed out of the farmyard. Never set foot out of the yard, he didn't. No, somebody took him, all right. Him and that Dixie dog both."

"Dixie?"

Lewis told about the coon-dog puppy.

"Do you think this Whitenaur stole the dogs?"

"I don't know if Whitenaur stole Dixie or not. I just know he stole my dog."

"That was in Virginia."

"Yes sir, three-point-four miles south of White Post, Virginia. That's the Burkholder farm."

"You reported the theft in Virginia?"

"Yes sir. Sheriff Lohr took my deposition. It was the sheriff who put me on to Whitenaur's stooges."

Writing: "That's L-O-R-E?"

"No. That's an 'H-R' in his name, not an 'R-E.' If you wanted to call him up, I'd be happy to reimburse you for your call."

"Did anybody see the dog being stolen? Any physical evidence?"

"No sir. It was Christmas day, you see, and the family was in to supper. Wasn't until I went out to do my chores, about five o'clock, that I knew Nop was missing and the Dixie dog too. I looked all over for him, even up on the road because I was afraid he got himself run over, but he wasn't to be found. This man Whitenaur—Nop licked his dog, Bit O' Scot, at the Innisfree Trial. Some men just naturally hate to lose and Whitenaur . . . I reckon he's one of them."

Sergeant Nelson underlined the sheriff's name. He sighed. "Mister Burkholder, I could con you along but you look like the sort of man who'd rather have the truth."

"I would."

"Well sir, it's like this. Dog theft is a category-five crime, crime against property. According to FBI statistics, category-five crimes are the fastest-growing crimes in the U.S. Suppose you come in here and report that somebody stole your license plate. The desk sergeant will take down your name, the number and that'll be pretty much the end of what we do. We don't broadcast the plate as stolen unless you report *both* your license plates. You can see why. One plate, we figure it probably just fell off." He held up two chubby fingers. "Two plates, we figure somebody stole 'em. It's the same way with dogs. I don't know how many cases of missing dogs we get in a year. Maybe four or five hundred reports. If there's no physical evidence, we figure chances are the dog ran off. If somebody sees somebody putting the dog into a car, then we look. Or if the dog's chain's been cut with bolt cutters."

Lewis was thoughtful. "Why would a happy dog run away from home?"

The sergeant underlined Sheriff Lohr's name again. He asked Lewis if he'd had morning coffee. Lewis had. Mark had too but would certainly take another. Sergeant Nelson went to the coffee machine where he chatted with a couple other detectives. He set paper towels on his desk so the cups wouldn't leave rings.

"Mister Burkholder, I got a dog. Cocker Spaniel. AKC registered. Hundred-fifty-dollar pup. Gave her all the shots. Had her spayed. The whole schmeer. Wife loves that dog. Every two, three days, the dog goes in the front room and takes a nice dump. Wouldn't matter so much if the dog dropped her load on the kitchen floor which is Armstrong tile or the dinette floor, that's natural oak, polyurethaned, but the dog goes into the front room, smack in the middle of the deep pile carpet me and my brother-in-law installed last fall. Every time, same place. It's starting to bleach the carpet from green to this sort of sick yellow, right in the middle of the floor. Now I hit that dog every time she craps but I can't see where I do a bit of good. If that dog was to run away from home, you think I'd report her? Hell, I'd keep the blinds down, in case she does come back she'll think we moved to Florida or something. My wife loves that dog."

"I'm sorry we took up so much of your time," Lewis said, rising to his feet.

Nelson beamed. "No trouble. Any time we can help."

Mark said, "Wait a minute. Wait a minute. You mean somebody can walk off with a five-thousand-dollar dog and the police won't do a thing about it?"

"Five thousand dollars?"

"I've turned down five thousand dollars for Nop."

Sergeant Nelson wrote "Nop" on his pad but didn't underline it.

Mark made a rather better job of explanation than Lewis had and Sergeant Nelson listened more attentively. Mark spoke of their long search, the reward posters, the rumors checked out. He told about finding Nop's collar with Lester Gumm.

"This Lester Gumm admitted stealing the dog? He stole him at Whitenaur's request?"

Mark didn't quote Lester's exact words. An exact quote would have seemed ambiguous, too weak to force this policeman to help them. Mark said what he _thought_ the words meant. "Whitenaur's our man all right. Lester fingered him."

Sergeant Nelson pursed his lips. "You'll pay for a call to Sheriff Lohr?"

"Yes sir."

Nelson hummed while the call went through and when he had the sheriff on the line, he spun his chair and hunched over so Mark and Lewis couldn't overhear. A few questions, a few minutes. When he hung up, his eyes were friendlier. "You're a fire chief, huh? What town?"

"White Post, Virginia. We have a good little department. Most of our volunteers are state-certified firefighters. We got us a Seagrave pumper and a Chevrolet brush truck—a one-ton with four-wheel drive and dual wheels. The brush unit will . . ."

"Uh-huh. Your sheriff says you're okay."

Lewis laughed. "He's got my vote."

Sergeant Nelson showed some laugh teeth. "No search warrant. With evidence like this, there's no way I could get a judge to sign a search warrant."

"I hadn't hoped for that," Lewis lied. Lewis paused, hoping alternatives would come to him. "I don't suppose you could accompany me to Whitenaur's house? I'd get my dog back and you could arrest him."

Nelson showed teeth again, as if Lewis had, once again, made a particularly lame joke. "Arrest?"

"Do you go with us or do Mark and me go alone?"

Sergeant Nelson wiped at his desk with his crumpled paper towel. He crushed his plastic cup and dunked it in his neighbor's wastebasket. He said yes he would and wasn't it a beautiful morning, nicest day so far this spring and did Lewis have a photograph of the missing critter. That was Nelson's word, *critter*.

He tapped the photograph. "That Mrs. Burkholder?"

"Yes sir. That's my wife Beverly."

"Handsome woman."

Lewis nodded agreement and thank you.

They all went in Sergeant Nelson's car. It was an unmarked cruiser with a dirty dashboard and plenty of body squeaks. For some reason, Lewis had expected something less ordinary and, face it, something a little cleaner. Sergeant Nelson kept one arm out the window and drove the narrow streets very fast, very smooth.

Lewis Burkholder had a lump in his throat. He thought Nop would probably recognize him.

They traveled north up the Strip: tire stores, fast foods, used-car lots, plenty of traffic lights. Sergeant Nelson talked about Cincinnati, how much nicer it had been when he was growing up. They passed roadhouses—just a few earlybirds parked on the gravel lots. The Red Lion, that was one of them. Billy's Temptation was another.

"This has always been pretty nice out here," Nelson said as they rode into Monte Verde Heights. "Plenty of money here after World War Numero Uno and they liked to build the big houses. It's still expensive too—never got run down. I always wanted one of them big old houses; figured I'd renovate it myself you know, but we never had the bucks. That's the place you want, 1412 Blandings Road, that brown job."

The house was stone sections alternating with stucco painted brown.

The house wasn't quite Tudor but yearned to be. The lawn could have used a little work—last year's weeds, this year's scraps of blown paper. Smeared cigarette butts decorated the long walk. The cedar shrubs were in their prime, healthy but rough.

The door kickplate was scuffed. Deep scratches around the keyhole.

It never occurred to Lewis that Doug Whitenaur might not have his dog.

"I'll do the talking, okay?" Sergeant Nelson pressed the buzzer.

"If he's not here, we can just stroll around back. He'll have his kennels in back and that's where Nop'll be."

Sounds inside. A door banged shut. Nelson took a notebook from his hip pocket, ruffled until he came to a blank page. His ballpoint was clipped to the cover.

127

"Wait a minute." Somebody clunked into the inside of the door, cursed and jerked it open.

Doug Whitenaur wore a powder-blue robe. He hadn't shaved and his cheeks were puffy. He was rubbing his stubbed toe on the inside of his calf. He squinted to honor the sun shining in his eyes. "What time is it?" The words came out like a frog's croak.

"After eleven. You're Douglas Whitenaur?"

With a sour look that didn't recognize anybody, Whitenaur swung the door closed until it collided with Sergeant Nelson's shoe. "I don't know you, do I? I closed the bars last night. I just got home a couple hours ago. Go pester someone else."

Lewis had his eyes on Whitenaur, like he was pinning him there, in that doorway, with his gaze. Lewis was primed to fire. "I've come for my dog," he said.

Whitenaur rubbed his eyes. Lewis got a whiff of his breath which was stale. "Burkholder," Whitenaur identified him. "What are you doing here?"

"You paid Lester and Grady Gumm to steal my Nop dog. They said you done it. Lester said you had the dog and I've come for him. It ain't fair what you done, Whitenaur. It ain't fair at all."

"It's eleven o'clock in the morning," Whitenaur said, like that was an answer. "I can't believe this."

Sergeant Nelson smiled a too-simple smile. "I'm Nelson, Sergeant, Cincinnati Police. Now, Mr. Whitenaur, you raise dogs and Mr. Burkholder he raises dogs too. Mr. Burkholder has come all the way from Virginia because he thinks you've got his dog. Photograph!"

Nelson had to repeat the command before Lewis heeded. Whitenaur was full awake now. His eyes were hurting but they were stopped down narrow. He wouldn't touch the photograph Lewis held out. "One of your dogs? One of your 'homegrown' Border Collies? Whatever makes you think I'd _want_ one of your dogs?"

"All the trophies my dogs took away from you."

"Take it easy everybody," Nelson said. "We can settle this very easily. Just let us come in to look for the dog and . . ."

Whitenaur laughed. He laughed and laughed.

Made Lewis mad. "Tyler Whitenaur wouldn't have approved," he said. "Your daddy wouldn't have thought high of what you've done."

Whitenaur took short breaths. Huffing. His hands folded into fists. "You leave Dad out of this!"

"Tyler Whitenaur was a fine dog handler. He was honest as the day is long. Everybody who knew your daddy thought the world of him."

Doug Whitenaur shrank before their eyes, "Oh hell," he said. "I haven't got your dog." He turned and walked back inside.

Sergeant Nelson looked at Lewis and said, "I'm sure I heard him invite us in."

"Uh-huh." For the second time that morning, Lewis lied. They all went inside.

The blinds were down and Lewis couldn't see much at first. He could smell stale beer, cigarette smoke, bad socks and a woman's perfume. He couldn't smell any dogs.

Whitenaur was at his bar (50s Danish modern) dropping ice in a drink.

He waved a negligent hand, "Go ahead. Help yourself. Knock yourself out. Ought to be fun for you, huh, Burkholder, searching Tyler Whitenaur's house." Fiercely, he hissed, "My Daddy was twice the man you'll ever be!"

For the first time Lewis wondered if maybe Nop wasn't here. He shook the thought off.

Somewhere in the back of the house a door closed and then water running.

Whitenaur downed half his drink and shook himself, miming the effect as the booze hit his stomach. For a moment he seemed a teenager, a boy who'd not yet put on the mantle of manhood. Lewis wondered how old he was. Older than Mark.

Footsteps behind them. A woman brushed by them into the kitchen. She was brown haired and in a hurry.

Whitenaur asked, "Do I call my lawyer?"

"Oh, I shouldn't think that necessary, Whitenaur."

A whine from the kitchen: "Dougie? Where the hell'd I leave my smokes? I can't find my damn smokes."

Whitenaur slapped on a man-to-man grin, "Try the bedroom, sweetheart."

"I already tried the bedroom. Why do you think I came out here?" She burst into the living room where the four men were, three and one. She had freckles on the backs of her hands. Her hands clutched her robe together at the throat. "One of you got a Marlboro Light?"

Lewis and Sergeant Nelson shook their heads. She said they were a pair of duds. Mark didn't offer his hand-rolled smokes because he was ashamed of them.

"H'lo, Marge," Nelson said.

"I know you?"

"Steve Nelson, remember? Goodies Saloon?"

"Oh yeah. Yeah. Well I hang out at Billy's Temptation now. I moved out to Edgeworth and Goodies is too far to drive. Sure, you and a couple other cops used to come in to Goodies." She pointed at Whitenaur, "Him and me met at the Temptation." She wrapped her arms around Whitenaur and made a child star's face: "Honey, let me have one of yours. They're awful strong but I need my smoky."

Whitenaur looked over her shoulder with a fixed smile while she rummaged his pockets. Puffed, coughed, returned Whitenaur's lighter.

"Honey, these men think I've stolen their dog." Whitenaur was repeating a charming anecdote.

"They think you stole their dog? Oh, really?" Marge was awfully amused until she coughed and lost it. She said, "Dougie honey, fix me up," indicating the bar. "I gotta go make weewee."

When her back was turned, Whitenaur made an ugly face and didn't care who saw it.

Whitenaur slapped his glass down. "You have ten minutes, Sergeant. Then you and your friends leave and don't come back. You hear me, Sergeant?"

Nelson backed out of the room and his nods were like the deference shown to royalty.

"The kennels are out back," Whitenaur added. "I don't keep animals in my house."

Lewis touched Sergeant Nelson's sleeve. "He's got Nop," he said. "Don't let him whip you."

"Shut up."

Lewis wanted to feel like Nop was near but his heart was too low in his chest to get a jack under it. He felt disloyal as hope died.

Behind the house where most of his neighbors had a swimming pool, Doug Whitenaur had a long row of dog kennels—twenty in all—chain-link affairs with frame walk-in doghouses.

Two dogs were in the runs, barking their frantic welcome: "Hello, hello, so nice to see you, welcome."

Not Nop. Lewis closed his eyes and opened them again but nothing changed.

One dog was Bit O' Scot. The other was a red dog. Lewis faced Sergeant Nelson squarely, "No," he said, "they're not mine. Neither of them is my dog Nop."

"Do you want to go through the kennels?"

"I can see the kennels, sir. Nop's not in these kennels."

"Are you satisfied now, Burkholder?"

"No sir. This man had my dog Nop stolen. I don't know where Nop is now and likely he's dead, but Doug Whitenaur is the man who had him stolen."

"Hey, Lewis," Whitenaur had followed. "Now you've searched the kennels, maybe you'd like to search the house? Look under the beds? Maybe I have your 'home-grown' dog under the bed."

Grimly, they went through every room. Mark opened every closet door. Though they didn't look under the beds, Lewis sorely wanted to.

Whitenaur led them down to the basement. The furnace room had a furnace in it. A storage room was full of crates and cardboard boxes bound with twine.

Finally, Whitenaur blocked their way. "No. You clowns don't come in here. This was Tyler Whitenaur's den and by God, you're not going to search it."

They'd found his point of principle. Here, he was willing to fight.

So they stood there like tourists before a museum room roped off. The mantel of the brick fireplace was crowded with trophies. Pictures of men and dogs on the wall. Shelves above the desk held more dusty honors: platters, loving cups, shields. All those dogs were dead now. Tyler Whitenaur too.

Wordlessly, they trooped back up the stairs. Wordlessly, they passed through the front room where Marge had built her own wake-me-up and silently toasted them. She had the TV on, some morning show. No sound.

Sergeant Nelson said, "Appreciate your cooperation, Mr. Whitenaur. Sorry we had to bother you." The sergeant was itchy, just standing there.

"Don't ever come back. This is my *home!*" Whitenaur invested *home* with such rage and self-pity the word shook like a badly cast bell.

Lewis wasn't going to offer any apology. No sir.

Doug Whitenaur swallowed and took a breath and, very sweetly, inquired, "Will I be seeing you at the Bluegrass this year, Lewis?"

Mark grabbed Lewis's arm. "Let's go," he hissed, and so they did.

The spring day was still bright and pretty. Nobody cared. Sergeant Nelson drove downtown faster than he'd traveled out. Lewis stared out the dirty window.

It was the lunch hour and the sidewalks were full of

lovely girls, around the fountains, in the light and shadows of the arcades.

At the station Sergeant Nelson skidded to a stop. "Okay. That's that. Maybe we all learned something." He was ready for them to be gone. "I went out on a limb for you, Burkholder, and I shouldn't have. Thanks, pal."

"Whitenaur stole my dog."

"Yeah. So you said. We went that way, Burkholder. That's it. Full stop. You bother Mr. Whitenaur again and you'll bump right up against me. Have a nice day."

Lewis chewed on that. He didn't have to like it, but he had to chew on it.

Lewis missed the I 71 ramp so they crawled through downtown Cincinnati at lunch hour. Plenty of exhaust fumes. Hot.

An hour later, outside of Lebanon, they picked up the gooseneck. Lewis said they'd sluice it out when they got home. He said they'd been away from the farm too long. Maybe they could drive straight home and Mark could see his family some other trip.

Mark said it'd be months before he got another chance. If Lewis didn't want to meet Mark's mother or brother, he could just wait in the truck.

Lewis said, "What do you take me for?"

So they headed north. Mark found some country music, but no matter how softly the radio played, it seemed too loud. The empty gooseneck clattered and bounced behind them. It had been a long time since breakfast.

Pulling their livestock trailer through Columbus's university district, they collected stares passing rows of townhouses and apartment complexes. "There's something you should know about my brother Scottie," Mark said. "Scottie's autistic."

"What's that?"

"That's like being retarded but it isn't the same thing."

"Oh."

"It's not hereditary, if you're worried about that."

"I hadn't thought about it," Lewis said. "I never had a chance to get worried if I wanted to. I just now heard about it."

"Over on the right. Pull on through the alley. The parking places are in back."

Modest brick apartment building with balconies on the second and third floor.

Mark assured Lewis that he could stay in the truck if he was scared of meeting Mark's mother. "I wouldn't want to put any pressure on you," Mark said. It wasn't much of a joke but it hadn't been much of a day. Lewis laughed.

A note on the door of 15B directed them to the laundry room and that's where they met her, in the basement stairwell. Her big plastic basket was neatly covered with a towel. Lewis touched his hat, mumbled something.

Mrs. Hilyer ("Call me Bebe") was a pert little thing with a beehive hairdo that provided another foot of altitude. She wore more than her fair share of makeup, but laugh lines radiated from the corners of her eyes like cracks. "Mark, you carry that darn basket. I'll put some water on for coffee."

"Ma'am," Lewis said, "we wouldn't want to be any trouble. . . ."

"I took the afternoon off so I'd be home when Mark showed up. I guess I can afford a cup of instant coffee."

Behind his mother's back, Mark grinned at Lewis's discomfiture.

A small apartment: just bedroom, living room, stove, refrigerator and sink against the living-room wall. Much of the floor space was taken up by floor-to-ceiling stacks of Avon cartons. "Just put the laundry on the bed. You goin' out to see Scottie?"

"Uh-huh," Mark said. "We'll visit with Scottie and then we're going straight back."

She busied herself at the stove. "Darn it, I was hoping you'd come back here after. I canceled all my evening visits so we could go out to dinner. You like Chinese?"

Lewis had to come up with the explanation. He couldn't tell the truth that he'd been whipped bad and wanted to get home where he could lick his wounds, so he concocted some lame explanation about livestock farming, how they couldn't leave the stock for too long, and so on.

Her sharp glance. "When Mark phoned, he said you were coming out here to find a dog?"

"Yes, ma'am. That was our hope. It didn't work out."

Her silence invited him to say more. His silence declined. They sat at the little dinette table before the window that overlooked the parking lot. She blew on her coffee to cool it. "I was sorry to miss Mark's wedding," she said. "I wanted to come out—Scottie started having seizures. There isn't much I can do about his seizures, except worry, but I didn't want to be far away. Mark brought Penny here a couple times. She's a great gal. Just great. So. You're a farmer. I'm a city girl myself. You see the boxes? 'Avon calling.' " She made a wrist gesture like somebody ringing a little bell. "That's me. The job calls for a strong smile and healthy kidneys. When you go into a woman's home, you got to accept her cup of coffee. It's good I'm a real coffee nut. You haven't had lunch, have you?"

Lewis opened his mouth but she was already at the stove. Her electric can opener whirred. "Chicken noodle all right? That's what I got. Chicken noodle. And I've got some cottage cheese too and lettuce for a salad. I don't dare put on an ounce of weight."

"Yes, ma'am." Lewis was dog paddling against the torrent of words.

"Before Mark went away to school, this place was pretty small. It didn't get bigger when he moved out because I took on two new lines, men's colognes and aftershave." She abandoned her stove for her cartons and the emerald-green bottle of aftershave which she set before Lewis. "Here," she said. "Free. Even a farmer's got to shave, right? Unless you'd rather have the lemon-lime." A small gold box was "bath salts for Mrs. Burkholder. Heather." She shook the box. "I use them myself." Her confidence faded as she smiled.

"Thank you, ma'am."

She put her hand on his. Feather-light. "Please don't call me ma'am. It makes me feel old as the hills. Call me Bebe."

Lewis's turn to blush. "Sure thing . . . Bebe."

She whirled into her bedroom and sorted laundry into

drawers. "I'm glad to meet you after so long, Lewis," she called. "Mark says you have a lovely farm. Maybe I'll get to see it someday." *Bam,* she slammed a drawer. *Bam,* another one. "I'll come for a nice visit when the baby's born."

She ate her cottage cheese with ladylike bites that were rapid. "You know about Scottie?"

Mark said, "I told Lewis just now. We didn't tell the Burkholders before. Penny wanted to, but I didn't want them worrying about the baby."

Lewis said, "It wasn't your place to keep things hid from us. I thought poorly of you because you hid your family from mine."

Bebe listened to this exchange with eyebrows cocked.

"Lewis is right. Scottie's no secret. He's not locked up in some darn attic someplace. Scottie's autistic."

"I suppose I heard about autistic," Lewis said. "I never knew anyone who had it."

"Scottie's eleven and he's not toilet trained and he doesn't speak. Scottie is in a world of his own. When he was first diagnosed, I used to think it was better for him to be in his private world, but now I think his world is pretty frightening and I'd rather he get out with everybody else. They don't know what causes autism. They used to think it was the parents and I'll tell you that was pretty horrible. It drove me and my husband apart. He's in Detroit last I heard. Nine years he's been gone and not so much as a Christmas card. Now, they think it's something chemical that causes it. I don't care what causes autism. I just want Scottie to get better." In a jiffy, she washed their dishes. She asked, "Will you keep on looking for your dog?"

While waiting for Lewis's answer, she dialed her phone. "I don't know."

She spoke into the phone, arranging a sales appointment for that evening. The next number she tried was busy. "I suppose it's the same on your farm? Never a free minute?"

"Well, I don't know . . ."

"You should keep on looking for your dog. Never give up. Mark, I got some shirts and a cap for you to take to Scottie."

The way she held the cap, it meant something, but Lewis wasn't sure what.

"Maybe your visit will do him some good. He was always happy when you visited him. I was going to go up this weekend, but if you're going, I'll give myself the weekend off."

Before they left she made two more appointments. At the door, she shook Lewis's hand. Her hand was paper-dry. "You sure the aftershave is okay? I could get you the lemon-lime. I'm sorry I missed the wedding. It isn't easy for a woman alone."

They could smell their livestock trailer fifty feet away. Nobody had parked near. Lewis rolled down a window to air the cab. "How long you say you lived here?"

"Since the old man ran off. The school's out the River Road, just past the State School for the Deaf and Blind."

They drove along beside the Olentangy River. The ground here was recently developed or brushy farmland waiting for the developer.

"It looks like good ground," Lewis said.

"You bet it's good. When I was in FFA, some of the kids lived up here. The farms were still farming then. Some places had fourteen inches of black topsoil. Beautiful."

"Well, it sure grows an ugly townhouse."

Row on row of new townhouses, making sterile what had been fruitful before.

Scottie's school was called the Nightingale School. The buildings had several decades on them and probably had always been one sort of school or another.

"Pull into that lot there."

Older American station wagons, badly rusted economy cars, none washed. Bumper stickers advised that NO NUKES IS GOOD NUKES and asked HAVE YOU HUGGED YOUR KID TODAY?

Scottie's dormitory was a one-story stone house. The door was latched inside, high enough so the kids couldn't reach it. The young woman who let them in was black, slender as a rail. "Hi, Mr. Hilyer. Good to see you again. Scottie's out in the playground."

"Hi, Linda. Here's some shirts and his mother sent along this sailor cap."

The woman took the shirts gladly but turned the cap around in her hand. "Scottie can't wear this," she said. "You can go to the Director and argue if you want, but Scottie can't wear this."

"I suppose my mother just hoped . . . you know."

Linda had a good smile. She introduced herself to Lewis as Linda Huss, Scottie's teacher.

140

Scottie Hilyer was a fine-featured blond boy, wearing a child-size crash helmet on his head. He was small for his age. He sat in the playground dirt.

A chunky black kid came right up to Lewis and took his hand. He beamed. "Bobble," he said. "Bobble, Bobble."

Mark ruffled the black kid's hair. "Hello, Woodie. Woodie's all right, aren't you, pal."

The kid swapped Lewis's hand for Mark's.

"Now, Woodie," the teacher admonished, "Mark's here to see his brother Scottie. When your mother comes to see you, Scottie doesn't bother her."

Scottie sat in the sunlight. A string of drool hung from his slack lower lip. He wrung his fingers like a terribly worried man.

"Scottie, you stop that." The teacher took one of his hands. He plucked it away and resumed the worried motions.

"He's got a whole world in those little hands of his. Unless we get his attention, he'll watch them all day. I wish he'd take a little interest in other people. I always thought he was happiest when Mr. Hilyer came to visit. Scottie hasn't really accepted any of the staff. Go, stay, talk, be quiet—I'm afraid it's all the same to Scottie. Isn't it, champ?" She put a hand on the boy's shoulder.

Peremptorily he shrugged away. His hands flew, knotting themselves, unknotting, wringing themselves out.

Something in the tension of his frail shoulders, his body hunched over his hands. . . . "Is he angry?" Lewis asked.

The teacher shrugged. "I hope so. I'd love to see one

141

sign that some other human being matters to him. Maybe Scottie's angry Mark hasn't been to visit him."

"I live in Virginia now," Mark said. "It's harder to come."

"I didn't mean to be accusatory."

The little hands flew. Mark went over and touched his brother's back. The boy flinched away. Mark hunkered behind the boy, keeping the contact less intimate and his hip touched against the boy's back so Scottie could pretend not to notice.

"How are you, Scottie? I missed you, you know. The original hardhat. Maybe we ought to take that crazy helmet of yours and decorate it. Just like the astronauts did with their names and their missions. You're a real space cadet, aren't you, Scottie, visiting worlds nobody's ever seen before."

He spoke to his brother for half an hour or so, sitting just behind his back, touching hip to rump, the narrowest contact. After a while, when his voice slowed, Scottie's hands slowed and when he paused Scottie's hands accelerated.

"You see," the boy's teacher said. "We can't *not* talk. None of us."

When Mark scooted around in front of his brother, the boy's fingers moved frantically, but Mark's calm voice slowed him. The two brothers sat in the dirt of the playground, one to one.

Lewis asked the teacher about the helmet.

"When Scottie has a seizure, he drops. Right there. He's had two concussions already. We'd like to reduce his seizure med but we don't dare. That's why his teeth are so bad. Dilantin destroys the enamel of the teeth, but Dilantin is the only thing that'll keep him from seizuring. You see that boy over there, by the swings? That's Billy D. A couple weeks ago he started hanging around with Scottie and paying attention to him, tugging him around the playground. We were all pretty excited because these kids don't relate much to their peers. It was the helmet. When Billy set Scottie in the sun, the sunlight made fascinating patterns and shadows through the helmet's airholes. That's what Billy was interested in."

Mark went for a walk—Scottie dangling from his back. Scottie crooned eerie sounds, like the cries of water loons on a misty morning.

Lewis sat still. As the shyest baby lambs will, if you sit quiet long enough, a few children came to Lewis. One crawled on his lap. Unknowingly, Lewis spoke to them in the same soft tones he used on skittish livestock.

The sun slid west. Mark said, "I suppose we better be going."

"Stay as long as you like."

"It's enough," Mark said. "Enough." He blew his breath out past his teeth.

Scottie was back in the dirt again, drooling, same as before, but his head was tilted back sharply so he could stare at his brother. His gaze was quite intense. His hands were still. One scuffed half of his crash helmet was in the sunlight, the other side was dark as the moon.

Lewis said, "Mark . . ."

"Hey, Scot. What's this? Are you crying?"

The little boy in the crash helmet cried because somebody he loved was leaving. Somebody.

While the teacher comforted Scottie, she was smiling too because she'd wished for such a sign, but her smile had tears in it too as smiles often do.

Courteously, Lewis didn't look into Mark's face all the way back to the truck and trailer.

They stopped for dinner at a HoJo's just out of Columbus. Lewis had hamburger steak, Mark had the clams. Lewis paid.

They lost their light while they were still in Ohio. Lewis filled the saddle tanks in Marietta, Ohio, because all-night stations are rare once you get into the mountains.

Mark slept for a couple hours. When he woke up, he lit a cigarette and made a face. They were in West Virginia. "We goin' on through?"

"Don't want to pay for another motel if we can help it."

Every now and again they'd pass a porch light, a pole light outside a barn. Every now and again they went through towns, mostly sleeping towns.

"You want me to drive for a while?"

The road bordered by trees. The headlights washing over the mailboxes, trees, oddly shaped bushes, overhead wires, the center line. The headlights caught the glint of broken glass and beer cans beside the road.

"I like to drive," Lewis said. "I can think things out when I'm driving at night. It's peaceful."

Lewis cracked the wind wing to let some of the smoke out.

Radio stations were few and far between and their signals were erratic. Mark sat with his hands in his lap.

At four in the morning they caught I 64 at White Sulphur Springs. "It'll be smooth sailing from here on," Lewis said. He squirmed against his seat to stretch his back muscles. "Look at that sky. It wants to be daybreak over there."

Mark rubbed his eyes.

"I think I'm gettin' things backward," Lewis said. "I ought to be feeling real bad about your brother Scottie, but I don't feel bad. I'm glad I met him. I'm glad he learned how to cry. I ought to be glad Nop is done. Looking for him, I mean. We gave it our all. Nop is dead. I better get used to the idea because I got a farm to work and a fire department and I've neglected Beverly. I ought to be glad we're finished looking for Nop, but I'm not. I feel awful."

PART 2

A dog is not "almost human" and I know of no greater insult to the canine race than to describe it as such. The dog can do many things which man cannot do, never could do and never will do.

JOHN HOLMES

Nop Loses His Balance

The Littlest Buckaroos began as an intermission act—a diversion while riders cleared the arena between the calf roping and the bulldogging. From the start, the TV folks loved them. The TV folks had seen more than one rodeo and believed that if you've seen one man bulldogging a twelve-hundred-pound bull, you've seem them all. A monkey dressed up like a cowboy riding a dog who's acting like a horse—that's a novelty. TV has never feared novelty.

Rodeo management believed TV could do them harm but little good. Rodeo fans don't need local coverage to pull them in, but unfavorable coverage can keep them away. Rodeo management worried that TV folks were antirodeo and, in this, were probably correct. If the TV folks owned animals, they were small animals, dutifully registered, licensed and spayed. Finicky eaters. TV folks weren't interested in large animals unless the large animals were in pain. Just let a horse go down or a bull break his neck and you could bet the TV cameras would be right on top of it.

So rodeo management shunted the TV folks toward the Littlest Buckaroos and everybody got what they wanted. The TV folks had their novelty and the rodeo got some surprisingly good coverage for a change.

At first when the interviewers came around, T.T. ducked out. Interviewers made him feel stupid and afraid. One reporter asked him for his training secrets. "That's why they call them 'secrets,' " he exploded. But T.T. got used to it. T.T. got glib.

At first, T.T. didn't like drawing a check made out to the Littlest Buckaroos, but the checks all cashed and when Good Ol' Red suggested the Buckaroos should gather the calves after every roping—instead of just working intermission—T.T. was agreeable, so long as his check reflected the extra work "center ring," as T.T. put it.

T.T. didn't spend all that money on himself, no indeed. He bought the monkey three distinctive cowboy suits. His "Tex-Mex" outfit was black leather chaps, leather vest and black sombrero with silver conchos on the hatband. His "Natural Cowpoke" outfit was a pair of tiny blue jeans, a diminutive red flannel shirt and a battered wheat-colored J. B. Stetson. The outfit the monkey preferred resembled a bullfighter's suit of lights—white pants, white vest, rhinestones all over his ten-gallon hat. T.T. called it "Nashville."

Since T.T.'s work was finished the moment he turned Nop into the arena, naturally he came to think the act's success or failure was determined prior to release. He attributed importance to the crowd's response to the monkey's outfit and studied each crowd carefully, changing outfits until the very last moment. Personally, T.T. preferred the "Natural Cowpoke," but most of the crowds liked "Nashville."

Rodeo management bought a pair of cap pistols for Festus to use. Child's replicas of the old Colt Equalizer in bright chrome with molded white plastic grips. T.T. wouldn't use them.

The calf roping took almost an hour. Nop had his work cut out for him. Single calves: roped, dropped, tied with a pigging string and released as the roper held up his hand to stop the clock. The calves struggle to their feet, trot on a few steps, bawl once or twice and hope their whirling brain will slow.

Cutting horses galloping past. The blaring lights and glaring sounds of the arena. A thousand people, roaring. Before the calf had quite settled, he'd find himself facing a dog with a monkey on its back. The crowd laughed and shouted. The dog hunkered down close to the ground and the monkey waving its arms and kicking its feet.

So long as Nop stayed back on the precise balance point, so long as he avoided the galloping horsemen and the rodeo clown (who thought, rightly, that Nop was stealing his thunder and spooked him whenever he could do so undetectably), Nop could do his work, bringing the calf back into the exhaust pen. A quick drink of water from the steel bowl at T. T. Raines's feet and back into the arena again.

An hour later an exhausted stockdog would reel out of the arena for the last time. Nop was glad to see his cage, back behind the horse trailers.

Sometimes, cowboys stepping out behind the trailers for a nip, a smoke or a piss would come over to talk to Nop. He liked the sound of their voices but didn't have enough left in him to respond.

One afternoon curious kids found the metal pen and poked sticks through the mesh and Nop went furious, snarling and howling until T.T. cursed the kids away.

T.T. fed his animals when he woke up—anytime between six-thirty and noon. Made little difference to Nop. Carnivores don't always bring down prey regularly. But the monkey suffered. He was used to eating very many times each day, no great amount at one time. When his breakfast got later and later, he became hysterical, sobbing and rattling his cage.

Matinee days they'd do twenty calves in the morning and twenty-five more at night. T.T. put out as much food as the monkey could eat and then took away the bowl. The monkey was alternately logy, full of food or so hungry he could hardly stand it.

The monkey began to lose interest which, in his case, meant failing to flail Nop with his little sombrero and failure to wave at the crowd. That afternoon, in Waco, when he managed to get both feet out of the straps, was the last time he went out untranquilized.

Animals speak the same language—just like a Frenchman and an Englishman speak the same language. There are occasions for understandings, occasions for great mistakes.

Nop had accepted T. T. Raines as Head of the Pack and T.T. didn't want him biting the monkey. Even when the monkey hurled scat at him or jerked his hair, Nop didn't bite though he would have dearly liked to.

When the monkey was tranquilized, he didn't have much personality at all; between bouts with T.T.'s needle, he was mean as hell.

Nop's coat had been pulled out in tufts. It looked like mange.

In Austin, May 8, T. T. Raines injected the monkey with one cc. of tranquilizer and sent him out in a leg harness so cunningly woven that no monkey (or man either, T.T. was heard to say) could possibly squirm free. The monkey didn't get free. Nor did he pretend to be a Little Buckaroo. He pushed against the roping horn and twisted in his leg loops and hurled himself about so violently that twice, as Nop made a tight turn at high speed, the monkey overbalanced him and they both went down in the dirt. Forty-three calves that day.

In Oklahoma City, May 10, they shared the Exposition Building with the National Quarterhorse Show and T. T. Raines went up to two cc.s because his act was looking foolish. Twenty-four calves that day.

May 11, still in Oklahoma City, T.T. tried three cc.s and the monkey drooped over Nop's neck as he gathered calves.

T. T. Raines quit drinking; he'd worried himself sober. Like many another employer, T.T. attributed his worker's troubles to moral failure. "Damn laziest monkey I ever did see," was how T.T. put it.

Forty-four calves in Kansas City, May 14.

T.T. sought out Good Ol' Red and made noises about

some other rodeo job. T.T. mentioned a vacancy on the cleanup crew.

"We were gonna eliminate that job," Red advised. "The Buckaroos need a little more excitement in their lives. They're bored." Really, the cap pistols were Red's idea.

Every evening Nop worked calves. Every other afternoon too. In between, when the monkey wasn't shrieking at him or hurling crap, Nop slept. When he slept, he dreamed of calves, dreamed of rounding them up, ducking horsemen and clowns, rolling with Festus's weak kicks, seeking the mouth of the exhaust chute, a quiet chute just across the arena, so small, so far. . . .

Nop was a young dog, not yet in his prime, and he was already strong. Nop was quick off the mark and usually the calf was moving before he quite knew he was being herded. Nop's body was relentless, graceful and hard. His exhausted brain spun as helplessly as the calf's.

Every time the monkey sat up and waved his white hat, the audience laughed. Nice ladies thought the Buckaroos were "nice." Men cheered them on with hollers and whoops.

Good Ol' Red said, more firmly now, "You take the cap pistols, T.T., and train Festus to use them. We'll put the spark back into your act."

T.T. took the monkey and the pistols to an empty horse trailer. He'd never trained anything in his life and he'd bought a bunch of bananas for training bait. The caps were extra loud and the first time the monkey pulled the trigger, he hurled the exploding toy away from him in terror. T.T. said, "Nice Festus," and fed him a hunk of fruit.

Hungry as he was, Festus soon learned to overcome his fear and, fueled by bananas, began to enjoy pulling the triggers.

May 17, the Littlest Buckaroos made their final U.S. appearance.

As it happened, the TV cameras were there (the news crew from WBBR, Sioux Falls) and they interviewed T. T. Raines and Good Ol' Red as they waited for the calf roping to commence.

Festus wore his "Nashville" suit, freshly dry cleaned. T. T. Raines hadn't tranquilized Festus tonight. Festus wore child's holsters, one on each scrawny monkey hip. The holsters were shoe white except for a triangle of jewels, green, amber and red.

T. T. Raines was staring a thousand-yard stare. He couldn't seem to focus on anything nearer than the far side of the arena and his speech was slurred, like he'd used a few tranquilizers himself.

"They say there's going to be a change in your act tonight?" the interviewer asked.

"Yeah." After a moment, T.T. added, by way of amplification, "I suppose so."

Good Ol' Red horned in, right in front of the camera, to say, "Our acts—we're continuously upgrading our acts. This is the first time we've tried Festus with cap pistols. It should, uh, enhance the illusion."

"How long did it take to train the act?"

Red jabbed T.T. in the ribs. T.T. tried to remember the question. "Couple years," he finally said. He took a deep breath. He gave a sigh of relief.

"Well, thank you, thank you," the interviewer said as the lights blipped out and all the colors softened again.

"Where's the best place to catch the action?"

Good Ol' Red directed the TV crew to one of the bull-proof panels, right beside the exhaust chute, where they'd get good closeups of the Buckaroos exiting.

When the TV men were gone, Red climbed all over T.T. "I don't know what you've been taking, T.T., but I tell you, I don't like it. I don't care what a man does on his own time, but . . ."

"Ain't takin' nothin'."

"Then what the hell's the matter with you?"

T.T. rubbed his face. "I purely don't know. I'm awful damn tired of worryin'."

The first calf out of the chute was older and bigger than most and when the roper dabbed his loop, the calf never went down but stayed on his feet facing the on-rushing cowboy. Cowboy slid right down the rope and the calf ran at him instead of away, veering wildly, and the cutting horse couldn't keep a taut rope. The cowboy slapped his Stetson into the dust in disappointment. "Bad luck, cowboy," the announcer said. "That was Bill Granger from Thermopolis, Wyoming. That was awful bum luck. And now, coming out of the chute, our own little pickup team. Maybe you heard of them. Let's have a nice hand for the Littlest Buckaroos."

The minute the Buckaroos came into the arena, the calf took off in a long diagonal and Nop changed direction, hoping to cut him off. That is, Nop's body changed directions, his mind was whirling like a piece of thistledown on a gusty day. Nop didn't really know whether this calf was real or a dream. He swerved violently and Festus ripped a hunk of hair out of his ruff.

The Littlest Buckaroos weren't having a bit of luck getting their calf and the audience laughed. Festus responded with a weak wave of his hat. When Nop came behind the calf, the calf stood its ground. It had been pushed around enough.

Lowered his head. Bawled.

Nop crept toward him. The monkey was quite alarmed. The calf charged and Nop dodged, monkey and all. The monkey squealed.

Nop came around to the calf's head and nipped at his nose.

Well, that did the trick and the stubborn calf backed down. The crowd hooted and cheered. Festus perked up. He waved his hat over his head to applause as the calf trotted toward the exit chute.

Someone yelled, "Ride 'em, cowboy," and though Festus didn't understand the words, he understood the sentiment and jabbed Nop in the flanks, just like a real cowboy. Festus was in good humor for a change.

Nop's tongue was out a yard and he was stumble-footed with exhaustion.

The TV camera had caught it all and hoped to use some of it. The cameraman thought the Buckaroos were "cute as a bug's ear." He hoped the monkey would wave his hat again or maybe fire his cap pistols like a real little cowboy. Just a little more footage.

When the monkey leaned forward and fired both pistols, one beside each of Nop's furry ears, the cameraman got footage.

Billy's Temptation is just another joint on the Strip. Friday and Saturday night draws leisure suits, darling little outfits and boozy foreplay. Other times Billy's Temptation inclines slightly to Leather—not Gay Leather, Ex-con Leather. Conversations along the bar have resulted in class-five felonies and a few class-four.

Billy's is Doug Whitenaur's hangout. He enjoys the status of a regular.

Sunday afternoons, in the back room, they set up a big-screen video projection system. The fans gather in the overstuffed booths or at the napkin-sized tables, lift a few, watch the game.

The bar is perfectly good wood, bleached white. The stools are covered with plump black Naugahyde. Everybody overtips. The waitresses wear black mesh blouses over black brassieres.

Johnnie Walker Black—that's a favorite. Chivas—that's another. A few sports order CogNac and that's how they pronounce it. Billy's Temptation is a sleaze joint and Doug Whitenaur can't get enough of it. He'll be here Wednesday, Thursday, Friday and Saturday nights—weekend days too, except when he's off to a dog trial.

Tyler Whitenaur wouldn't have been caught dead in a place like this. Which is not the least of its attractions.

Doug Whitenaur's inheritance takes care of him—he can buy most of the things that are for sale; but his wealth is cumbersome too, like a thick cocoon drawn tight around the skin: too warm, often itchy, terribly dull. He avoids most of the frequent Whitenaur family gatherings, and those he can't duck, he arrives late and leaves early. The uncles and cousins ask him about the stockdogs—such a source of family pride while Tyler Whitenaur was alive. Their questions make him squirm. Yes, he was still running the dogs. No, not so many as his father had. Actually, he'd won all the trials his father had. Except the Bluegrass. Right—he hadn't won the Bluegrass. True, Tyler Whitenaur had won the Bluegrass three times. You could say that was quite an accomplishment, yes. Doug meant to win the Bluegrass this year. After that, maybe he'd give up the dogs altogether and he'd turn to his kinsmen and say, "Since you're so damn concerned about the dogs, maybe you'd like to start running them yourself," and he'd make some excuse and quit the family table with its too curious, too empathetic questions and hurry to Billy's where he could loosen his tie and set both elbows on the bleached bar: "Johnnie Black, water back, for God's sake make that a double."

Doug Whitenaur wanted to be free. Free like the players who made the whispered deals, head to head, along the bar. Outlaw-free. Free like his pals Hack and Sandy.

Sandy had taken up weightlifting in prison and stayed with it afterward. He was short but didn't seem so because of his massive neck and deltoids. Sandy read *Playboy* magazine and took that authority's advice on consumer goods, autos, fashions and sex mores.

Sandy's hair was that color. His eyes were green.

Though he wasn't particularly handsome, he was convinced otherwise and such was his confidence he had considerable success with the mousy secretarial sorts who came in on Friday night to sample low-life thrills. Sandy's teeth were capped and he flashed them. His partner, Hack, was ten years older—near forty—with dead black hair combed over one side of his face and a pool-hall complexion. Hack was tall and ate antacid tablets like candy. Hack had a mean streak. He never talked much. Would jab his finger at Sandy and say, "He does the talking. I carry the mail."

Doug Whitenaur saw Hack and Sandy as graceful predators swimming through a sea filled with fat, slow tuna. Doug didn't wish to be one of the tuna.

Doug admired them. He bought them drinks. He never invited them to his home and wouldn't think of lending them his car.

Sandy had done time for grand theft auto. Cops don't frequently prosecute for grand theft auto but they were willing to make an exception in Sandy's case. Sandy had been arrested several times for procuring but nothing came of it. Hack took a fall for assault. Too much prosperity ruined him. He'd been making collections for a loan shark and doing pretty well for himself. Hack, a buddy and a couple girlfriends took off one weekend for the track, Hack in the back seat drinking and munching Tums. Just outside of Louisville, the driver got in an argument, mocked Hack, laughed at him, something. . . . Hack climbed over the back seat and commenced working him over with a whiskey bottle. When the car hit the abutment, they all went to the hospital—Hack, subsequently, to jail.

Doug Whitenaur sent drinks to the booth where the two were watching NBA finals on the big screen.

Not a big crowd today and Doug knew most everybody. He sucked on his Johnnie Walker and was about as happy as he ever got. The Bluegrass was coming up next month and Lewis Burkholder didn't have a dog to run against him. Tough titty, Lewis. Although having Burkholder's dog stolen was just a drunken notion, and nobody had been more surprised than Doug when Grady Gumm took him up on it, it had worked out pretty good (and humiliated Lewis Burkholder in the bargain). Doug took full credit for the theft. He was becoming, he thought, "streetwise."

Sandy wore a light blue shirt, trousers of the same color and a corduroy jacket. All his lapels were extreme. He lifted his Gucci loafer from the seat so Doug could sit.

Hack was engrossed in the game. He had money riding on the Lakers. The flesh was tight on Hack's pale cheekbones and his knuckles were the size of half dollars. They formed a thick continuous ridge across the back of his hand. Absently, he picked at the label of his beer bottle.

Sandy's fingernails were extremely long, almost as long as a woman's. Sandy did no manual labor. Manual labor wasn't his bag. "How you makin' it, Mr. D?"

Sandy owned a blue TR-7. The right front fender was primer brown. Sandy liked to brag his car was a classic but it wasn't. He admired Doug Whitenaur's De Lorean because *Playboy* admired it and the sportscar gained status

161

in his mind when its maker, John De Lorean, was indicted on cocaine charges.

"Funny thing happened to me the other day," Doug said. "Cops gave my house a toss."

"They what?"

Hack looked away from his game. "You?" Hack never cared so much for Doug as Sandy did. Most of the time Hack didn't know if he liked Sandy either.

"Yep. Cop name of Nelson. Sergeant Nelson."

"Stocky dude with big teeth?" Sandy pointed at his own fine choppers.

"That's him. I'd closed this joint the night before and Marge came home with me . . ."

"That pig."

"So what else is new?" Doug's contempt for the woman was deeper than Sandy's. "Like I was trying to say, it was eleven o'clock in the morning when Nelson comes banging on my door and I was in a real fog, you know how it is."

Hack grunted. "I heard about Nelson. He's put a few players away."

"Ah, he's nothing. Soon as he left my house, I got on the horn to my lawyers and they climbed on the chief of police and he personally hung Nelson out to dry." Doug smiled a wicked smile. "That clown didn't even have a warrant."

"I didn't know you was that way, Mr. D," Sandy said. "I always thought you were a civilian." His look was curious.

"Think what you like," Doug said and was glad to say

it. After a moment he asked if anyone wanted another drink. Sandy yes. Hack no. Doug was having such a fine time. Good whiskey, good company—conversation to pass the time—what more could a man want? Doug decided to break one of his self-imposed rules. He decided to let one of his lives leak into the other. "You know anything about dogs?"

Sandy said, "I had a dog once. Pretty little Collie dog. When it got run over, I cried for three days. 'Course," he excused himself, "I was just a dumb kid."

"Good dog's worth money," Doug said.

Sandy shook his head. "Not to somebody who can keep a De Lorean," he said. "You can't get more'n twenty, say half a yard, for a dog. There's a creep downtown buys them, a white truck, he . . ."

"Five K," Doug said quietly.

"Five thousand dollars? One dog? Come on, Mr. D. You and me go back, how long?"

They'd known each other for six months.

"The department store downtown. I heard that was you, Mr. D."

Doug Whitenaur went cold. His money was nobody's business but his own. He felt like someone—a stranger—had put greasy hands on him. "Grandad sold out to a chain years ago," he snapped.

Sandy ignored the signals. "Still, you ain't exactly hurtin', are you? Maybe you got a little extra dinero you want to put out on the street? You and me and Hack, maybe we could get something going . . ."

Hack interrupted. "I'll take that drink now. I'll take a

Kahlua and cream. For my stomach. The Lakers are down nine, Sandy. There goes five hundred dollars." He popped a Tums. "Sandy, I think we better take that Toledo deal. I think we better get on it."

Sandy made a face. "Man, I dunno. . . ."

They spoke right through Doug Whitenaur who wore the expression he thought a deaf man might wear.

"Sandy, if you don't want to back me up, I can get somebody else."

Doug stood and said he'd get Hack's drink, so excuse him. Some details of their life fascinated him. Many details he didn't want to know. What if he said to Hack, "Hack, I'll go along to Toledo," wouldn't Hack be surprised?

Standing at the bar of Billy's Temptation, creasing a ten-dollar bill, Doug Whitenaur felt his belly lurch, like a dropped elevator. Because he knew, in that instant, how close he was to full membership in Hack and Sandy's dangerous world. He was a predator too. The thought filled him with joy, though no joy, not a smidge, showed on his hardening countenance.

The TV stayed with the Lakers while the fans filed out of the stadium and Billy's patrons were calling for fresh drinks and settling wagers. When Doug returned to the booth, Sandy was staring off into space and Hack was watching himself rub his flattened knuckles. Doug was feeling pretty good. "Lighten up, can't you?" he said. For comic relief, he told them the full story of Lewis Burk- holder's dog, putting a bold face on his own part in the theft. "Five thousand dollars Burkholder was offered for that dog. Isn't that a kick?"

Sandy listened because he didn't want to think about

164

Toledo. Hack scootched around in the booth watching "Wide World of Sports."

Doug described Burkholder's arrival at his house with his son-in-law and Sergeant Nelson. He made them all seem like fools.

Hack said, "That's what you're talking about, isn't it? Look, dummy, on the tube! Isn't that a Border Collie with the monkey on his back?"

Doug Whitenaur got up like someone had jerked all his strings. He went over directly in front of the screen where nobody could see through him. Softly he said, "I don't believe this." Then he smacked his palm and said, much louder, "I don't believe this at all."

VIDEO: Nop and the monkey begin their outrun toward the stubborn calf.

AUDIO: Crowd noises. Announcer (Voiceover): "But you know what they say about the best laid plans. Though the Littlest Buckaroos have rounded up hundreds of calves without incident, here in Sioux Falls, something happened."

VIDEO: T. T. Raines. The harsh sungun washes out his features. He's pasty faced but his eyes glint like hard coal. A super I.D.s him: T. T. Raines—Buckaroo's Trainer.

AUDIO: Announcer: "How long did it take to train the act?"

T. T. Raines: Long pause. "Couple years . . ."

VIDEO: Calf squares off against Nop.

AUDIO: Crowd laughter, hoots and cheers. Announcer (VO): "The dog was having a little trouble with this calf, but nothing he hadn't handled before. . . ."

VIDEO: Zoom to Nop's face. His eyes are fixed in the

Border Collie stare, his tongue hangs out. There's foam at the corner of his mouth. The monkey is rubbernecking, quite uninterested, until the calf charges and Nop leaps sideways to avoid him. The monkey tears at Nop's ruff, terrified.

AUDIO: "But no animal, no matter how carefully trained, is entirely predictable. . . ."

VIDEO: The dog nips the calf and turns it. The calf trots directly toward the camera. The monkey waves his cowboy hat and swats the dog. Dust puff on the dog's flank. The calf weaves but the dog stays right behind it, hunkered down. The monkey draws cap pistols and fires them simultaneously. The dog goes into the air like a VTO aircraft.

INSTANT REPLAY: In slow motion, the monkey sets the pistols beside the dog's ears and tugs the triggers. Smoke from the exploding caps. The dog half turns and sinks back on its haunches. He leaps straight into the air, twisting to snap at his tormentor. The monkey, saddle and stirrups, slide around to the dog's belly. When the dog hits earth, he's running for the far side of the arena. The monkey bounces along underneath, hindering him, making him buck. One swipe of his teeth severs the girth strap, and rider and saddle are dumped in the middle of the arena. The dog accelerates.

AUDIO: The audience is roaring with laughter and cheering. The laughter stops when the dog nears the bull-proof barrier. Everyone realizes that a bull-proof barrier is not necessarily a dog-proof barrier.

Though the barrier was six feet tall, Nop sailed clean

over it. Left and right, people were falling off their seats and Nop went through that crowd like Israelites parting the Red Sea. Up, up the tiers. The camera zooming in and out of focus as it tracked the black-and-white streak. At the top of the coliseum he hurled himself down the aisle behind the very last row of seats, and people came out of their seats like cheese peeling away before the knife.

Pistols drawn, security guards race up the aisles. Nop dodges. Cornered, he jumps for a security man and twists by when the man raises his arms to guard his face. A cowboy lunges at him, misses and loses his Stetson. The hat sails away over row after row. Camera focuses on the cowboy, his outrage, his dismay.

Nop can't find an exit. Since he hasn't bitten anyone, his pursuers are emboldened, pulling at his fur, clutching for his neck, snatching at one flying leg. Nop disappears under three men, like a football pileup, but squirts out of the pile, unrecovered.

T. T. Raines and Good Ol' Red wait in arena center, bellowing for the dog.

No luck in the stands, so Nop forces his failing legs down the wide aisle, full-tilt, feet speeding to keep up with his body.

Men beyond the bull-proof barrier, security men.

Once more Nop launches himself over the barrier, out, out, far above the packed earth of the arena. The camera zooms in to catch him, midflight, his tail arched over his back like a drag chute.

He hits, goes to his belly, spots an opening between Red and T.T.

T. T. Raines makes a heroic dive, wraps arms around Nop and clamps him fast. T.T.'s throat is right next to Nop's foaming jaws but Nop must not bite man, must not bite!

The camera zooms back as the security men close in.

AUDIO: Announcer (VO): "Nobody hurt. (Chuckle) Except hurt pride."

VIDEO: The camera shows us the cowboy climbing down the rows of seats to recover his hat. People are laughing at him. He's burned up.

In the arena so many security men surround Nop, you can't see the dog at all.

AUDIO: Announcer (VO): "Even the monkey got off with just scratches. The end of the Littlest Buckaroos. Kind of sad, isn't it? We'll be right back. Stay tuned for a look at spring training."

VIDEO: Cut to commercial for a razor blade that gives a "macho shave."

Doug Whitenaur's words chased each other out of his mouth, tumbling. "Him, that's him. That's the dog I was tellin' you about. Lewis Burkholder's Nop dog. Two times that dog beat my imported bitch. Five thousand dollars that dog's worth and it's in a rodeo. A rodeo, for God's sake."

Sandy said, "Mr. D. You may have a very great knowledge of these kind of dogs but how can you be sure that dog's the five-thousand-dollar dog, huh?"

Hack swiveled his head like watching the ball at a tennis match.

"Because he beat me! That's how! Five thousand dollars. If you want to own a dog that'll run against that Nop dog, that's what it'll cost you. Did you see those brown patches behind his ears?"

Hack grinned. "That dog ain't worth five cents. Not five cents. Dog runs loose like that they gas it. That dog might have bit somebody."

"Aw, Hack," Sandy said. "Who's gonna hurt a dog like that?" He tossed off his drink and his ice cubes clinked against his teeth. "A valuable dog like that?"

Hack gave him the ha, ha. Hack couldn't stand sentimentalists. "Maybe they don't know that dog's worth five large. Maybe they think that dog's worth nothing." The drink stirrers were little plastic devils. Hack picked his teeth with the tip of the devil's tail.

Doug Whitenaur's jaws wobbled. Dogs—he knew about dogs. Hack's doubt was making him small. "I say that's Nop. That's the same dog Lewis Burkholder ran against me in Maryland. Five thousand dollars is what that dog's worth."

Hack was awfully bored with the discussion. He wanted to get at Sandy again. They had to decide the Toledo business. The job called for two men. "So buy the dog," Hack said.

"What?"

Hack's mouth curled and rolled like he wanted to spit. "You say the dog's worth five thousand dollars. Fine. I believe you. 'Deed I do. You think the rodeo's gonna keep that dog after what he done? They'll sell him for peanuts. The cops already tossed your place and came up empty. Do you think they'll come back and toss you again?"

Sandy said, "Hack's got a good idea there, Mr. D. Buy the dog. If you call up that rodeo, maybe they won't kill him."

Doug Whitenaur paused to think it over. "That's Burkholder's dog. I'd swear it."

Sandy plinked a dime on the table. "There you are, Mr. D. For the phone call."

Thou art a beaten dog beneath the hail,
a swollen magpie in a fitful sun,
Half black—half white
Nor knowst'ou wing from tail
Pull down thy vanity
     How mean thy hates
Fostered in falsity,
     Pull down thy vanity,
Rathe to destroy, niggard in charity,
Pull down thy vanity,
     I say pull down.

     —Ezra Pound, from Canto LXXXI

Penny Hilyer pressed her hands in the small of her back and straightened. "Any more tomato plants want to get planted, I believe they'll have to plant themselves."

Beverly tucked a wisp of hair under her kerchief and smudged her sweat-dampened forehead. "You just take a seat in that lawn chair. I'll be finished in a jiffy."

"Oh, Ma, I hate to be so darn helpless." And she did look awful helpless and awful uncomfortable as she waddled down the row. Some girls show early, some show late. Beverly had been lucky herself, but then, Penny had been such a small baby. "It'll be over before you know it," Beverly said.

"The last week of this month seems so far away. I'm so darn big! Some of the girls at the Lamaze classes are still slim and they're looking forward to the baby and, my, they just couldn't be happier. I'm fat and my feet hurt and I'm always bursting into tears." She sat heavily and hoisted her legs with a grunt.

The early June soil was warm and loose under Beverly's fingertips. She pocketed several small stones. She set the plant—this one already had a couple star-shaped blossoms.

Beverly loved tomatoes but the smell of the plants made her sneeze. She hoped they weren't planting too early. Winter had stayed late this year. Still, it's human nature to expect the usual and if everybody waited until absolutely all frost danger was past, nobody would have tomatoes until August.

The tractor muttered along in the river field. Beverly could see Mark and Lewis putting up the last of the first cutting hay. Most years, this time of year, rainstorms chased each other up and down the valley and it was very difficult to get the hay up dry. This year it had been hot and sunny. Many farmers were already predicting drought.

The river field was the brilliant green of pond scum. The tractor chugged along like some legendary creature, a centaur or a modest dragon.

Lewis hoped to make better than two thousand bales, most of it alfalfa with some orchard grass mixed in. Lewis had thought to hire somebody to help Mark on the wagon but Mark wanted to try it alone—pull the bale out of the chute, toss it back, get it stacked and return in time for the next. The dense grass had slowed their ground speed and, so far, Mark had managed.

The forsythias had come and gone, the dogwoods bloomed white or pink, the bees covered the honeysuckle.

Garden dirt always cracked her hands, so Beverly wore an old pair of Lewis's work gloves in the garden. Now, she peeled them off. She walked the row, stepping heavily with her stout brogans around the tomato plants, ensuring root contact.

"I hope they're done soon," Penny complained. "We have a class tonight."

"If they're still in the field, I'll drive you."

"That's not the point, Ma. That's not the point! The husband is part of it all, don't you see? It makes the birthing easier."

Beverly hated the effrontery of new words. *Birthing,* indeed. "When I had you, I took the gas and your father waited in the waiting room and it never hurt you, not that I could tell."

Penny's eyes filled with tears. The corners of her mouth fell, "Oh, Ma . . ."

"Now I've done it! Honey, I didn't mean anything. I think your classes are just fine. If Lewis and me were to have a baby today, I'd hope to do the same as you're doing."

"I know, Ma. I honestly don't know what comes over me," she said, wiping her eyes with the balloon sleeve of her cotton dress.

The pale blue sky floated a couple wispy clouds. The

trees were tremendous with leaf buds. In the afternoon all the young lambs came up to the barn galloping through the pasture, dancing and kicking their heels.

"They've stopped the tractor." Beverly shaded her eyes. "Looks like they're putting the tarp over the baler."

Penny wallowed to her feet. "I'll bring the ice tea out to the barn."

"Oh, I can do it."

"Ma, I am not completely spastic or crippled."

Beverly bit her too sharp tongue. Her daughter waddled (there really was no other word for it) away.

Tractor and wagon chugged toward the barn. Mark sat on top of the hay bales, legs crossed, like a mahout.

The oats and corn were in the ground. It looked like the best first cutting since the dry year of 1978, the young lambs throve and there were only two cases of mastitis in the ewes; so why did Beverly Burkholder have that awful feeling in the pit of her stomach?

Her daughter's pregnancy was normal (knock wood), her husband had finally come to appreciate his son-in-law, even the Stink Dog (worked and exercised everyday by Penny) had regained her old vitality. So why did Beverly worry herself so bad? She got up during the night and crept out of the bedroom with a spare blanket for the couch in the front room, where she'd toss and turn the night away without Lewis ever noticing.

Not that he noticed whether she was in the bed or out of it.

The pot roast was nice and tender. She'd had to cut up the potatoes pretty good because this time of year some are sprouting and the ones that aren't sprouting are full of black spots. Women who bought their potatoes at the supermarket didn't have Beverly's difficulties because the packers used (she'd heard) some sort of chemicals to retard potatoes' sprouting instincts. Virtuously, Beverly forked a dark slice out of the boiling water. Beef, potatoes, and a fresh green salad: lettuce, beet greens, and some early radishes sliced thin. Just before she served the salad, she'd cover it with chilled Kraft blue cheese dressing, Lewis's favorite.

When Penny set down the empty pitcher, Beverly asked her about class.

"Oh, Mark can take me. Daddy says soon as they get this load in the loft they'll be coming in for supper."

Both men's clothing was covered with hay chaff and Beverly had them whisk each other with the little broom that hung right beside the back door for just that purpose. "I don't see why you should make more work for me," she said sternly.

Mark giggled and made a face. When he broomed Lewis, he whacked the back of the older man's neck like a barber might.

Both men were loose and easy, a little bulkier in her kitchen than they needed to be.

"Now you-all hurry and wash. Penny's got her class."

"Don't rush them, Beverly. It's only half an hour to Strasburg. Let 'em digest their food." Shoveling it in. Pot roast and meat gravy on the mashed potatoes. Plenty of pepper but no garlic. Every time Beverly used garlic it came through her pores for days.

175

"You should have seen ol' Mark tossin' those bales." Lewis laughed. "You know, down on the east end of that field it's a little sparse, so I put her in high range and the bales came humpin' out of the chute and Mark was jumpin' around back there on that wagon like a, like a . . . kangaroo."

"They were coming quick." Mark was shoveling food in no better than Lewis. Beverly thought Mark had had better table manners when he first came to her house. Then, he didn't eat any more than a bird.

Beverly brought out some gingerbread and took the Cool Whip out of the fridge. "You know, Lewis," she said, "the Stevensons have a Jersey heifer that'll be freshening in August. If we were to have a cow again, I'd milk her and there'd be plenty of good milk for the baby."

Earnest. Penny leaned forward. "Ma, I told you I mean to breast feed."

"Well, you aren't going to breast feed forever," Beverly snapped. In her day only poor folks breast fed their infants. Beverly blushed for her daughter.

Softly, Lewis said, "If you're interested, I could just go down and take a look at that cow."

"Never mind. Penny says she don't care." Spoken hotter than she meant to.

"Well, it would be nice to have real whipped cream again," Lewis said, examining the tines of his fork.

"If we don't need milk for the baby, a cow's too much to fool with," Beverly said. "Are you done with that gingerbread?"

Lewis scraped his chair back. Tossed his wadded paper

napkin beside the plate. "I guess I'll go take a look at the mastitis ewes," he said.

"I'll want to take a shower before we leave," Mark said. He checked his worn wallet. The bills he counted were mostly singles. "Penny," he said, "how about a movie afterward?"

Though the pregnancy had overfilled her body, Penny's eyes were more beautiful than ever—whites like new china, the blues of blue sapphires. "I don't know. I get so tired. I was up at six this morning with Stink. She's ready to trial. She's so eager, she wears me out."

Lewis out the door. Mark in the shower. Penny in her bedroom collecting the notebook and diaper materials for her class.

Four plates, four dessert plates, two coffee cups, two glasses for ice tea, silverware and pots. Beverly washed. The pot roast to the refrigerator. Plenty of meat for noontime tomorrow. The mashed potatoes were a waste. Wished there was something she could do with them but Lewis didn't care for potato cakes and Beverly never baked potato bread.

She slipped a scrap of pot roast to the Stink Dog who'd come from behind the stove with a purposeful grin.

Once the kitchen was clean, Beverly turned on the TV set. The evening news. She left the sound off. There was plenty in this world she didn't need to know. The pictures showed numbed civilians picking through the ruins of an airstrike. Some country, today. Beverly poured herself a glass of ice tea though she didn't want it.

Mark and Penny were running late. Their VW putted

off down the road and Beverly winced for Penny when they crossed that rough spot by the culvert.

Beverly Burkholder poured her ice tea back in the pitcher and rinsed her glass. She did something she did maybe twice a year and poured herself a glass of beer. One thing she didn't like about beer was once you opened it you had to drink the whole bottle or it'd go flat.

The beers were Mark's but Beverly didn't think he'd mind if she took just one.

When she went out to the screened front porch, she carried a magazine as well as her beer.

The frogs were beginning to chirp. Tiny things, most of them not much bigger than your thumbnail.

She thumbed through the *McCall's* magazine but nothing caught her eye. She set it on the white wicker table. That table had been Lewis's mother's. Idly, Beverly pulled open the drawer. The curled paper of pins she found sent a chill down her back like the woman, dead these fifteen years, had spoken to her. The grass in the front yard needed mowing. The lilac, done blooming, needed pruning before it made buds for next year. So much to do. So very much to do. Beverly Burkholder sipped at the beer and licked foam off her upper lip, neat as a cat.

She heard the water running as Lewis scrubbed up. Mastitis is one of the smelly diseases.

"Nice evening," he ventured. After a bit he noted, "I'm gonna save both sides on that whiteface. She raises two big lambs every year and I'd hate to cull her."

"You don't want to keep any ewe who can't raise

twins," Beverly lectured him. "Here," she said. "I can't drink all this."

Lewis smiled his smile. He said, "It's not like you, Beverly," and took the bottle. "I guess the boys at the fire department won't mind if I show up with beer on my breath." He laughed. "A few of them will have six-packs in their car."

Beverly did not like Lewis's new smile. She thought it was long-suffering, all-accepting, generous, humorless, full of love and completely passionless. She said, "The fire department again, tonight?"

"You know we're putting a new tank in the Seagrave pumper. Now that we got the old one out, we might as well sand right down to the metal and repaint it."

"That's three nights this week, Lewis. I suppose you're going to have Mama and Daddy over for Sunday dinner?"

"Sure. You know how happy they are about the baby."

"Lewis, Mama never cared about anything beyond her own front door in her whole life and Daddy is tight as an old man's bowels. Why do you think I ran away with you, Lewis? Why do you think I married you?"

So Lewis sat down. And now he took a good drink from his beer. "I don't have much time before I have to leave," he said.

"That's all right. I know how busy you are."

"If I don't go up there, Mike Pearson and his brother will do all the work. I hate to have other men doing my work."

"I said I know how busy you are!"

"Maybe if I call, I can catch Mike before he leaves

home. I guess they can get along without me once." He laid down his jacket on the back of his seat.

"Go if you have to!" Beverly said. Beverly had a way of making one last circle around things once they'd been decided.

She could hear him on the phone, explaining. Why should he have to explain? Other men missed one fire department work session after another and never called to explain. Why should Lewis explain?

"Ol' Mike Pearson wasn't much pleased." That same smile. "I told him he'd just have to handle it by himself. He said you shouldn't forget, the ladies auxiliary is making plans for a chicken barbecue opening day of trout season. Betty Pearson wants you to call."

Beverly sighed. "Well, there's another afternoon wasted."

"You're touchy tonight."

"How would you know. You haven't spent an hour alone in my company in weeks."

The frogs chirped. The humans were silent. Stink scratched on the door and Lewis got up to let her out. Playing to her audience, Stink rolled around and rushed back and forth showing diligence in sniffing.

"Stink looks good."

"You know Penny entered Stink in the Bluegrass?"

Lewis's forehead showed mild surprise. "Good for Penny. I don't expect Stink'll do much, but it'll be good for Penny to run her."

"And Nop. Penny didn't want to. I entered Nop myself." That knocked the saintly smile off Lewis's face in quite a satisfactory manner. Next instant, Beverly was overtaken by remorse. "It's only thirty dollars entry fee, Lewis. It seemed important that somebody show a little faith." She touched his arm. She might as well have been touching a block of wood.

"Nop's dead," Lewis said. Both words took enough space for full sentences. "Thinking Nop was alive made me the biggest fool I ever been. I hurt people because of that dog, Beverly. Ignored Mark, ignored my own daughter, Penny, ignored this farm—which is the only thing puts food on our table—ignored the fire department. Beverly, I feel real strong about this. After that business out in Ohio, I took a good long look at myself and I didn't much like what I saw. I'd come to value that dog too much, Beverly, and it wasn't the dog I was valuing so much as I was my own pride. That dog was going to make me a big man. Two in a row at the Bluegrass Trials. First with Stink and then, one year later, with Nop. Oh, I was full of myself, I was. I was wrong, Beverly. I thought I was right, but I was wrong." He swirled the beer around in the bottle and set it down without drinking. "It's gone flat," he announced.

In a voice younger than her years, Beverly asked, "How about me?"

Lewis said, "If Penny wants to run Stink in the Bluegrass, that's fine. But I want you to write them and tell them Nop is dead and gone and he won't be running in the Bluegrass or any other place."

"Lewis, we haven't been together as man and wife since you came back from Ohio."

181

Lewis Burkholder was so disappointed. She didn't understand him, didn't understand the Big Lesson he'd learned either. He repeated his confession, watching her face, hoping to catch himself when he began to go wrong. He didn't care for a woman drinking beer. There was something sloppy about it. He concluded, "And I was driving my own pregnant daughter and her chosen husband out of the house."

"Lewis"—she shook her head—"you weren't that bad."

"Sometimes I think the best thing ever happened to me was losing that dog. Losing that dog was bettern' losing Mark and Penny. You know what Mark said to me the other day? He said he was real happy on the farm and he wished his brother, Scottie, could see it once. I told you about Scottie."

"Yes, Lewis. Lewis, when was the last time we went dancing?"

He thought. "Oh, it wasn't so very long ago. Not so long ago."

"Lewis, would you bring me another beer?"

"Beverly, I'm not sure Mark's gonna like you guzzling all his beers."

Her eyes gave him all the answer he was likely to get. He counted the beers in the fridge, four left. Even if Beverly drank them all, they wouldn't do her too much harm. He tried to think if Beverly had ever been "high." One time, when they were on their honeymoon, in a little Italian restaurant in West Virginia. Bottle of red wine. Big old streaky candle. Red checked oilcloth for a tablecloth. The food hadn't been much, but the red wine had been sweet as her lips and . . . "Here." He handed her the bottle uncomfortably.

She looked at him, nibbling the inside corner of her mouth. "Maybe you should go to the firehouse, Lewis," she said.

"By God, maybe I will." Proud as a schoolboy, he snatched his jacket and marched to his pickup and roared off and all four wheels left the ground for a moment at the rough spot near the culvert.

"Changed my mind." That was what he said to Mike Pearson, all he said. And then he kept them at it until they had the tank well scraped and sanded though it took until well past eleven o'clock, about an hour later than Mike had wanted to work.

"That's got it," Lewis said. And jumped in his truck and roared home as fast as he'd come.

There were a few things he had to say, but Beverly's pillow was gone from the bedroom and her reading spectacles and glass of water too.

Every night, before they retired, they each took vitamin C tabs because Beverly thought they were good medicine. Lewis made jokes about them. No vitamin C's lying on the night table tonight.

Lewis went into the front room. Beverly was all wrapped up on the couch. He put his hands on his hips. There were a lot of things he might have said.

He slept badly, tossing and turning in sheets Beverly should have changed twice a week instead of once a week like she did.

When the sun came up, Lewis rose from the bed that had been as uncomfortable as any he'd known. Snatched his jacket and rubber boots and started down the winding lane that ended at the river. The wild irises in the ditch were ready to open. The wild irises were smaller than the ones Beverly cultivated but more vivid. He left dark green tracks along the grassy path. A red-winged blackbird jumped up in a flurry and Lewis paused to see if he could spot her nest.

The farm was better for his having worked it. Isn't that enough to ask of a man—that three hundred acres of the earth flourish under his hand?

The Stink Dog chased after him. Penny must have let her out. The speeding dog knocked dew off the grass heads, casting a perfect rooster tail of exploded droplets behind her.

She still ran funny. Like it hurt her.

"Stink! Go home! Get back! Get back, darn you! Go home!"

He had to shout again each time she paused for another backward glance, but Stink obeyed and Lewis was alone. Just like he liked it. Fool dog ruined his walk. The river was mud brown, carrying the lifestuff of the upstream pastures. The raw smell smelled like an open grave. A dead bird tumbling, hung up on a snag, rotating, bobbing. A wood duck, with brown-and-white speckled breast— nature's bounty, freely given.

The smoke column from the kitchen chimney was straight and strong. He hesitated, but said the heck with it and went to get a bucket of grain. This morning he'd take some steers to market. At least he'd be off the farm.

Eight good young five-hundred-pound steers. They'd

bring top dollar from farmers who'd pasture them over the summer and resell them at the state graded sales in the fall.

"Soo, soo!" And he rattled the grain bucket and called. One of them raised his head for a moment before resuming grazing. They didn't care for grain this morning, thank you.

Lewis could have gone in and got Stink, but he'd promised that he'd never work her again and, by God, he was a man who kept his promises!

When he went out to the left, the steers moseyed right. When he came up close, they'd split to one side or the other. Like all young steers, they loved to run. Like all farmers, Lewis didn't.

After forty-five minutes, they were lathered and he was sucking for air. Twice, he almost got them in the chute before one animal broke and the others followed the escapee's lead. He swore. He threw stones.

When Mark came out to help, Lewis hollered at him too. "Over to the left! Head that red steer. Don't you know livestock at all? Pay attention!"

Heart pounding, breath coming in gasps, Lewis closed the gate on the animals and sagged against the gatepost. Mark looked like he meant to say something. By God, he better not! Not a word!

"I'll get the gooseneck."

"When you back up, give the wheel a little turn so the trailer comes uphill."

"I've loaded cows before."

"Have you now?"

Lewis flogged the frightened animals aboard with a nylon stockwhip, popping its tassel at their ears.

The exhaust burbled under the pickup like fog.

Mark stood at the window. "You want any company?"

"It only takes one man to get these steers to market and only one man to unload them. I'd thank you to get something done on the line fence."

Mark scratched his head. Probably he was thinking that digging postholes in rocky ground would make a bad day.

Lewis ate at the little luncheonette at the livestock market. He talked to men he knew. He waited for the auction. He got eighty-two cents a pound for his steers and remembered when he'd let good steers go for twenty. He saw spirited bidding on an orphan lamb someone had brought in. Bleating. Dashing about. That was something he didn't like about the livestock market—the two-day-old calves and the great big old cows, down on their feet so they had to unload with electric prods. Man who'd use a cow until she couldn't walk before bringing her to market. Lewis couldn't see much in that sort of man.

He drank several more cups of coffee than was his custom. He spoke to a few men he knew and was introduced to some he didn't.

The first half of the way home he drove very fast, the second half slower. When he turned into his own road, he was creeping along.

Beverly was in the kitchen. "Where's Mark and Penny?" he asked.

"They went on into Strasburg."

"Two movie nights in a row?"

"Lewis, I asked them to go."

Heavily, he sat at the Formica table. He twirled his cap between his hands. DEKALB SEEDS. That was the legend on his cap. "Got a pretty good price for the steers today," he said.

She had her back to him, wiping the stove. Her shoulders shook.

"Oh hey! Hey! Don't cry, Beverly."

And he put his hands on her shoulders, just like he had every right to comfort her.

"Lewis, I've missed you. Lewis, what's to become of us?"

"I been right here, honey."

Dabbing at her eyes with a paper towel. Blew her nose a good honk. She was awful embarrassed and her smile trembled. "I'll be fine," she said. "Just fine."

And Lewis was shamefaced and all thumbs. He hitched an awkward shoulder, "I'm sorry Beverly. I shouldn't have run off last night the way I did."

"Oh, it wasn't that," she said. "I just hate to see you give up hope."

"I haven't given up hope for us."

She turned half away. "Lewis, when I heard you coming down the road, I put It in. You know."

He kissed away her salty tears.

She was the one to lead the way into their bedroom. She faced away from him while she undressed, just like she always did. When she caught him looking at her, she blushed.

"I never seen such a one as you," he said, softly.

She tossed back the coverlets and slicked under and tucked the covers up to her neck.

"Your hands are cold," he said, chafing them between his own. Her long back curved against his belly, her dear shoulders. The freckles just below the tip of her collar bone. He kissed her there. The skin tasted good.

Suddenly, she turned around to face him. "What do you mean, you never seen such a one as me?" she demanded. "You said you saw Mary Beth Rivercomb like this. You said the two of you, you did this."

"How long ago?"

"Seems like yesterday to me. I'd sit there in that old schoolroom watching the two of you mooning over each other. Darn, it'd make me mad. Her giving you the coweye."

"She never did have no breasts to speak of," Lewis said, holding Beverly's with both hands.

"You said she had a pretty . . . behind!" she accused. Her breath was a little quicker and her hands around his back, why, they were warm enough.

"Oh, it wasn't too bad."

"Lewis, you haven't seen another woman since you and me hitched up? On all those trips, hauling the stock, you never looked at anyone else?"

"Um," he said. "Nothing wrong with your behind. Or up front either."

"Lewis. You tell me the truth. Don't . . ."

"Beverly, there never has been anyone but you."

"That'd be all right then." And she spread her legs and

pulled him over on top of her and, once more, they became man and wife.

They had a scandalous good time, completely wasted the long spring evening, and when Penny and Mark came home, oh, it must have been after ten o'clock, they pretended they were already asleep.

Next morning, first thing, Lewis went outside and fired up the John Deere. He got his greasegun, a couple spare filters, a plastic tube of bearing grease and as soon as the oil was warm, he shut her down and opened the drain plug.

Mark came out, barefoot, tin cup of coffee in his hand. He hadn't bothered to button his shirt which hung open as a vest. "You sure know how to make a racket," he said.

"Sun's up, ain't it? It's gonna be a pretty day. Look at that. No clouds. You can hand me that oil spigot if you're tired of doing nothing."

"You gonna have some breakfast?"

Lewis punched the spigot into the oil can and inverted it. "You know," he said, "I had myself convinced that the whole search was foolishness—that Doug Whitenaur was an innocent man. Somebody stole my dog and I'm sure that it was Whitenaur that did it. You get anywhere on that fence yesterday?"

They worked on the equipment all morning, readying it for the next time it'd go into the field. And the morning was just as Lewis had predicted, and over supper of ham, brown beans, coleslaw and hot biscuits, Lewis complimented Penny on the work she'd done with Stink. "She's still got a bad hitch in her stride, but she's running free now. Maybe I'll try her out this evening."

Beverly laughed. "Lewis, Stink is Penny's dog now. Why don't you get a dog of your own?"

His coffee cup just halted on its way to his lips. He put it down. "I suppose that's good sense. I suppose I could buy me a started dog. Yesterday, those steers tore me every which way but loose."

Penny said that he could get a pup if he wanted. Stink could handle the farmwork until the puppy was trained.

Lewis said he wouldn't want to have a new puppy. Not just yet. He'd get him a year-old dog, one that knew its flanking commands and could fetch but wasn't ready to start driving. A year-old dog would be best.

The phone rang. "Lewis, it's for you." Beverly covered the mouthpiece. "Long distance. It's Ethel Harwood."

"Hello, Ethel. How you been?"

"Lewis, I'm down here in Pike Road, Alabama. The Alabama State Trials."

"Uh-huh. Any good runs?"

"So far it looks like Ralph Pulfer has it with that Shep dog of his. John Bauserman's still to run and Lewis Pence, but Shep's going to be hard to beat. Lewis, the reason I'm calling—I just heard you lost your Nop dog."

"That was months ago. Before the New Year, Ethel. He . . ."

"I just heard it today. Bill Dillard told me. I thought it was just a coincidence at the time. I thought I saw Nop but couldn't be sure and I was darn sure you wouldn't sell him to a rodeo if you wouldn't sell him to me. He had one of his ears broke down like he'd been in a fight and a nasty scar on his leg but he had the little tufts of brown behind his ears. I thought about it afterward and I was sure it was him."

Lewis's throat closed like he was choking.

"Lewis? You still there? I was at the National Quarter-horse Show in Oklahoma City. May tenth, 'twas. Your dog, Nop, was in the rodeo there. I'm not mistaken, you know. Nop. I'm not about to forget the best stockdog I ever saw."

A Love Knot

Fourteen years is a very old Border Collie. Their lives are faster than ours, and their memories are faster too. It had been just six months since Grady Gumm took Nop from Burkholder's farm. Sometimes a scent or a motion or the color of a leaf would remind Nop of his lost life and then he'd feel a pang of sadness, but he never knew why he felt the pangs or what they meant.

That night in Sioux Falls spelled finish to Nop's career as a rodeo star. T. T. Raines dragged him out of the arena by his collar and his feet barely touched the ground and the world faded in and out in the rushing of his blood. Nop scarcely felt the blows or the parting kick that lifted him into his cage. "Get in there, you worthless . . ." Nop managed to bare his teeth and T.T. booted the wire cage, in case Nop doubted his anger.

But T.T. was no more willing to lose his meal ticket than the next man and, next morning, despite jibes from other cowboys, he returned Nop and Festus to the arena again. The monkey jabbered with fear. Nop showed teeth. His ruff stood up and a growl rolled around in his throat. When T.T. laid into him, "to teach him a lesson he'll not soon forget," Nop snarled at T.T. and, if it hadn't been for the choke chain, who knows what he would have done.

T.T. was no longer pack leader. T.T. had no more right to order him around than any other cur. Nop would have died before he let that monkey on his back again. T.T. tried. He beat the dog and the monkey too, but Nop was stubborn and the monkey was no more willing than the dog.

Good Ol' Red felt a little guilty about the cap pistols, which T.T. might not have thought of on his own, but the economy being the way it is, he offered T.T. a job peddling peanuts and beer.

A pet store downtown gave T.T. twenty-five dollars for the monkey.

"You're lucky I don't shoot you in the head," T.T. informed Nop as he dragged him into the animal shelter.

The woman volunteer behind the counter sighed. The dog was an older animal and had been in some nasty fights. Worse, he resisted his lead and growled.

"He's a Border Collie, Mr. Raines?"

"Yes, ma'am."

"Are you sure you want to leave him with us? Have you tried to find him a home yourself?"

"Lady, I'm with the rodeo. I don't know anybody in Sioux Falls."

Nop's feet found no purchase on the linoleum floor. Colors: blue-gray linoleum, light blue walls. The desk towering over his head was unpainted plywood. Odors:

Lysol, urine, feces and fear. The fear smell was so strong it made his eyes water.

"The reason I ask, Mr. Raines—an older dog like this one—we aren't always able to place them for adoption. Most people wish to adopt a puppy. Many of the older dogs—well—they have to be put to sleep."

What the volunteer might have said is that ninety percent of the older dogs were destroyed. A hundred percent of the shy dogs or frightened dogs or those who growled or bared their teeth. They kept animals five days before one of the volunteers gave the injection.

Nop had supported T. T. Raines for two months, asking nothing in return but a dry place to sleep and a little dogfood. When T.T. looked at Nop, he pictured himself passing a cup of beer up the aisles and spilling sticky beer on his wrists. Sometimes human memory is not much longer than a dog's.

The volunteer made a note on her form. "Does he have papers? Sometimes it helps if a dog has papers."

"Naw. He's just a mutt."

Stubbornly, Nop dragged against his steel lead, choking himself, gagging.

"And what shall I put down for your reason?"

"Reason?"

"Why must you leave your dog with us?"

"Uh. I'm allergic to him. Thought I wasn't, but by God, I'm sure allergic to this dog."

The volunteer wrote the word. "You've been to a doctor then?"

"A doctor?"

194

"For allergies. You went to a dermatologist?"

"Naw. It's him all right."

"Quite often people think they're allergic to their pets when it's something else—simple hay fever, perhaps a dust allergy."

T.T. scratched under his arm. Grinning, he scratched his crotch. "I'm allergic," he said.

"I see. We'll do what we can."

"You can keep the leash and collar," T.T. said magnanimously. "I got no further use for them."

"Yes." When the volunteer took the lead, Nop dropped to his belly, tail tucked underneath.

"I hope you can give us a donation," she said. "Our suggested donation is five dollars. It goes toward their food."

T.T. had drawn his last Buckaroos' check. There wouldn't be any more where that came from. "Lady," he said, "you know what I do for a living? I sell beer and peanuts. Do I look like a man with money to burn?"

And so the volunteer took Nop back to his cage. He walked beside her willingly enough and went inside without protest. The volunteer owned four dogs of her own: two Golden Retrievers, a Lhasa Apso and a mutt. She hardened her heart against Nop's brown eyes.

Nop retired to the very back of his cage and closed his eyes. For hours he dreamt and sometimes his legs would twitch as he gathered woolies on the green fields of his mind.

The cages were separate and the shelter had no common run, so Nop never got to meet any of the other dogs.

Every hour or so, one desperate Schnauzer barked an alarm call, "Someone near the house! Intruder! Help! Help!" The Schnauzer's bark had the precise effect of a burglar alarm on a Sunday afternoon on a deserted street, going on and on. After two days, the Schnauzer had his injection and the shelter was quieter.

People came in to search for lost pets or to adopt a pet. The shelter had several puppy litters and most people headed straight for the cute wriggly things.

If a farmer had come in looking for a dog, the shelter would have directed him to Nop, but no farmer came.

Three days. Adequate food was provided but none of the dogs had much appetite. The cages were kept clean.

Nop stayed in the very back of his cage with his nose between his paws. Like the other dogs he always knew when people came into the shelter. Some of the dogs whined or ran back and forth or barked a welcome. Some dogs pushed their paws through the mesh, trying to make contact. Nop lay quiet.

The face that stopped before his cage was a child's face. They looked at each other for a long while before Nop gave a tentative wag of his tail.

Two faces outside the mesh. The boy's father peered into the gloom. "No, Timmy, not this one."

"But, Daddy, he likes me."

"Look at his eyes. You see how they glow? This dog has vicious eyes. Come look at the puppies."

Nop's tail went still.

On the fourth day of Nop's stay at the shelter, T. T. Raines got a phone call. T.T. was then in New Jersey where the rodeo was booked into a vast sports coliseum.

T.T. took the call in the office. He was wearing his apron and little paper cap.

Mr. Doug Whitenaur said he'd seen the Littlest Buckaroos on TV and wondered if the dog—after that unfortunate incident—maybe he was for sale?

T. T. Raines thought.

Mr. Doug Whitenaur said the dog reminded him of a real good dog he'd seen once. Dog belonged to a man called Grady Gumm.

"I'll be damned." Though T.T. had mixed feelings about Grady, the mention of his name put things on a more familiar plane. "That's the dog. That was ol' Grady's dog before he sold him to me. Look, I'll tell you true. I ain't got the dog with me this minute. I got somebody, uh, takin' care of him for me. How much you thinkin' of payin'?"

Doug Whitenaur thought he'd pay as much as two hundred dollars for the dog.

"Two fifty." Damn, T.T. was havin' a bit of *good* luck for a change.

"I'll wire the money. You get the dog out to the airport and there'll be a ticket for him."

T.T. laughed. "I never heard of no dog riding an airplane. Soon as I get my two hundred fifty dollars I'll call my friends and have them take the dog to the plane. Send the ticket to the Sioux Falls airport."

The director of the shelter didn't care for T.T.'s long-distance adoption, but the volunteer argued. T.T. was the original owner and, she added, "The dog's already been here four full days."

"Oh my. Oh dear." The director put his hand to his

mouth. Like the other volunteers, he liked the dogs he so often had to put to death.

"Mr. Whitenaur handles Border Collies at trials. Mr. Raines said that about him."

The shelter director seized on that bit of evidence with relief. "Very well then. Would you . . . I'm afraid we have no way to get him to the airport."

Nop rode quietly on the floorboards. This woman was not his master but she was capable and he would obey. He trotted beside her into the terminal, oblivious to the passengers, all the new sights and sounds, and lay at her feet at the ticket desk until she got things straight.

The clerk brought out a molded plastic crate and Nop entered through the little chrome-plated door and it was latched behind him.

The clerk set it on the luggage belt. Nop whined when he started moving in a way he'd never moved before. The cage brushed through a heavy curtain and tipped and slid down the chute into a big room full of other luggage but no other dogs.

At the bottom the crate tottered but ended upright. Other suitcases clattered on top of it and Nop lost much of his vision when a red two-suiter blocked the door. He scratched at the metal.

Noises—motors—tractor motors, the whine of electric forklifts, the whine of rubber wheels.

He was swooped into the air and set on a baggage cart. The jerk dropped him on his haunches.

He heard roars, men's voices, a tremendous thundering sound. He smelled rubber and scorched kerosene.

The volunteer watched from the observation deck as

the luggage was lifted into the belly of the airliner. She raised a hand in farewell. "Good luck, doggy." If people who loved animals didn't man the shelters, who would? That was her thought as she turned away.

Nop's flight was loud, terrifying, uneventful; buried in the dark beneath the baggage of Flight 167 he flew from Sioux Falls to Cincinnati.

He had a tough time keeping his feet on the spinning baggage carousel and sprawled when someone jerked him roughly to the floor.

A face pressed right against the door of the crate. "You *are* him," the man said. "You're Nop!"

Nop's ears perked at the sound of his own name but his eyes were blank as mirrors. Border Collies give affection easily, but he'd seen a few things.

Leaving the airport, Doug Whitenaur drove too fast. Whitenaur felt happy and godlike. The two best stockdogs in America and he owned them both! He wouldn't be able to trial Nop (the trial world was too small), but that squarehead, Burkholder, wouldn't be trialing him either.

Owning him would be enough. Keeping him out of competition. "Like," Doug said, "a dog in the manger," and laughed and pounded the steering wheel. Somewhat off key, he sang: "And nothing can stop the Army Air Corps." Pounded the wheel again. He was halfway home, speeding down the Strip, when a thought occurred to him.

Slid into the parking lot beside Billy's Temptation and clipped Nop to a steel lead. Nop followed him inside, well mannered but dubious. Hack and Sandy were gone somewhere. Toledo, someone said. Billy, the owner, was genuinely offended Doug brought a dog in his place. Billy thought Whitenaur was showing great disrespect.

Billy's anger made Nop very nervous and he might have bitten the owner if Whitenaur hadn't snubbed him up tight.

Getting 86'd from Billy's Temptation drained every bit of pleasure from Whitenaur's coup. What use was this dog if he couldn't brag about it?

He could breed Nop and Bit O' Scot. Though he could never run the dog, he could run the bitch and her puppies. He'd send the most promising pups out to Jack Knox in Wisconsin or Bill Crowe in Virginia or maybe to Bruce Fogt. Whitenaur was no trainer, he was a handler. He belched. His stomach was full of gas.

He pushed Nop into the kennel right next to Bit O' Scot. He didn't think to put out food before he left and the only water was rain water that stagnated in the gutters. The water looked awful and smelled worse but Nop was very thirsty.

The bitch pressed against the chain-link fence that formed their common boundary.

Like many breeds, Border Collies are great snobs and prefer their kind to any other. Nop smiled. He sniffed. He dropped into the invitation-to-play.

Her ruff was blue merle. Both her ears lay flat along her skull. Her tail was fluffier than Nop's and her eyes were sweet dark brown. She laughed at him and made a mock lunge.

Nop's tail curled over his back and he forgot. Forgot

fear, anger, exhaustion. His spinning brain slowed to a stop.

"Thou art she," he said, panting with joy.

"Thou art fool," she replied, tossing her head disdainfully. She then sniffed at a dark spot on the floor. What an interesting spot! How rich in fascination!

Nop sat slack-jawed with disappointment.

Bit O' Scot ("Bit") was a long-bodied bitch. Her chest was not as broad as Nop's; she was built more sleekly. The tip of her tail was blue merle.

She extracted every iota of interest from her feigned fascination and put her nose to the wire.

Two dark wet noses touched and Nop lost his heart.

Her scent was rich with new and good things, redolent of her warm heart, her joy in her own speed. She withdrew and licked at her flank. So glossy! So neat!

Nop marched to the far corner of his kennel, without taking his eyes off Bit. He hoisted his leg against the stanchion, somewhat more jerkily than he'd intended because it had been a long plane ride.

They had no bones or toys in the kennels and this afternoon, like so many others, there wouldn't be any food either.

"Dost thou work woolies?" Nop asked. He'd not seen her that day, so long ago, at Innisfree.

"I do. I chase them about. They do as I wish, even the rams. In my home country my master was Jock but I was sold and my master is Douglas. I wish I was back in my home country."

"Dost thou work woolies, work woolies, work wool-

ies?" Nop had no word for many. He knew the difference
between herding a great flock of sheep and working three
sheep at a trial but had no word for his understanding.

"The master has no woolies. I travel to woolies. When
I do work well, Douglas gives me food. When I do badly,
he puts his hands to me and hurts."

"Oh, I will work woolies too," Nop said, happily, because there was no way he could understand Whitenaur's intent to never work him again. If a dog is trained
to work woolies, why, working woolies is its work and a
dog must do its work; that was how Nop thought. Sometimes he was much too direct for the world he inhabited.

Until recently, Whitenaur had owned two stockdogs:
Bit and another imported dog, Sweep. Sweep was a red
dog. He'd been a brace champion in Scotland.

In brace trials, two dogs are worked at once, like a
mirror image. Until Sweep's arrival in this country, Whitenaur hadn't known that the dog was trained to reverse
commands. For Sweep, "come by" meant "go right" instead of "go left." Thus, with one command two dogs
would go out on both sides of the sheep. Whitenaur didn't
have patience to work the reverse commands or retrain
Sweep. He fooled with him for a month or two, placed
badly in a couple trials and sold him for half what he'd
paid for him.

"I only keep winners," he said at the time.

Sweep's buyer—who was about to own a brace champion for less than two thousand dollars—said, "We'll see
what we can do with him. Perhaps I can work with reverse commands."

"Better you than me," Whitenaur sneered.

And Sweep's purchaser agreed but bit his tongue.

Sweep and Bit had been kennel mates and when the big friendly dog was taken away, Bit sorrowed for days.

Now, despite her show of indifference, she was de-lighted to have a pal again. Perhaps they couldn't nip and race around each other, but they could lie side by side and doze and commune.

She wasn't alone anymore.

In the next few days, Whitenaur came out to the kennels frequently. He spent time admiring the two animals and, by extension, his own ruthless cleverness.

Whitenaur enjoyed the symbol more than the fact. He never was genuinely fond of his dogs.

Nop and Bit loafed through the long drowsy days and once in a great while an insect came into the cage and they'd chase it with great ferocity, and once a black wasp stung Bit and after she killed it, angrily, she licked at her sore paw for an hour and complained bitterly about the pain.

They attended to the few noises that drifted to the ken-nels from the suburban street. At night they watched the halo that glowed over the distant city.

It rained and cleaned the runs. Twice Doug Whitenaur hosed the kennels down.

They lay side by side, on each side of the heavy mesh.

One morning Bit woke before her habitual time and began to pace.

"What worries thee?"

She snapped right back at him. "It is none of thy con-cern, dog." She sat and licked her vulva.

She was restless and snappish and kept herself extremely

clean. Nop had never bred before but the smell from the next kennel took him by the nose. He drooled. He pressed against the wire mesh. He invented conversations but forgot what he meant. "How lovely is thy tail, thy black nose, thy . . . What a stud dog am I, that chases woolies, I . . . Thy teeth, how sharp, how able to crush the large bones of thine enemies . . ."

And she'd snap at him when she was too greatly annoyed and Nop would retreat, quite abashed, quite chagrined. "Thou art cruel."

"Thou ruffian, why should I not be cruel? Thy manners and thy fur, they both offend me."

That evening when Doug Whitenaur came by to feed he was wearing blue velour pants and a light yellow ruffled shirt. "Well now," he said. "Well now. The two best stockdogs in America."

Though there was no guarantee that their pups would be special, the odds were good. When he stepped inside Bit's cage, she was so pleased she jumped up, muddying his pants legs and he smacked her down hard, a reflex. She cowered and an angry Nop hurled himself at the chain link.

"Maybe you'd like a beating?" Whitenaur inquired, savagely. "Maybe you'd like to feel my hand?"

Nop growled. Bit whimpered and cowered away.

It was Nop's lucky day. Doug Whitenaur was due at a party in forty minutes—his family again—and now he'd have to change clothes. "Just you wait," he threatened.

The entire incident flew right out of Whitenaur's mind and, though he was slow to feed the next day, he didn't beat either dog and, in fact, inspected Bit to see how far along she was in her heat.

Bit's scent was driving Nop crazy. Her aroma was perfectly delicious, familiar, unfamiliar and exotic. It befuddled him. No more did he pounce on the insects that happened into his run. The loudest street noises didn't penetrate. He was quite carried away.

He thought of tall cool rooms with plush pillows. He thought of spring grass before it was cut for hay, when to stand in it was to be blind in a green world. For the first time in months he thought of his mother's nipples, so white and supple and how they felt when he nursed and pushed at them with his feet, a perfect little eating machine.

The heat cycle takes twenty-one days. The bitch will accept the male dog for four of those days.

One morning Doug Whitenaur came into Nop's kennel, grabbed his collar and dragged him in with Bit.

Bit was on Nop in a flash, snarling and nipping.

He went over on his back, presenting his belly. He wagged his tail when he thought it wouldn't offend too greatly.

Whitenaur stayed for just a moment. He had more important things to do than watch dogs mate.

He left them together.

For several days Bit was as kind as Ivan the Terrible, nipping Nop when he came near, flying at him for the slightest provocation. He tried to play and sometimes he could intrigue her into a romp for a moment but, quickly, she'd lose interest and lick herself or slash at him and push him into the farthest corner of the run.

Neither of them ate very much though both were terribly thirsty. Nop sprinkled his urine all over the shared kennel, creating a wall from his own body through which no bad magic could come.

Much of the time she ignored him, treating him like he was a nondog, like he was a crude, overlarge object placed in her kennel by mistake. She even objected when he sniffed at her fresh urine. She'd rush on him growling until he retreated.

Nop admired her so. Her silky fur, her grace, her perfume, the gay set of her tail. His brain was slack and helpless. They rarely spoke. Their present preoccupation was too rich for talk.

Nop became erratic. In sparse droplets he urinated incessantly. He invited play. He feigned indifference.

One morning she woke him with a nudge of her nose. Nop rose and made the obeisance to the dog god with which he started every day.

She wagged her tail. She grinned. Her brown eyes were full of fun. Before he was quite awake, she nipped him on the very tip of his tender nose, turned and ran.

He bounced after her. Her scent had been musky, slightly acrid and hot. This morning it was clear as a distant church bell. She was what she was. Nop pranced around her, high on his toes, like a dancer. His shoulder bumped her and, wonder of wonders, this morning she did not bite him or growl or insult him. "Thou art he," she said.

How Nop pranced! How they circled! When he rolled her over in their rough and tumble, she allowed him to grasp her by the ruff and allowed too his dominant growl.

She got up, feigned indifference, thumped idly at her ear with her foot and Nop circled; something to be done, something to be done. He wrapped his forelegs around her and hugged her.

She threw off his embrace. "Thou fool," she said, but there was no sting in her words.

His circlings grew narrower and quicker. His tongue lolled. She held her tail to one side, exposing herself as if by accident. He embraced her and slipped back when she turned. He hugged her around her ribs and she simply walked away, dropping him onto his forepaws. He growled but she ignored him.

Again she stood, again he hugged her and his loins moved precisely.

Bit grunted. She panted. She grunted again.

As his excitement grew, he knew less and less until he totally became dog instinct—not the specific instinct bred into stockdog but the ancient instinct that guides the Miniature Poodle and the Great Dane alike. Nop was witless in the power of his brilliant instinct.

Nop became her mate, fastened himself upon her, created the tie.

While his dogs mated, Whitenaur was having a glass of champagne down at Billy's Temptation. A couple regulars had got hitched and the joint was closed for the reception. Drapes were drawn across the front window. The sign on the door said PRIVATE PARTY.

Toasts were drunk to regulars who'd moved to New York or the Coast. Epic drunks and epic feuds were remembered fondly. Like the holidays—when regulars brought kids into the joint—the reception transformed an ordinary gin mill into something rather more important —a club, a loyalty, a community, a better family than one's own blood.

Someone said, wonderingly, "There's people here I never saw in daylight before."

Hack was at the bar banging down free champagne.

Sandy was circulating, putting his arm around the men, hugging the women. He never got too close to Hack; Doug noticed that. "Howdy," Sandy said and plunked himself down and his champagne glass was untouched— Whitenaur noticed that too.

Doug was feeling light and fast and very much on top of things. He was in the know. "Didn't go well in Toledo?" he asked.

Sandy made the same kind of face Hack made when his stomach was bothering him. "Buy me a drink," he said.

And Doug said, "Sure," and popped his fingers and, surprised, a waitress came right over.

When Sandy had his Chivas (rocks, water back), he said, "Better times," and upended it.

Doug wanted to hear about Toledo, but Sandy started an involved tale about some businessman he knew ("He's straight, honest to God. Pays quarterly taxes, everything") who needed a loan ("Just a little cash-flow problem. He's good for it, Mr. D. Thirty thousand dollars. You know what the vig is on thirty K? You and me, Mr. D. You put up the scratch and I make collections"). Sandy was sweating underneath his hairline.

"You want another drink?" Doug popped his fingers

again but didn't catch his waitress this time. He said, "How about Hack? Would he be in on it?"

"You'll have to ask him yourself," Sandy said.

"So what went wrong? I thought you two were palsy-walsy."

"Hack fronted everything. The Holiday Inn, the Hertz car—he's the one has a credit card. The deal didn't go down." Sandy shrugged. "So what. Why's he so hincky with me? Toledo wasn't my idea. This ain't our line of work, that's what I told him. . . ."

"Telephone for Doug Whitenaur. Mr. D?"

The waitress handed the phone to Doug and said, "Make it quick, okay? This is a business phone."

"Uh-huh." Whitenaur took the phone into a corner to hear better.

"Mister Whitenaur? This is Nelson. Sergeant Nelson. Police Department."

"Speak up. We're having a party here."

"Whitenaur! That man's here after his dog again! Lewis Burkholder!"

Though the policeman's voice was loud, Doug held the earpiece glued to his ear like grim death. "What? . . . He? . . . When?"

"Right about now. He just left the station. Probably on his way to your house."

"Oh God!" Doug felt the champagne washing around his belly lining. "Why, well, stop him!"

"Man claims you got his dog. Man drove all the way from Virginia because he claims you stole it. He had that other guy, his son-in-law, with him."

"Arrest him!"

Bored. "He hasn't broke any laws. I shouldn't be calling
you. Why should I give a damn? Talk to your lawyer.
Maybe your lawyer can arrest him." *Clunk.* And the buzz
of the phone was louder than Nelson's voice had been.
Whitenaur's ear was red and he wiped the sweaty instrument on his pants leg.

The way his heart was pounding, Doug Whitenaur
hoped he wasn't having a heart attack. He took slow,
deliberate breaths. It's interesting to note he went directly
to Hack, not to Sandy.

The look Hack gave him was neutral and cold.

"Hack, I need to talk."

Hack's dip of the shoulder meant "So, talk."

"Hack, I got trouble and I want to hire you guys to
make it right, but we can't talk in here and you can't sit
around playing hard-to-get. Follow me."

And, somewhat to Hack's surprise, he found himself
following Doug Whitenaur outside into the parking lot.
"I understand you could use some fast cash," Whitenaur
began.

Hack clenched the plastic champagne glass in his hand,
just popped it into pieces.

"Five hundred for you and five hundred for Sandy.
Both of you. There's two of them so I'll want two of you
and you'll have to get over to my house fast as you can. I
want that dog out of there. If they don't find the dog, they
can't do squat. No dog, no evidence."

"Whoa now, slow down, Mr. D. Just what . . ."

"I told you before. I had that dog stolen. Hack, you're
such a wise guy. 'Buy the dog, Mr. D. They already

tossed your place, they won't do it again.' Well, wise guy, the dog's owner is on his way to my place right now and if he finds that dog, I got trouble." His laugh was a whinny. "Oh boy, I got trouble."

"Cool your jets, partner."

"I wouldn't have the dog if you hadn't opened your smart mouth! This key fits my kennel. Take it. Take it. There's two dogs, a bitch and a male. It's the male you want. Don't get the bitch by mistake. I'm running the bitch at the Bluegrass. Take the male."

Hack said, "You want me to steal your five-thousand-dollar dog?"

"I don't want that dog in Cincinnati. I don't want that dog within a thousand miles. I don't want to hear about that dog again." He closed his eyes. When he opened them, he was very reasonable. "All right. I made a mistake buying the dog. Get rid of him."

"You haven't spent all your five hundred yet."

Doug spoke through his teeth. His eyes were big as frog's eyes. "Burkholder and his buddy. This is the second time they traveled all the way here to make trouble and I am sick of it."

"We don't do hits. I don't know what you heard about me and Sandy, but we don't do that kind of work. Somebody wants a little protection, somebody's having a tough time with his collections—that's what we do. Sometimes we . . ."

"Don't kill them! God, what do you take me for?"

Hack swallowed his spontaneous answer. He was pretty broke. "Seven fifty for me. You got to have Sandy?"

"There isn't time to get anyone else."

"Five hundred for Sandy. We could go out to your place and take care of the dog and if we was to find anyone trespassing out there, I suppose we could . . . discourage them."

Doug's eyes were frantic. "I haven't got cash. Cards. I got a gold American Express. . . ."

Hack allowed himself to be amused. "We don't generally take plastic." He patted Doug's arm in quite a familiar way. "I'll bet you're good for the money. I don't suppose we could borrow your car. Sandy's car is in the shop again." And Hack waited until Doug Whitenaur laid the keys of his expensive silver sportscar right in his palm.

Nop was weary and he was sore. Bit wanted to play. She romped around him, gruffing and growling, grinning her silly grin.

She barked and sang, "Thou art he. He thou art. He art thee."

Nop whimpered. He wasn't *that* sore but he wanted sympathy.

"Poor Nop." All kindness, she lay down beside him and helped him groom himself.

With good appetite, she ate from the red plastic bowl. When she had it empty, she teased it on its edge so it would roll—a toy. She batted it, pounced. With mock ferocity, she worried the empty plastic dish.

Both dogs heard the footsteps coming around back. Nop's ears cocked like hairtriggers. Unfamiliar steps.

Both dogs settled down to bark. Bit loudest, because it was her home.

"Shut your yap!" Hack snapped.

"Yeah," Sandy agreed.

Nop sat back on his haunches and snarled. Bit backed from the kennel gate growling disapproval. "Which one's the girl? Whitenaur said to take the male."

"How should I know? There, the one in the corner." Sandy hunkered down and crooned. "Good doggy. Nice doggy."

The dogs settled down to a determined steady alarm.

"Get in there. You're the one likes dogs. You get him."

Sandy stepped cautiously inside and unclipped a dog lead that hung beside the gate.

"Come here," he said in a soft voice. Nop was dubious but Bit came right over and climbed all over Sandy, licking his face until he was slick.

Sandy offered his fingertips and, stiff-legged, Nop came over for a sniff. This man was friendly, and yet, and yet . . .

"Grab hold of him," Hack advised.

"Nice dog. Good dog." Sandy slipped his hand under Nop's collar and lifted his forefeet off the ground so he couldn't bite.

Hack swung the door wide. Bit ran to the rear of the kennel, growling, and Sandy yanked Nop outside.

"Don't you let go of him."

"He'll be all right as soon as I get him on this leash."

And so it was. When Nop felt the familiar pull at his collar, he retreated into his customary obedience.

Bit whined. Nop dug in his heels and threw her a look: her beautiful fur, her gay tail, her muzzle.

"Come on now, doggy."

Nop got right on the floorboards, on the passenger side, and laid his muzzle on Hack's foot. It was how Nop always traveled but Hack didn't know that. "Dog trusts me. How stupid can you get."

Sandy was revving and gear shifting and driving quite sportily. He was happy as a clam. "What a great car! Just great! When we get this over with, maybe we can take a little spin. I told you Mr. D would come through for us."

Hack thought Sandy looked like a college kid. He thought Sandy looked like a jerk. "Are you the one who likes dogs? Weren't you the one who had a cute little Collie once? How long did you say you cried when that dog got killed? I forgot. Was it two days? Three days? Come on, you can tell me."

Sandy said, "Aw, Hack! Don't!" He slowed the car.

They were in the rough part of town and the pavement was broken and full of potholes. Storefront churches, chili joints, low bars—all the usual commerce of street life.

Hack mocked, " 'Aw, Hack! Don't,' " making the words sound like a little girl was speaking them. God, he hated sentimentalists. Sentimentalists wore their hearts on their sleeves until the deal went down and those same hearts—just try and find those hearts then. Hack had had some experience with sentimentalists.

"How about here?" Sandy pulled into the mouth of an alley. Piles and heaps of broken cartons, toppled garbage cans. Two green dumpsters were labeled for the exclusive use of Holman's Bakery. Sandy left the motor running. "This is as good a place as any," he advised.

For the sheer hell of it, Hack didn't make a move. He popped a Tums. His foot was warmed by the dog's jaw.

"Well, you gonna do it?"

Hack let his disgust leak through his eyes until Sandy looked away. Sandy said, "I'll hold him until you get a tire iron. Must be a tire iron in the trunk."

Standing beside the car, Hack whacked the tire iron into his hand. *Whap.*

Nervously, Sandy said, "Man, get it over with. We got to get back to Mr. D's house and bounce those two farmers."

Whap.

Nop got very excited. He showed his teeth. Sandy said, "See, look at him. He's a bad dog. Real bad." He had Nop's collar and was pressing him against the floorboards. Nop struggled in earnest, but a forty-pound dog can't escape a hundred-eighty-pound man and Nop's mouth was smeared with cigarette butts and floor filth.

When Hack dragged Nop out of the car, he held something. A bad thing.

Nop couldn't slip the choke collar. Though his feet were dug in and his claws scraped and hooked the cobblestones, the leash dragged him forward. Nop's teeth were bared and he was very frightened.

"Nice doggy. I ain't gonna hurt you. Come here, doggy."

His claws clicked in the alleyway. High walls on either side. Piles of rubbish, higher than a man—higher than any man, even his old master. Hack steadily dragging him through the spill behind a big square dumpster, overflowing, redolent.

"Hurry it," Sandy yelled.

"Just a little farther. Nice doggy," Hack murmured, his eyes boring into Nop's and the bad thing—a black rod with a bend in it—the bad thing hanging from his hand.

Rags, pile of tin cans. Broken glass. Breathing rags. Paper bags. Burst paper bags.

Nop bolted past Hack and hit the end of the leash with his whole body's weight and strength, and it was enough to jerk the end of the lead out of Hack's hand, almost.

Nop flipped on his back. He had no more wind in him. Breathing rags.

Hack lifted the bad thing in the air.

Back at the car, Sandy shading his eyes. "Get it over with," he yelled.

"Dog," Hack said quietly, "you got guts."

Nop had no more breath for escape or defiance. He looked up.

The bad thing rose and fell. Rose and fell. The noise was awful and there was more noise when Hack hurled it into the garbage.

When Hack came back into the sunlight, Sandy said, "Where's Mr. D's tire iron?"

"Don't press your luck," Hack said.

If Lewis had been watching when "Wide World of Sports" featured the Littlest Buckaroos, perhaps things would have turned out differently, but Lewis never saw

the show and when Ethel called to say she'd seen Nop in
a rodeo, Nop had already been with Doug Whitenaur for
three weeks. Things moved quickly then. Ethel called the
president of the rodeo association (an old friend) and,
shortly, Lewis had T. T. Raines on the phone.

T.T. had nothing to hide. "Sure I bought that dog from
Grady Gumm, fair and square. And I sold him to Doug
Whitenaur. Made a few dollars on the deal, if you got to
know."

Trembling with excitement, Lewis thanked the man.
He grinned. He whooped. He did a jig of sheer joy. How
rare it was to be this happy, like a kid again. Joy throughout his whole laughing body.

The women needed the pickup, so next morning the
two men rolled toward Ohio in Mark's old VW. Lewis
slept most of the way. The excitement had taken a lot out
of him.

Lewis didn't expect much help from the Cincinnati
P.D. and got less. Sergeant Nelson didn't want to hear
about Lewis's stolen dog and wouldn't listen to what
Lewis had to say about Doug Whitenaur.

"Whitenaur is a big man in this town," Nelson had said.
"You just stay away from him."

Well, that made Lewis hot and he said some things to
Sergeant Nelson that maybe he shouldn't have. And when
he stormed out of the police station he was still hot, got
lost in traffic, crossed the river to the Kentucky side and it
was ninety minutes later when he finally pulled into Doug
Whitenaur's driveway and parked behind the silver De-
Lorean.

In the course of his affairs, Lewis Burkholder had upended rams, wrestled hogs, pinned calves and subdued a crazy-hurt horse or two. But today was the first time he fought a human being since he was in the service, some thirty years ago.

TEN

Strays

"What kind of a man is that? What kind of a man? Oh, this noise, this shouting." She pressed her hands to her ears. Nop cocked his head, curiously.

She looked and smelled like an old woman. Her sorrowful feet burst through the sides of her tennis shoes and her red hair lay flat and wispy against her skull.

"Such a man. Such a terrible man. To bring a doggy here, to my resting place; my place by the warm grate from Holman's Bakery and raise the club high up and smash the garbage. Crazy world." She rocked and moaned.

Nop lay where Hack had pushed him down, belly flat on the cobblestones. The leash was wrapped around the dumpster leg, and scattered, flattened garbage lay where Hack had killed it with crushing blows. Nop was panting. He knew the blows had been meant for him.

She looked like a pile of rags. Like she was no more than one of her own flopping, bulging shopping bags. Her eyes were green and shot with redness and tired.

"Doggy, what am I to do? Perhaps the crazy will come

back? With crazies, you never can tell." She shook an admonitory finger at Nop, who responded with a weak wag of his tail. She was rattling on—rudely awakened and terrified by the senseless attack on the privacy she'd reserved for herself among the overflowing garbage cans and trash. "Doggy. Doggy. I had a nice doggy once. I called . . . I can't remember what I called the doggy. Jack hated the doggy." She leaned close to confide, "Jack was the one took my doggy up on the roof and threw him off, though he always claimed it was an accident that my doggy just wandered too close to the edge." She paused. "You have the same eyes my doggy had. Kind and sweet."

She rolled onto her hands and knees and pushed, arthritically, to her feet. "I ain't stayin' here," she said, shaking her head vigorously. "No siree. This was a place once: safe and warm, and I haven't been attacked in this neighborhood but it's ruined now." She rubbed the place off her hands. "Ruined," she said, passing final judgment.

She hooked the twine handles of her bags on her arms —she adjusted herself.

"What day is it?" she asked Nop. "If it's Thursday, I'll have my SSI check at the Belvedere, but if it's Wednesday, I'll make the trip for nothing and I hate that. Well, I won't name names, but that Negro behind the desk, he's as bad as my husband Jack. Worse!"

Nop didn't know what day it was but he wagged again, vigorously, to show his concern. She paid him no mind, just walked on past, tottering on the uneven cobblestones.

Though Nop whined, she didn't turn around. When she

turned out of the alley, he barked. He jerked on his lead, jerked again. He dug at the leash with his claws and the hurried knot fell apart. Nop raced after the woman he'd chosen, his metal leash bouncing and jangling behind him. She hadn't gotten far. Nop streaked past a couple pedestrians and skidded to a stop beside her. She didn't look at him.

It's hard to say why dogs pick friends, but in his heart, Nop was sure he'd picked one. He just had to make her see it his way. He smiled. He walked handsomely. He was very charming. He wished she'd pick up the lead.

"Doggy," she muttered. "I ain't got no doggy. My husband, Jack, killed my doggy. Tried to kill me too. I'm too poor to have a doggy. You find yourself someone else."

Nop adjusted himself to her slow pace. It gave him plenty of time to look around, to inspect the street and the street life: loafers and hookers, hustlers and housewives returning from the convenience stores with groceries clutched protectively under their arms. A couple disco skaters spun by on rubber wheels, oblivious, headphones covering their ears.

More people looked at Nop than looked at the woman. People didn't like to see the woman because they were afraid she'd ask for something beyond their powers. Nop walked very close to the woman, at heel, so none could mistake his affiliation. He had chosen this woman on the strength of something buried deep in her green eyes.

She spoke to an audience of her own. She spoke about her husband, Jack, who'd been a sailor when she met him

("Just the cutest little sailor boy. And his baby blues, oh, I never could resist him"). She said it had been a love match. She also said it had been accursed. She waited at each corner for the light to change and sometimes hadn't reached the far curb when the light changed again. Her dress rustled; her broken shoes scuffed. She paused at a wire trash basket and fished through it.

"Nothin' today, Susie Q." The hotdog vendor, whose cart occupied the corner, called to her, "I ain't got rid of yesterday's buns yet."

She grumbled.

"That your dog, Susie? Why don't you leave him with me and I'll heat him up! Yeah, I'll turn him into a *real* hotdog."

Susie Q (for so she was called by others and herself) waited patiently.

"All right," the vendor said. "All right. I was just gonna throw them away anyway." With more generosity than grace he handed her two stale hotdog buns.

"My teeth," she mumbled. "You know how it is."

"Yeah. I know." He was looking away, like he was hoping to spy a customer, but it was because he couldn't stand watching her eat. It was the same thing every day. If he threw the buns away, she fished them out again. If she was early, she got them before they got thrown away. She said she couldn't eat hotdogs.

Nop wagged his tail and grinned, charming as a boulevardier. She didn't exactly feed him the piece of bun. She let it drop. He sniffed and looked up at her.

"Go ahead. Don't say I never gave you nothin'."

Though it was unappetizing, Nop gobbled it down. He

was anxious to cement bonds between them. He'd been too long friendless, too long alone.

"Dog's gonna hook his leash on somepin'," the vendor observed.

"I ain't got time to take care of no dog," Susie Q said. She waited until the vendor offered her a napkin; then she dabbed carefully at her lips. "Thank you," she said. "You are a real saint."

" 'S all right," the vendor said. He'd feed her but he wouldn't look at her. "I'll undo the leash," he said. "Then the dog won't hook himself on nothin'. He could strangle."

She tucked the steel lead in a shopping bag that held two skirts, a holey wool sweater, a copy of *Cosmopolitan* (August 1980) and a statuette of Jesus Christ of Nazareth, six inches tall. She always set it at bedside, when she had one.

She also carried an envelope with her Social Security card, birth certificate, high-school transcript (Woodrow Wilson High, Flint, Michigan), a certificate of marriage to one Jack D. Cunningham and several letters from the VA hospital where he'd been for three years now—Parkinson's disease. Though she had always loved him, and, in a way, depended on him, he'd beat her and hurt her and drank too much and fooled around with other men's wives and she didn't mind that so much on account of not being a jealous person but she certainly didn't want her own husband killed on her doorstep, or, God forbid, in the kitchenette of her little apartment by some jealous husband not as forgiving as she.

When Jack was admitted by the VA, her world fell

apart. She'd been a fifty-year-old housewife. And now what was she? The VA put Jack in the hospital but wouldn't give her anything and the SSI check wasn't much to live on and one month, when the check was late, or maybe stolen from her mailbox, they evicted her right into the street.

At first she tried to get back. She'd made the laborious rounds of the various bureaucracies. She sought papers to prove who she was, papers to prove her need. From one office to another, and a crowded bench of supplicants ahead of her at each office. She'd taken to dozing off in the offices instead of pursuing the papers they said they wanted but seemed to lose or require in triplicate as soon as she had her hand on them.

She began to think of papers as talismans, rare bits of magic that opened guarded doors. On the street she'd been robbed time after time—perhaps eight times in the past three years—by street kids who believed the rumor that shopping-bag ladies always had wealth stuffed into their sacks of belongings. She'd been hit and knocked down and her clothing strewn all over the pavement, but the only thing she ever cared about was her little statue and her precious envelope of papers.

She'd lost track of her relatives. She thought she had a sister somewhere in California. She'd never made any particular effort to trace her because her sister was married and had kids and a house and a car and everything she was supposed to have so why would she need Susie Q?

She walked slow but Nop stepped along, precisely at her side. From time to time she spoke to him and he listened, quite intently. She shot him a glance, occasionally, when she thought he wasn't looking.

Invisibility was her protection. When she walked into the train station, nobody asked her her business, even when she went into the ladies' room with a black-and-white Border Collie at her heels.

Three other women like her, at the far end of the rest room where they wouldn't bother fastidious travelers. One woman dried her face with the automatic drier. Susie Q took a corner sink where she stepped out of her ruined shoes and with her hands hoisted one leg into the bowl and ran water over her toes.

One black woman, one white woman, one Puerto Rican. America, the melting pot.

Susie asked Alice what day it was. She didn't know. Marietta, the PR, didn't know either but the question reminded her of the House of Naomi, the women's shelter where they asked you all sorts of tough questions before they told you they had no vacancy in any of their programs.

Alice said she'd ask the attendant when she came back. The others urged her not to ask because "it's better she doesn't notice us. Better."

Marietta was afraid of Nop and moved away as far as she could. Alice admired him. She said he was a nice doggy and invited him to come over for a pat—an invitation which Nop declined because he didn't wish to abandon his friend.

During winter months a half-dozen women gathered here and slept fitfully under the down-turned hand driers.

The cops let them stay until 5 A.M., and they were proud of leaving the room as clean as they found it.

Susie Q removed her blouse to wash her upper arms.

At the sink in her worn brassiere, she scrubbed. This was one of her important daily rituals and one of the few events that made her feel good.

Usually the women who came here didn't speak to each other—each ashamed, each afraid. But Nop provided the excuse for a curious normalcy. "He's a nice dog," Alice said. "I used to have a dog like that when I lived out in Kansas. It was a black Labrador Retriever. My daughter . . . he was great with my daughter."

"I hope your daughter is well," Susie said.

"Yeah," Alice said, sadly. "I hope so too."

Marietta was humming a sad tune. She was arranging her things around her and making a place to sit.

Alice told Susie about her former life. She'd been married three times ever since she was "just a child of fifteen." She'd never been lucky with men but she'd never been locked up in no "loony bin" either she said, with a sly thumb poked at Marietta.

Like most states, Ohio had deinstitutionalized many former mental patients. After years of custodial care and the frailest connections to the community at large, most of them ended up like Marietta, on the street.

Fresh off the train, a couple of perfectly ordinary women came into the room. They didn't react to the ladies but one of them gave Nop a funny look.

"She's gonna make trouble," Alice said after the white swinging door closed.

"It's the dog," Susie Q said. "Thought the dog was going to bite her. He's a good dog, look at him."

Nop wagged his tail and panted. Nop lay with his snout between his paws. Cold tile under his belly. White fluorescent lights. Mirrors. Strange smells. Every time a train departed the station, Nop could feel the vibration through his belly. The women couldn't, but he could.

The two women gossiped for a while. When they couldn't think of anything to say about people, they said something about the dog and that kept conversation flowing. It was a nervous business, conversation, because they weren't practiced. They were in the same boat. That was the gist of what they said. Each listened to the other and began to think that since the other person was destitute and on the streets and still seemed decent, that maybe she was too.

The attendant came into the ladies' room and said, "You can't keep a dog in here."

Nop got to his feet and eyed her.

Rather airily, Susie Q said, "He's a thoroughbred, you know. A genuine, uh, thoroughbred dog. I believe we'll go over to the Belvedere and collect my check."

Her feet hurt like blazes and she was pavement weary but she'd washed and had a conversation with another soul and she had a dog that depended on her. Fancy that. A dog that depended on her. She snapped her fingers, "Come on, King," she said and Nop followed her right away. "See," she said, "he knows his name already."

They walked down the street, side by side.

The Belvedere Arms was built in the 1880s as housing for unmarried immigrants. The Belvedere was a "workingman's residence" and said so on one substantial cornerstone.

The architect who designed the Belvedere (and similar residences in Cleveland, St. Louis, Toledo and New York) had a strange conception of what an unmarried immigrant required. Rooms lined four sides of a central airshaft. The courtyard below may once have provided a sort of immigrant street life but now it was a place to toss bottles and nobody dared walk across it.

The Belvedere's windows never opened. Above the first floor the panes facing the street were frosted glass, like bathroom windows. The building broadcasted a fey, massive sense of modesty.

The Belvedere was an SRO, meaning single-room occupancy, meaning the city used it as a dumping ground for the homeless, aged, mad and helpless. The hotel housed the newly destitute and those whose destitution was a way of life. It housed the same people who'd been institutionalized by the state previously. It housed paroled convicts, welfare mothers and elders and Medicaids.

The Belvedere was absentee owned, absentee managed and only the black man behind the desk was concrete. "Hi there, Susie Q. Come for your check?"

The tall desk was paneled with looks-like-wood paneling. A brace of fluorescents buzzed overhead. It was the bright focus of that lobby that smelled like booze, medicine and defeat. Mounds of rags dozed on the hopeless couches. It was safer down here than upstairs in the rooms and, who knows, maybe someone would have something to say.

A couple of the desk clerk's pals occupied a red vinyl couch which was dragged so close to the front of the desk that Susie Q had to step over outstretched feet.

"Yeah," she said, and there was a shrillness in her voice Nop hadn't heard before. "I didn't know what day it was, whether it was Thursday or not, so I didn't know if to come."

The clerk was pure beef in a navy-blue shirt and hip-length white leather jacket. His two pals were of the same mold but a weaker casting. Any of them could have hurt Susie Q. To give them full credit, they had never done so in the past.

The clerk held the envelope to the light. He drawled, "Mrs. Jack Cunningham. That you, Susie Q?"

The woman chittered. She put her hand over her mouth to hide her bad teeth. Nop's ruff and the hackle line along his black back erected.

"That's me. Sure that's me. I get my checks here and I always take a room, too, you know. The check isn't all it should be, but it's enough so I get by."

He let the letter dangle from his very fingertips like maybe it was some disgusting thing. It was just beyond the woman's farthest reach. "We're supposed to mail this right back if the correct person—the addressee—don't pick it up. Says so, right here on this envelope: Do Not Forward. That's what it says."

The woman set down her bags and dug inside, dropping clothing on the filthy floor. "Mrs. Jack Cunningham," she whispered. "That's me. I got proof. I got a marriage certificate right here." When she found the envelope, she clutched it like salvation. She placed it precisely before the clerk. "Me. I'm me," she said.

"I don't want your cruddy papers," the clerk said. "You may remove them."

Susie blinked. She didn't understand. The man flicked the precious documents off the desk. She scuttled for them.

Disdainfully, he poked his finger into her SSI envelope and ripped it open. "You got a check here for one hundred twenty-eight dollars and fifty cents, Susie. How long you want a room, week or two weeks? You ain't got enough here for a month."

Her documents were pressed against her breast like a letter from her dearest love. She gaped.

"The week is sixty dollars, less ten percent for cashing this, comes to thirteen dollars call it seventy-three, suppose we'll call it an even seventy-eight fifty, means I owe you fifty bucks. Sign and you get your money." Plain black ballpoint beside her check.

She didn't know whether to go backward or forward. Eventually she'd sign the check and take what was offered to her and a room key. She always had signed, eventually.

Nop didn't know that. He didn't follow the words of the conversation, but he understood the ritual perfectly well. The man was threatening his friend, and he reacted like any honest dog when a packmate is threatened. He set his feet and coiled and bared his white teeth. His tail shot out straight behind him, and with all his hair standing on end, he looked like a much larger dog than he was. He made a sound in the very back of his throat which was meant to let her know he was with her and meant to tell her enemy that a stud dog was dealing himself in.

It was the last thing the desk clerk expected. Susie Q was shocked too. The clerk took an involuntary step backward and both his pals jerked their legs back as far as they could get from that dog's jaws.

Nop slipped sideways where he could keep a balance point between all three men.

"Goddamn," one man breathed hurriedly, "goddamn. Goddamn."

In the far shadows of the lobby, somebody sneezed.

"That dog," the clerk stuttered, "you get that dog . . ."

She said the name like a prayer. "King!"

It was seven feet from the floor to the surface of the Belvedere's desk. Nop made the jump, caught with his elbows and pulled himself up. His snarling face wasn't twenty inches from the desk clerk's own. The clerk opened his mouth wide but no word came out.

"I'd like you to meet my dog," she said. "Him and me are great pals, don't you know. He's a real thorough-bred." She snapped her fingers. "And don't you know he'd tear out your throat just like that! Like that!" She snapped her fingers again.

"Get. Him. Off my. Desk."

"How much did you say the room rate was? For one night? I don't like it here. It's dirty and it isn't very safe. Do you think people stay here because they want to?"

231

The clerk had both his hands clutching the desk. Nop stayed at the ready and his eyes blazed like fire opals.

She ignored the clerk's silence. "I suppose it'll be twelve dollars for one night. My, you do get a pretty penny. Twelve dollars from one hundred twenty-eight dollars and fifty cents leaves me one hundred sixteen dollars and fifty cents."

His hand groped through the cash drawer. His eyes never left the dog. The dog was actually drooling. Drooling with lust to kill. "Please," he said.

"One sixteen fifty," she said, as merciless as she was proud.

His fingers found the correct bills and laid them down beside that damn animal's feet, that damn thing that never moved, just drooled and glared. She took quite a long time to count the money and then, recount it. She endorsed with a flourish. "My full name is Mrs. Jack Cunningham," she said. "I am known to my friends as Susanna. You may call me Mrs. Cunningham. My key?"

Room 228, second floor rear. Since it was a simple skeleton key, likely the key fit other doors and other keys fit the lock of this room.

The iron army cot had a mattress pad, one sheet and a pair of skimpy blankets. Blue light filtered through the frosted windowpanes. A gunmetal wall locker, a sink, a kitchen chair, its yellow seat pad mended with gray tape. No mirror. Susanna was disappointed. Some of the rooms had a mirror.

Nop sniffed carbolic, vomit, feces, urine, fear. Fear from the night sweats, fear from D.T.s. Fear of cells. Fear of rape. Fear of loneliness. Death fear.

He was still nervy from facing the desk clerk and the smells were so strong they made him sneeze and sneeze again.

"Next time," Susanna muttered. "Next time we'll get one with a mirror."

Nop's hackles stayed up. They just wouldn't come down. He growled once, very softly, and dribbled a bit of urine on the doorframe, to make the room his.

"Now look what you've done," she said. She smiled. "Well, I suppose dog pee isn't the worst thing been spilled between these walls."

A shout in the hall. Some drunk screaming and another man yelling at him to shut up, shut his face.

The bathrooms were in the halls. Between certain hours they were dangerous.

Nine days ago her check ran out and she hadn't lain in a bed since then. She longed for the narrow cot, but decided to go out again. She had an animal to feed.

She took only one shopping bag, the one with her envelope and money. Usually she was afraid to leave her possessions in the room, but today she felt rather devil-may-care. On the street, in her best dress, she looked just like every woman except for her broken shoes.

She marched right into the Greco-American Deli, as if she had every right. The waitress asked her to sit in back but she parked beside the door. "I got my dog fastened up out there," she said. "I got to keep an eye on him."

She had the hamburger steak (medium) and the tomato soup (bowl, not a cup) and a big piece of lemon meringue pie. All that food made her nauseous but she still managed to choke down the coffee that came with the meal (double cream, double sugar) because who knows what tomorrow will bring? She had them fry up a burger pattie. "It's for my dog. If you come over here, you can see him. He's a thoroughbred dog."

The waitress went to the window. "That black-and-white thing?"

"That's him."

"I'd never keep a dog in the city. It's cruel. I got cats."

"Well, he's good protection. A woman alone."

"Here's your burger. It's only sixty-five cents on account of it's plain."

"Thank you." And Susanna left a twenty-five-cent tip beside her water glass, just like every woman might.

Sitting on the curb, she broke the burger into bits and fed it to Nop. When Nop had gobbled every piece, she let him lick her palm clean and actually laughed when his rough tongue tickled. She laughed. Think of that.

Though Nop had passed through cities, going to and from trials, he'd never stayed overnight in one. The noises. The smells. Long after the woman fell into an exhausted slumber, he paced the room from locker to sink, cot to door. With a thump, he'd lie down, but with every siren or outcry from the bowels of the hotel, he'd be up and pacing again.

Border Collies learn well. They are able to think on their own. Now, Nop didn't know what to think. His world had been Lewis, the farm, the woolies and Lewis's family. Occasionally, as a great adventure, he'd travel to a stockdog trial, but his life was fairly well ordered and quite predictable and he'd created his understanding from that order.

At Grady Gumm's, his understanding had been useless. At the rodeo, his understanding had made him take on an impossible job, trusting for relief that never came.

The dog pound had been stupefying fear.

He remembered Bit O' Scot's fluffy, impudent tail and that image finally put him to sleep.

Hours later, a key rattled in the lock. Nop was on his feet, fully awake. Someone behind the key: bad. Susanna snored and tossed. Nop could smell the bad outside the door. The man eased his key against the tumblers and Nop growled pretty loud.

Froze.

Nop growled again. The key slipped back out of the lock and someone swore under his breath and footsteps went off looking for an easier victim.

Nop didn't go back to sleep again that night. Across the doorway he lay with his nose between his paws and waited. This was his work. He was not very certain of anything, but he knew work.

At dawn, Susanna woke because it was the time cops usually asked her to move on. She lay on the bed with her hands under her head staring at the ceiling, enjoying the luxury of a fed body and two skimpy blankets.

It was never completely quiet at the Belvedere and it wasn't quiet now. Some of the street people were up and moving out. Some of the night people were stumbling home. The Belvedere's rest room was the most ill-smelling place Nop had ever been and he'd sniffed his share of feces and dead meat. When Susanna laid him down before her stall, he waited without demur. The smell was very bad. It was making him hysterical and he was glad when she was finished.

She tossed the room key on the desk and the desk clerk tightened his lips and his two pals pulled in their feet and sat like two schoolboys on the red couch.

"Don't come back here with that dog," he said.

Susanna tossed her head. "I wouldn't be caught dead in this dump. I'm gonna go out and get a good job." She didn't look back.

The House of Naomi didn't open its doors until eight, so she and Nop sat outside among her shopping bags, sharing a cup of takeout coffee (double sugar, double cream). Nop liked it quite a bit.

The House of Naomi was a women's shelter, run by private charities. It offered counseling, long-term residence in a clean dormitory and, ultimately, a job-referral service. It had just twenty-four beds.

Every women's shelter in America has to turn away applicants and if the House of Naomi accepted only the most promising women for its program, who could blame them?

A street-cleaning machine broomed the gutters. Nop growled.

People marched past on their way to work: attaché cases, lunchboxes, crisp clothing, shiny shoes, severely tailored suits.

"That'll be me, doggy. Every morning, down at the

old bus stop. Same time every morning. Exact change—
I'll have it ready in my hand. I'll take my seat and
I'll unfold my newspaper and read the news and the
sale ads, too. 'Hummm. Maybe I'll get a new coverlet
for my bed. My, there's a special on a coffee service.'
Ridin' the bus downtown to my job. From my apartment to my job and, in the evening, back again. Oh, I
wouldn't want a fancy place. Nothin' too grand. Just a
studio apartment without too many cockroaches and only
one key to the front door. You'll have all the canned dogfood you can eat."

The shelter's staff was arriving now. Susanna smiled her
best smile at everyone who climbed the stoop and when
one woman said "Good morning," Susanna followed her
right inside, shopping bags, dog and all.

A sign advised all APPLICANTS. WAIT HERE PLEASE and
Susanna took a chair in what had been the front parlor
when the building had been a family home. Cheerful paint
covered all the walls and the window seats and speckled
the glass in the Edwardian bow windows.

Plastic chairs filled the waiting room like a bus station
or airline terminal. Drawings and amateurish watercolors
were taped to the walls with Scotch tape.

Susanna waited, very nervous. Surely if the House had
a vacancy, this room would be full of women. Surely she
was too old. She wondered if they ever took women with
bad teeth. Her teeth were horrible. She had to admit it
herself, how ugly they were. Nop put his nose on her
foot. Absently, she petted him. "Well, we're here anyway."

She heard voices in the rear of the house. Must have been a swell house once. This whole neighborhood must have been pretty ritzy. Just look at it now! She smelled food. Coffee? Burned bacon? The clink of cutlery, a swinging door bumped open and the chatter of voices sounded pretty happy, all of them. Her stomach grumbled. That's the trouble with eating one big meal like last night—you stretch your stomach and are twice as hungry the next day.

A woman strode toward her, hand outstretched. "Hello," she said. "I'm Chrissy Holt. I handle admissions at the House."

Nop's eyes moved but his body stayed perfectly still.

Susanna Cunningham heaved to her feet. She almost forgot her name. She almost introduced herself as Susie Q but remembered in the nick of time. "Susanna Cunningham," she mumbled.

The woman's smile was big enough but didn't mean anything personal. "Will you follow me? You can leave your things—they'll be safe here."

Susanna examined the younger woman carefully, storing up details: blond hair brushed back and secured with a band—wedding ring and engagement ring. Susanna wished she still had her ring but something had happened to it. Stolen? Pawned? She felt like a child. The woman wore glasses with upswept frames, like elf eyes. Perfect makeup. Perfect teeth. Nop touched his bare nose to Susanna's ankle and the sudden cold broke her fear. "Yeah. You got a good face," she said. "Stay here. Stay here, good doggy."

Down the hallway, made a turn, paused at an office where a sullen youth was wielding a broom. "You're not finished, Leon?"

"No'm."

"I suppose I can use Miss Coolidge's office. I do hope you'll speed it up."

Leon didn't say a word. He swept a sweep. The admissions lady made an irritated face, just like Susanna couldn't see it. That is a bad sign. When people don't think you can see them, they can't see you.

The admissions lady jerked drawers, searching for forms.

Susanna, in a yellow plastic chair before the desk, wished she were somewhere else.

"There! That'll do it." Again the bright smile. The woman uncapped a ballpoint. "Susanna Cunningham. Is that a Mrs. or a Miss?"

"Oh, it's Mrs. I don't have no wedding ring, but I'm a married woman, all right."

She wrote it down.

"History of employment?"

She wrote it down.

There were questions about drugs. "No ma'am. I never used 'em."

Questions about alcohol. "I used to take a glass of port, sometimes, when we had a big dinner, you know, Thanksgiving or Christmas, before my Jack took sick, but I never took no strong drink besides that."

"Never?"

"No ma'am. I never liked the smell of it."

She asked a good many questions about alcohol and Susanna answered them all honestly. She said she'd never been a drunk and she'd never sold her body either. The woman seemed quite interested in alcohol but indifferent to whether she'd sold her body or not.

The woman's smile held more warmth now. "Tell me something about yourself, Mrs. Cunningham. You don't have to hurry. Just use your own words."

Susanna didn't get it. She'd heard the words but just didn't understand. "Wait a minute," she said. She hurried out of the room, back to the parlor where she'd left her precious envelope. Nop stood up and stretched. She squeezed his furry head. "Wish me luck, doggy," she said. "Wish me luck."

She poked her envelope at the admissions lady. "Take them," she said. "It's all there. Social Security, marriage certificate, all of 'em."

The woman held the envelope but didn't look inside. "Papers can help us, Mrs. Cunningham, but they're not the whole picture. They don't help me get to know *you*. Please, tell me what you hope the House of Naomi can do for you."

"You can put me up."

The woman's expression didn't change for good or evil. Susanna knew she'd been too blunt. She took a deep breath. She wasn't used to this kind of conversation. "Mrs. Holt, I'm fifty-three years old and I been without a home for three years. My husband, he's in the VA and he'll never be coming out and maybe it ain't such a bad thing he won't. I got a high-school diploma, in the commercial arts, and I used to be a whiz at the typewriter.

'Course that was when I was a kid so I don't know how many words I'd be able to do today. I was still at home with my parents when I met Jack, you see, but I got my diploma before I'd marry him. I been confused."

The woman cut in: "Any history of institutionalization?"

"No ma'am. I'm not nuts, I'm just poor. But I been 'confused,' you know how a person gets."

The admissions lady showed no sign that she ever got confused or that anyone in her circle ever got confused.

Susanna hurried on, "I been living best I could on the SSI check, just one day at a time, winter, summer, spring. The other day I kind of woke up and I wasn't confused so much anymore and I said to myself, 'Susie . . . *Susanna,* you better take hold of yourself or you're gonna die out here on the street and nothin' to show for your life but regrets.' So I figured I'd come to you. I know you got the counseling and I know you got the job training. If you don't have no room in your House, then I'll stay on the street and just come in for the training but, lady, I got to have something more'n I got."

The eyes behind the upturned elfin eyeglasses looked at her for the longest time. Very slowly she nodded. "Well, Susanna," she said, "I think we'll take a chance on you."

Susanna's heart stopped. A chill spread from her forehead through her cheeks, from the pin bones of her shoulders to her fingertips. Though she'd asked, she hadn't really expected anything. Hope can kill you faster than any criminal can. "I . . ." she said. "I . . . thank . . . job."

The admissions lady rubbed her hands briskly. "You're

in luck today," she said. "We rarely have openings, but just last night one of our women left the shelter. Went to Missouri, actually. Her daughter has a home in Springfield and they've been corresponding." She clapped her hands. "Peggy's bed is empty and Susanna can have it." She picked up the envelope. "We'll need to get your SSI transferred to us so I'll need your papers." She performed legerdemain and made the papers disappear. "We won't rush into the counseling. We'll just introduce you around and make you comfortable. Have you had breakfast?"

Susanna didn't trust her speech. She shook her head no.

"I could use a cup of tea myself. After breakfast we'll get you some fresh clothes. I hope we have something that'll fit."

And she ushered Susanna right through the swinging door into a big room full of women, old and young. There would be many marvels to explore here but none so marvelous as seeing women conversing with each other, neither ashamed nor afraid.

"You'll get your tray over there. Mrs. Johnson? Is the kitchen still serving?"

Assured that it was, the two women stepped right over to the kitchen window and there were good smells and large brown plastic trays and the cook was asking her how did she like her eggs?

The admissions lady poured a cup of water from an aluminum tureen and dunked her tea bag. "We don't allow pets here at the shelter," she said. "I do hope you understand."

Eggs. Susanna had to decide what kind of eggs she

wanted. She couldn't let herself get confused. "He's my friend!" she blurted.

"A pat of margarine for your toast? Grapefruit juice or orange juice?"

"I don't . . . whatever you're having."

"I already had breakfast, Susanna. We'll find the dog a good home. I'll have Leon take him. You won't have to say good-bye. It'll be easier that way."

The cook wanted to know how Susanna liked her eggs. "Scrambled? Scrambled eggs be all right?"

"Yes. Please. The orange juice, please. Please."

"Susanna, where would you like to sit?" The admissions lady gestured to the whole wide world of a room.

So many women. So many empty chairs. But no space for her dog no matter how small he made himself. A tear splashed on her plastic tray. "Wherever you want me to sit would be fine," Susanna whispered.

The Village of Lost Dogs

DOGS WANTED: Strays, mean and unwanted. Will pick up. No charge. Chip Ralston, Elite Kennels, Goshen, Oh.

FREE TO GOOD HOME: AKC Female
Cocker Spaniel. 6 yrs. Spayed and all shots.
Loves children. Relocating. 864-5679 after 6.

The White Truck came to the lot behind Shakey's Pizza
Tuesdays and Fridays. It was Nop's bad luck today was
Friday.

The city dog pound didn't give you zip for a dog, Leon
knew that. The White Truck didn't give you much, but
more than zip. When Mrs. Holt told Leon to take the bag
lady's mutt to the pound right away, Leon started thinking "White Truck" and about the fifty dollars he hoped to
get for the dog.

Dog didn't want to go with Leon. He lifted his lip and
growled way back in his throat like he meant to have Leon
for his next meal. Dog fluffed up to about twice his natural
size and got down on his feet, like he was gathering himself for a spring and growled. It took Mrs. Holt to catch

hold of the dog. Dog had seen her and the bag lady talking friendly so he mistook Holt for a friend of his and let her come up and pet his head and get a couple fingers under his collar so he couldn't bite. Then Leon came back into the room and dragged the dog outside, out where the radio cab was waiting. Held that sucker in the air so he couldn't get hardly no air and his eyes popped out of his head and his tongue hung out but he was still growlin' like he meant to have himself a slice of throat meat. Leon beat the dog—smacked it hard but the dog wasn't gonna learn his lesson. Dog thought he was tougher than Leon —a grown man. Dog thought he was really something.

The cabbie took one look at the snarling, drooling animal and shut the trunk lid.

"That dog'll tear things to pieces back there," he said. "There's wiring that runs through the trunk and the gas pipe too. I don't want no crazy rabid dog biting things in there."

"How the hell I gonna carry him?" Leon demanded.

"Man, that's your problem. You think of a way so he don't tear up my cab and you and him can ride. Otherwise . . ." He shrugged.

Leon sat in the back with both feet on the dog and the choke chain snugged up tight, so that his shoes shoved the dog into the floorboards and the collar pulled the opposite and the dog's breathing got thin. He commenced to choke so Leon let off a little pressure. "You just lay still," he said. "Man in a White Truck waitin' for you. You and him gonna have a fine time."

The White Truck was a one-ton Ford F-350 with dual

wheels and a box body. A '78; it already had two hundred thousand miles on it. The box was white, the cab was white. It had the usual line of running lights and, on each side, a six-inch ventilating grate high and forward. No lettering on the door and no lettering on the body either.

The lot had belonged to "Joe The Motorist's Friend" until Joe closed up shop. The realtor who handled the empty store let the White Truck park for twenty bucks a week.

A skinny man sat on a kitchen stool behind the truck's rear doors. His hair was cut short, in a neat crew cut. He wore a translucent green polyester shirt and a string tie, anchored by a five-dollar gold piece.

When Leon's cab stopped, Skinny got off his stool and threw the rear doors open. Inside, the truck was wall-to-wall cages. Cages with oak doors and dogs' faces pressed against the gratings. Big dogs' faces, little dogs' faces— their snouts, tongues, ears.

Leon walked stooped over so it wouldn't look like he was choking the bag lady's dog. Skinny thumped a cage, smartly, to drive the dogs back, grabbed Nop and hurled him inside with a smooth, practiced motion. He relatched the cage. He left a narrow crack open for ventilation when he closed the truck's outer doors.

"Twenty dollars," Skinny said.

Leon winced. "Twenty dollars ain't much. That's a good dog there, worth forty dollars easy."

"Dog's been bit. Half his ear gone. Ain't many people looking for a lopped-eared black-and-white dog with no papers. Twenty."

"I hate to take that for this dog," Leon said. "This dog's a family pet."

"He looked like he was, the way you were holding him. Twenty dollars is twenty more'n you had before."

Leon reached for the bill.

Skinny retracted it. "I generally get somebody to sign me a bill of sale." He furnished a printed pad. Skinny had already written the date in the space labeled DATE and "Cincinnati" under TOWN OF PURCHASE. He'd written "mongrel" in the place labeled BREED. "Just sign at the bottom."

Leon signed the book, "Joe Louis." The man gave up the crisp new money without examining the signature. Perched on his stool: "If you happen to run across any nice Cocker Spaniels, we got a contract for them. I'll give forty dollars for any female Cocker in good health."

Leon got back in his cab and went away.

Nop shared his cage with a dozen other dogs. A young Irish Setter lay up front near him. A Pomeranian huddled in the farthest part of the cage whimpering and scratching the mesh. There were many other dogs—and a few cats —in the truck, but Nop couldn't see them through the plywood walls and floors.

The truck bed was splotched with droppings. The dogs had tried to keep their mess in one small area but some hadn't been able.

The inside of the oak gates were gnawed white, and all the black paint had been chipped off the wire mesh by the teeth of many, many dogs.

The crazy Pomeranian cried and whimpered. A sinking

feeling came over Nop like a poisonous fog. He had lost everything.

The Irish Setter had worried brown eyes. Young dog— younger than Nop. Timidly, he asked, "Dost thou have a master?"

Nop saw everything he could see through the narrow crack. It wasn't much. Asphalt—the man's right shoulder blade.

"My master will come and bring me home," the Setter said.

The sun got up higher.

Some air moved between the rear door and the vents, but not much. The stink got bad. Occasionally, Nop heard footsteps. The Setter's tail would start to go; he would hesitate and he'd sigh and put his head on his paws.

"Man, you only give me twenty dollars for these Lhasas? These are pure-bred dogs, man. Pure-bred. AKC."

"I don't suppose you'd happen to have the papers."

"No, I don't. But you can tell from looking at them. I mean these dogs are nicer'n what you find in a pet store. . . ."

The door swung open and the Lhasas went into the cage. This time, when the skinny man closed the door, the crack was narrower, so Nop couldn't see any part of him.

Others arrived. A woman brought half a dozen dogs. "Don't worry about these," she said. "These are family dogs. They won't bite."

"Good week, Hilda?"

"Fair. I'd like to get a little more for the Cocker. I know you're looking for Cockers."

"Forty dollars for the Cocker. Twenty apiece for the others."

"They closed down the Bendix plant. Whenever they start laying people off, there's plenty 'good home' dogs."

People came with dogs. The skinny man passed out crisp new bills. Once, he went into Shakey's and bought himself a slice of pizza. When he took up his post, Nop could smell it.

"I am so hungry," the Setter complained.

The Irish Setter had been taken from a backyard in Dayton, three days ago. Though his owner had paid two hundred dollars for him as a pup, the White Truck had given thirty.

Single dogs. Dogs in groups. Several more dogs were tossed into Nop's cage: Beagles. They stayed together, shivering with fear.

Promptly at noon, Skinny closed up shop and the White Truck moved to its afternoon location.

The open door had provided some ventilation. Nop began to pant.

The Irish Setter told Nop about his master, master's wife, master's children. The master's cat hadn't been stolen and the Setter resented that fact. "The cat will drink my water and eat my meat," the Setter complained. "The cat will romp with the master's children."

Nop said, "Masters take you up and then they leave. I have experienced this myself."

"My master will bring me home," the Setter said stoutly.

One of the Beagles threw up. Nop's bowels were full but he didn't want to go here. He'd hold it.

The mesh was loose and clattered and several dogs whined and dogs in the next cage got in a fight, snarling and crashing against the plywood.

Another two-hour stop in a vacant lot. More dogs. Twenty dogs in Nop's cage, several sick, one or two crazy. When Nop moved at all, he moved on his tiptoes hoping not to offend these strange dogs and provoke a fight.

At every stop, the door crack provided a little light but it was pitch dark on the road—the odors of the dogs, their hurried breathing.

Skinny threw a Brittany bitch in. She'd been pulled off a litter of two-week-old puppies. She whined, searched the cage, gasped, licked her tight dugs, searched again.

It was after dark when they drove around back of a small-town dog pound. Skinny had the keys to the pound, took three dogs and left money in the usual place.

Badly embarrassed, Nop squatted to relieve himself.

One more stop, another pound. The dog warden was working late and helped Skinny load. Sure he had a nice Cocker bitch but she'd been picked up that morning and her owner would probably be by for her. She had a collar and a name tag. The owner had simply forgotten to buy the county license.

"We need seventy Cockers," Skinny said. "National

Institute of Health. Forty apiece. For all the owner knows, she wandered off and got run over."

The dog warden said no, he couldn't do it. The township paid his salary, he said. Come back next week. He'd keep her in back where she wouldn't get adopted, but he'd have her if the owner showed.

"Next week we might not need Cockers," Skinny warned darkly.

Nop and the Setter were young enough and healthy enough to command some floor space to lie down, side by side, nose to nose. Other dogs piled up in the back of the cage. Dog noses went crazy. Dogs who didn't like being touched lay under other dogs scarcely able to breathe.

The White Truck headed out, trundling down the interstate, full of life.

Every human child must learn the universe fresh. Every stockdog pup carries the universe within him. Humans have externalized their wisdom—stored it in museums, libraries, the expertise of the learned. Dog wisdom is inside the blood and bones. Humans trace their ancestors through books and records. Nop's ancestors were what he knew.

Nop hadn't lost his balance but his balance point had shifted, throwing everything out of proportion, and he no longer knew what to do.

Whispers, stirrings in the bone, hints.

In the far reaches of Nop's brain there were memory traces from the old times: before dogs had names, when shepherds were rough and their dogs rougher, when the dogs lay outside stone hovels half buried in snow and God help the luckless intruder who stumbled upon them.

He heard whispers in his blood.

Further back before the Romans came to the island: back when dogs ran free.

The Irish Setter described the bed he lay in every night. Folded blankets tucked inside a wooden crate, just outside the childrens' bedroom door.

"Long ago," Nop said, "we made a covenant with man. We were the first animal to make covenant and brought him the cows, sheep, horses: all the others. We hunted his meat, guarded his flocks, his home and his children. On our bellies we went into narrow dens after creatures with sharp teeth. We have hunted foxes and wolves and bears and lions because he wished it. At his behest we have killed our own kind. We will die for him. Free dogs made covenant with man: we made him master."

The Setter said, "My master scratches my silky ears. Sometimes I chew his shoes because they smell so wonderfully of him. He punishes me for chewing his shoes. Am I here because I chewed his shoes?"

"We made no food covenant," Nop went on. "We are not woolies that would die without shepherds to tend them. Free dogs hunt their own meat. We only asked that the master keep us in his wonderful eyes. But masters no longer keep us. They have forgotten the old time when they were alone and terrified on the darkening plain. They have forgotten their first ally against the night. Oh, they are so foolish! Like young puppies turned loose with stock, they rush here and there, exciting themselves for no reason but excitement itself. Like puppies, they are hurtful one moment, forgetful the next. They do not keep us in their eyes. They do not trouble to see us."

The Setter nuzzled Nop's ear. He said, "Do not forget how to love."

"I have no master," Nop said. He lay still, but his muscles were cable taut and hard.

The Setter babbled about his master, but more desperately now. The Britanny bitch still searched the cage for her missing puppies but less hopefully. Some dogs had become comatose. One of the dogs voided his bowels on the others piled beneath.

The White Truck rolled down the interstate, beside families going on vacation, salesmen seeking a vacancy sign, eighteen-wheelers with their cargoes of foodstuffs and machinery. The White Truck slowed at an off ramp. A few minutes later, the floorboards rumbled and bounced above a dirt road.

Skinny got out to unlock a gate and again to relock it behind him. A moment later, he cut the ignition and they could hear other dogs barking. A curse. A blow. After a couple of dogs were silenced, the others fell quiet.

All in a rush, the rear doors were hurled open and the cage doors unlocked.

"Come on out of there. Come out, sweet babies."

A bearded man and Skinny standing in the middle of a receiving pen. Nop lay still as a stream of dogs hurried out of the cages, some of them jumping right over him. Dogs landing on the ground. Small dogs hesitating to make the leap, pushed by those behind. "Hurry, sweet babies. I don't have all damn night." Spiky gray beard.

Khaki shirt. Wide heavy belt buckle. In his right hand, an orange-colored stick.

Several dogs made obeisance, groveling in the dirt. A Poodle sat up and begged. The Poodle wore a red ribbon behind her ear and a smear of fecal matter on one white flank.

The Setter stepped up forthrightly and offered his paw. The big man ignored him. "How many Cockers?"

"Fifteen, Mr. Ralston. The dog warden at Burnsville had a Cocker but wouldn't let it go."

"Fifteen aren't seventy."

"I can only buy what they bring me."

"I'm gonna have to get on the horn. If we don't have the Cockers by next week, NIH is gonna start shopping around."

"There's that dog auction in Pennsylvania."

"That's Friday, a week. And everybody there bidding up Cockers because they know I'm stuck for the NIH contract. Harvard called yesterday. They're looking for black Labs. Older animals: eight, nine years old. Aging research."

"We already got a couple Labradors."

"Uh-huh. Harvard'll pay three hundred. Bitch or dog, no difference. We can give fifty for them."

He leaned over, peering at the bundles still in the truck. "I told you once, I told you a hundred times, this trip's a stress on dogs. When you buy unhealthy dogs, they don't make it. I see, three, no four, ain't moving and one of them's a Cocker. That's a hundred bucks worth of dead dog you hauled back here."

Skinny set his mouth hard but didn't say anything.

Nop lay just as still as the dead Cocker. Give him an opening and he meant to take it. Dogs swirled around the two men, some squatting to relieve themselves in the dirt. A few cowered against the farthest corner of the pen. The truck was backed into an old milk barn. The central aisles were open and the old stalls were covered with wire mesh. A jumble of old corn planters lay in one corner. Cobwebs connected wooden beams.

Elite Kennels could house three hundred and fifty dogs in the converted barn. When the barn was full up, they locked dogs outside in an old metal corncrib.

The bearded man took an involuntary step backward. "Hey! This bastard's alive!"

"Which?"

"This one. Black-and-white Border Collie." He held his orange-colored stick like a weapon. "Troublesome, cunning beasts. Come out of there, sweet baby, or I'll tickle you."

Nop bared his teeth soundlessly. He couldn't see any opening in the pen. Wire higher than he could jump. Wire overhead.

The stick just touched him. *Terrible*. The shock from the cattle prod knocked the wind right out of him. The bearded man touched him again (*Terrible*) with the rod designed to move a full-grown bull. "You ticklish, sweet baby? You want to bite old Chipper?"

Chip Ralston grabbed Nop by one leg and hurled him into the dirt, scattering the other dogs. Nop's tongue lolled out of his mouth and his near legs twitched spasmodically. He wanted to rise to his feet. Oh, how he wanted to.

Ralston took a deliberate step forward, cattle prod extended like a sword. "I hate a vicious dog," Ralston said. He patted the wire pliers in his hip pocket. "Dog tries to use his teeth on me, I'll have his teeth, or I'll tickle them until they don't get up no more. Sweet baby." The prod paused a half inch from Nop's skull, then withdrew. Ralston's big chest heaved. He wiped his forehead with the back of his hand. "Mercy," he said. "I can't lose my temper like that. Old blood pressure goes straight to hell. I want that dog on the first truck going out. Junior's taking a load to Detweiler Labs in the morning. If I see that dog again, I'll lose my temper and Detweiler won't pay two hundred dollars for no dead dog."

Nop's coat was covered with dust and dog droppings. Skinny dragged him into a big cage, next to the receiving pen, with the thirty other dogs scheduled to go out at 3 A.M.

The two men sorted dogs. They had a pen for Cockers, another pen for purebred bitches of breeding age. A few young, fashionable dogs were put aside for the pet stores. Most, like Nop, would go to research. The Britanny went in Nop's pen.

"What about this one?"

Ralston ran his hand through the Setter's lustrous red fur. The Setter wagged. "He's got a nice pelt on him. Put him out in the corncrib with the bunch for the furriers."

Nop's left side was paralyzed. The other dogs in the pen didn't have anything to say. They knew they were going to die and what more can a dog say than that?

Skinny fed and watered the other dogs but didn't bother

with Nop's bunch. He cut all the lights when he left the barn. In the dark the steady pulsation of dog hearts, dog brains, dog breathing.

Bit by bit, the feeling returned to Nop's legs and as soon as he could hobble, he prowled the pen seeking an opening. His pen mates didn't object. They'd seen others make that tour before.

After three, a camper-bodied pickup backed into the barn and the lights came on again, making the farthest reaches of the barn bright as day. The driver wasn't anyone Nop had seen before. He kept the orange electric prod in his hand until the dogs climbed aboard the truck.

The truck rolled south. Each dog was alone with its thoughts. They made one brief stop at a vet's office to collect health certificates for interstate travel. Since the vet who signed the papers didn't inspect the dogs, the stop didn't take long.

The dogs were silent. Nop's ancestors were silent. Nop had found his new balance point. He was a free dog: without covenant.

When the sun came up, the driver stopped for breakfast. Out of habit he parked in the very back of the lot. Thirty minutes later, still sucking bits of Egg McMuffin through his teeth, he backed up to the loading dock of Detweiler Labs: Quality Pharmaceuticals.

Though Detweiler did manufacture some pharmaceuticals, its principal business was testing other manufacturers' products, especially products suspected of being carcinogenic.

A large steel cage stood on the south end of the concrete

257

platform and the pickup camper backed right up to the sliding gate with no gap, not the tiniest. Dispiritedly, the dogs came out. When the kennel truck pulled away, they were quite alone.

Some dogs stretched. Some yawned. Some shivered. Nop prowled. Experimentally, he gnawed the mesh, but it was much harder than his teeth.

The rush of trucks grumbled on the nearby highway. A few cars rolled by in front of the low brick building; birds woke in the dewy grasses and sang their cheerful songs. A dog scratched his fleas. Another took up the thumping beat.

A golden light lay over the fields behind the lab.

At 7:30 Detweiler's lowest paid workers started arriving. They hurried up the concrete steps at the far end of the dock and were buzzed inside. Though there were thirty dogs, just a few feet away, no worker spared them a glance.

Lewis fought his fight just before three o'clock on a Thursday afternoon in June. Just a hundred miles south, that weekend, they were to run the 24th annual Kentucky Bluegrass Open Sheep Dog Trials, but Lewis wasn't thinking about that. He just wanted to get his dog back.

Stiff from travel, he and Mark climbed out of the VW. "That's his car," Lewis said. "That De Lorean sportscar."

"I guess Whitenaur's home."

"I surely hope so. Once we have Nop safe, I mean to give that gentleman a piece of my mind."

But nobody answered the doorbell. Nobody answered

when they pounded either. Mark put his head against the door to listen. "If he's in there, he's awful quiet."

"That's his car parked in the driveway. Of course he's here." And Lewis rang the doorbell with no better luck than Mark had. A curtain fluttered in the house next door. In this neighborhood, years could go by without neighbors talking to each other, but they shared a common fear of burglars.

"Nop'll be in the kennels. I believe we'll just go back there and liberate him." Lewis liked the word and repeated it. "Yes. We'll liberate Nop."

Mark said that they'd need something to bust into the kennels. He got his hardened-steel fence pliers from the VW. They could snip their way in or, failing that, use the hammer face to shatter the lock.

The neighbor's curtain fluttered again as the two men started around the side of the house.

Hack and Sandy were waiting for them, Sandy with a dog lead wrapped around his knuckles. Hack carried no weapon except his hands and his rage.

"My name is Lewis Burkholder," Lewis began. "Mr. Whitenaur has my dog. Nop is a black-and-white Border Collie with a patch of brown behind . . ."

"Wow," Sandy said, stretching the word until it wobbled.

Hack's hands hung at his sides like live animals taking their last precious seconds of rest. His eyes had a funny, blank shine.

Lewis took a breath and began again. "My dog, Nop, is in the kennels here. I intend to examine those kennels and take my dog home and if you interfere with me, it will go hard with you."

Lewis's body was settling and he was swelling and growing squat as his center of gravity dropped.

"You ain't goin' anywhere, hayseed. Mr. D says he don't want you comin' 'round no more. He is sick of your face." For emphasis, Sandy smacked his mailed fist into his palm. It sounded like a cleaver hitting a carcass. Hack glided forward, intent on Mark.

"I shan't be turned away," Lewis said.

"Makes no difference," Sandy grinned. "Your dog is dead. Right now that mutt is lifting his leg in dog heaven."

Lewis grew still. Sandy cocked his fist and showed all his teeth.

"Good," Hack grunted and broke Mark's nose. Mark windmilled at him and the dark-haired man stepped back out of range and jabbed at Mark's ribs.

Every year, Lewis had to upend his rams for the sheep shearer. His rams averaged close to three hundred pounds. While Sandy's punch whistled by overhead, Lewis reached down, grabbed behind Sandy's leg and jerked it out from under him. His free hand lifted Sandy's rib cage and Lewis's shoulder was behind the shove. Sandy's ankle twisted as he fell and his wind whooshed out of him.

Hack glided around Mark, whistling soundlessly, like a workman intent on his task.

Mark cautiously tried to match the other man's jabs. He didn't quite know what to do with the fencing pliers but used them to block some of Hack's fast punches. His nose hurt bad. All his face above his mouth swelled like a painful melon.

Split seconds, shifting distances, pain and blood. Lewis had Sandy wrapped on hands and knees. He rammed Sandy's head against the wall of the house. The sound seemed loud to Lewis but you couldn't have heard it at the street.

Mark's jabs were ineffectual and Hack batted them aside. Mark hadn't landed one good blow. Hack stepped back, dropped his arms and shook them out. Lewis rammed Sandy's head again. Sandy said, "Uh." Hack grinned and shook his head like an indulgent father watching favorite offspring at play.

Lewis flung Sandy at the house and hurt him bad.

A siren growled. It wasn't far away, already in the driveway.

Lewis had Sandy's left arm bent behind his back and Sandy's neck in a choke hold. He knelt on one of Sandy's legs.

Hack straightened at the siren. He said, "Hssst!" and wiped his mouth. Freed from the barrage of blows, Mark paused for a heartbeat or two before he smacked Hack on the side of the face with the flat of the fence pliers. Though the pliers didn't break bones, there's plenty blood in the face and it shot out where the pliers landed.

Hack said, "Oh. Cops. Cops, you idiot." Hack touched the blood spurting through his fingers into his dangling hair.

The cops was one cop, Sergeant Nelson, who watched

Lewis grinding Sandy's face against the concrete for a moment before announcing cheerfully, "What have we here? Mr. Hackemeyer, hello. Burkholder, if you keep rubbing Sandy Allbright's face into the cement, it's gonna damage his credibility. Leave off! Break it up!"

Mark's face was gray and he hunkered down with his back against the house. His legs were trembling and he had to sit flat on the pavement with his legs stuck out in front of him.

"Let him up, Burkholder. I won't tell you again!"

Lewis let his hands drop and leaned back on his knees. "He killed Nop," he said in a voice the color of lead. "He killed a dog that was a friend of mine." Lewis got to his feet but never quit looking at Sandy who was bloody and swollen. "I'm not sorry I did this," Lewis said. "If you put me in prison for it, I'm not sorry."

"That bastard hit me with that thing," Hackemeyer said. "That's a deadly weapon."

"Not deadly enough, Mr. Hackemeyer," Nelson said. "I know you."

That bit of information hung in the air while Hackemeyer wiped at his bloody hair and Sandy crawled into the bushes to toss his lunch and Lewis knelt beside his son-in-law touching his temples. "Don't even try to breathe through your nose," Lewis advised. "No sense even trying."

"Mr. Whitenaur, he's a particular friend of yours?" Nelson asked Hack.

"Yeah," Hack replied. He was offended trying to comb the blood out of his hair. "Whitenaur hired us to watch his home. He thought these two farmers might try and trespass."

"What about the dog?" Nelson asked.

Sandy turned one ruined eye to the cop. His face looked horrible. His eyebrows had been scraped right off. "There's one dog won't yap at anybody again. And what of it? A man can kill a dog anytime he wants to, right? No law against that."

Sergeant Nelson said, "Some of your caps are broken, Sandy. It's gonna cost you to get them replaced."

Sandy's hand went to his mouth. Tentative and amazed. His eyes filled. "Oh, I'll get you, hayseed. One day . . ."

Lewis said, "I believe Mark here's going into shock. I took the advanced first aid, you know. This is a life-threatening situation."

"Call the ambulance," Sandy said. "I want X rays. I'm gonna sue you, hayseed. Count on it!"

"I call an ambulance, it's official," Nelson said. "I'll bet you don't want it official."

Very quick off the mark, Hack said, "That's right, Sergeant."

Nelson eyeballed him for the longest time before nodding once, like he and Hack had entered into an agreement between professionals. "I'll take you two in my car. Burkholder, you follow."

Lewis helped Mark walk. Sandy had to make it on his own.

Lewis drove by habit and reflex. A great calm came over him. What had been was foreordained and likewise that which was to come. His ears registered Mark's breathing.

"You just relax," he said. "There ain't that much wrong with you." Quite unconsciously, he used the strong calm voice of Lewis Burkholder, Chief, White Post Volunteer Fire Department.

"I'm sorry, Lewis," Mark said. "It's a shame."

"Oh, don't you worry about Nop," Lewis said from the center of his great calm. "Nop loved the farm. In two or three days his soul will drift on home. I expect it'll take a day for him to find his way through the mountains."

In the lead car Sergeant Nelson said, pleasantly, "You boys just moved up on my list. I believe you bobbed right up to the top of it."

Sandy moaned. "I think my ankle is broken."

Hack sat as far away from Sandy as he could.

"How'd you come to meet a man like Whitenaur?" Nelson asked.

"Old friends. Mr. D and us are old friends."

"That dog you killed was stolen," Nelson said. "The dog was worth felony money. You boys just hit the jackpot."

"You gonna try and nail us?" Hack asked, angrily. "You just go ahead and try."

Sergeant Nelson drove without the siren.

After a bit, Hack said, "The dog isn't dead, you know."

Sergeant Nelson pulled into the emergency entrance of Doctor's Hospital but didn't get out or open the door. He faced his prisoners through the steel mesh of the cage. "Spill," he said.

"Off the list," Hack bargained. "Not on your list anywhere."

Sandy cursed. He said Hack was a punk. He would have said more except Hack grabbed his wrist and twisted it.

Tersely, Hack told Sergeant Nelson how he'd left the dog chained to a green dumpster behind Holman's Bakery. "I gave the dog away," he said and chuckled. His stiff, bloody hair fell over one eye. "Mutt like that? Five thousand dollars for a mutt like that? He looked like he'd lost every fight he ever fought. I gave the dog to a red-haired bag lady. I never killed him. I just found him a home."

Sandy was stupefied. "Why?" he asked and the question came from some place in him deeper than pain.

"Because he had more guts than you do," Hack said.

And Nelson opened the door and Sandy went right into Emergency and Hack snarled, "I don't need no doctor. I just need a shampoo," and his figure got small until it was gone.

The intern took Sandy before he took Mark and Lewis felt a slight perverse pleasure that he'd hurt his enemies more than they'd hurt his kin. Sergeant Nelson took the seat next to him.

"These emergency rooms are awful sad," Lewis said.

"You get used to 'em," Nelson said. "They didn't kill your dog. They gave it to a bag lady. There's a red-headed bag lady named Susie Q. Sounds like the one. I'll get your dog back."

Lewis said, "Don't be foolin' with me now. This isn't a foolin' matter."

So Nelson told Lewis just what Hack said and added he didn't think the man was lying.

Lewis chewed on that for a few minutes. "All right,"
he said slowly. "So why are you helpin' us now? You
might have helped us earlier and saved considerable grief."

"I warned Whitenaur," Nelson answered.

"I figured you had," Lewis said gravely. "Wasn't anybody else knew we were in town."

The intern came out to say they'd taped Mark's cracked
ribs and set his broken nose. They wanted Mark to stay in
the hospital overnight for observation.

"You're worryin' he has a concussion?" Lewis asked.

That was one of the possibilities, yes.

"You just hang on to him until you're sure he's right."
Lewis knew he'd be the one to tell Penny and Beverly.
The prospect didn't please him overmuch.

Sergeant Nelson told Lewis about the trouble Whitenaur had made after Lewis came looking for Nop before.
Nelson said he was on his way to Whitenaur's house when
the police dispatcher reported a burglary in progress and
four burglars fighting, trying to kill one another.

Lewis laughed. It wasn't particularly funny but he had
been dry so long. "Nop's alive," he said. "That's the good
news."

They phoned the city dog pound from a booth right in
the emergency room but no Nop. Nelson called the Ohio
State animal officer and asked questions and made a few
more calls. No Nop.

Nelson said he'd put the word out on the street. Finding
Susie Q would be "duck soup."

Lewis took a room at the downtown Holiday Inn. He
showered, changed and went right back out again. Lewis

checked the city pound himself. Not everybody knows what a champion stockdog looks like. No Nop.

He waited until he had eaten dinner (Salisbury steak, medium rare with baked potato and sour cream and the blue cheese salad dressing) before he called Beverly. When he said Nop was alive she said, "Thank God." She said she had prayed for Lewis.

"I don't have him yet, Beverly," he said. "But we're close. Sergeant Nelson said finding him would be duck soup."

Lewis downplayed the fight and made Mark's injuries seem quite minor, but Beverly's voice got quiet and distant all at once. "Lewis, what have you done?"

Lewis's excuses didn't really help.

Beverly said some of the things a wife says to a husband on these occasions, infrequent though they may be. Lewis hung his head. She said, "Lewis, where would we be if you got hurt or killed? You're not a kid anymore."

"That man bragged he'd murdered Nop."

Undaunted, she replied, "But he hadn't, had he?"

No answering that.

After a bit, when she was in a better frame of mind, she forgave him. "Phone in the morning, as soon as Mark is released from the hospital. Don't dawdle now, or you'll miss us."

Beverly, Penny and the Stink Dog were setting off for the Kentucky Bluegrass Sheep Dog Trials. Yes, they had the camper on the pickup. Neighbors had helped them load. Yes, they had somebody to feed the livestock.

"Once you find Nop, you can just drive down and meet us there. Lexington isn't far from where you are. Lewis, Penny's so darned excited."

"Don't worry her about Mark. He isn't hurt bad. I'll put him on a bus tomorrow and send him home. He should rest up." Lewis laughed. "He'll need his strength for when the baby comes."

Finding Nop was not duck soup. That night, the Cincinnati P.D. had two murders, an arson and several burglaries to handle. Nobody had time to look for a bag lady and a stolen dog.

In the morning the hospital released Mark. Mark's cheeks were black and blue. "It was a good thing you had a hammer," Lewis joked. "You needed it." Mark said he'd be glad to get back to the farm.

By eleven o'clock in the morning, the cops traced Susie Q to the Belvedere. Though everybody remembered her and her dog, nobody knew where they'd gone. Lewis lay around watching afternoon TV. Waiting was hard for him.

Eight-thirty that night, they finally traced Susanna Cunningham to the House of Naomi. Nelson called Lewis to fill him in. "The address they got for this Leon character isn't current. We'll have to catch him tomorrow morning when he comes in to work."

"Saturday?" Lewis asked.

Sourly: "Yeah. Saturday. That's my day off. Me and the wife had plans."

So Lewis ate dinner in the Holiday Inn again.

Home Box Office was showing *Atlantic City* with Burt Lancaster. Lewis'd always liked Burt Lancaster because he'd been a real athlete before he became a movie star. It shocked him to see Burt looking so old. That night Lewis slept badly.

At a quarter to seven, the morning of June 12, Lewis Burkholder was waiting in Mark's VW outside the steps of the women's shelter. Just one year ago, he'd been in Lexington watching the first dogs run. Eighty dogs ran on qualifying day and the top twenty would run in the finals, Sunday. Last year Lewis ran the Stink Dog. It had been so green, so very green: the long horse pasture, lifting away. The wild Texas sheep they brought in special, just for the trial.

Nelson rapped on the car window and Lewis let him in. Nelson wore a red-and-black checked hunting jacket and his tan Hush Puppies were spattered with flecks of white paint. "My wife really loves you, Burkholder. Thanks for the wonderful day off."

Lewis turned away wrath. "It's gonna be a nice morning," he said. "You ever see a sheep dog trial?"

Nelson hadn't. Lewis told him about the Bluegrass Trial, which is the Kentucky Derby of all American trials.

"All those guys come flying in for this trial? First prize is five hundred bucks? Don't make sense to me, buying a five-thousand-dollar dog to win a five-hundred-dollar prize."

"There's plenty of other trials with bigger prize money. But the Bluegrass—well, it's special."

"That diddybop comin' down the street now. Five'll get you ten, that's your man."

Leon readily admitted selling the dog. The dog was too

vicious for the pound, Leon said. "White Truck don't care if a dog is mean. They take all kinds."

"Which white truck?"

"White Truck, man. White Truck. Parks down behind the Shakey's Pizza."

"A dog dealer?"

"Sure, what you think?"

"What's the dealer's name?"

"How should I know? White Truck, man."

When Sergeant Nelson called the state animal control officer, he learned about the White Truck. He learned about one or two other dealers, too, but White Truck was the worst. "A real piece of work," the animal officer said. "Elite Kennels runs that truck." And he provided an address and a little free advice: were it him, he wouldn't announce his visit in advance. Nelson was so determined to salvage some of his day that the two men rolled through Goshen, Ohio, by half past eight.

No sign advertised Elite Kennels. One sign beside the gate said:

NO TRESPASSING. ATTACK DOGS.

In black stick-on letters another sign claimed:

DANGEROUS DOGS. NO VISITORS. TRESPASSERS WILL BE DAMAGED.

"Where's their hospitality suite?" Nelson asked, gruffly.

Lewis was all keyed up and his laugh was sudden and loud. Nelson gave him a look to prove it wasn't that funny and climbed the gate.

The road crossed the top of a knoll and the whole place was laid out below them. The fields were overgrown and choked with brush and scrub cedar. Most of the fences were down. A big old barn with a metal corncrib and, some distance away, a newish house. "It's been some time since this place was farmed," Lewis observed.

"Yeah, I suppose so." Nelson was listening to dogs barking. He had his hand on his hip, not so far from his off-duty revolver.

The farmhouse was a low brick rancher. It wasn't very big but everything was new and neat as a pin. The windows were covered with aluminum screen-and-storm combinations and the roof guttering was bright. The brick walk was bordered by low wire guards so nobody would step off and crush the new grass.

A bearded man opened the door. Lewis hated him on sight. "You can't read?" Ralston asked. "You want to see what my Dobes can do to your throat?"

Wordlessly, Nelson flashed his I.D.

Ralston didn't take it for granted. He studied the card, "Cinci, huh? You're a long way from home. So?"

"You got a federal license, pal. Federal law says law officers got a right to go into your kennels."

"I think I'm gonna electrify that gate," Ralston noted. "Wouldn't be too hard to do, just use a regular charger and insulate the hinges. You know how many kooks I get up here? You think the law protects *me?*"

"You picked up a stolen Border Collie, black and white, in Cincinnati yesterday morning."

Ralston twinkled like Old King Cole. "Jesus Christ, no! My drivers always get a bill of sale. Every dog. You mean some thieving bastard sold us a stolen animal? Mercy."

"Yeah, yeah. We go down and look through your dogs and pick up the dog and we're out of your hair. Let's go."

Lewis disliked Ralston's beard, which reminded him of the spike on a German helmet. He disliked the neatness of the man's haircut and thought Ralston spent too much time in front of a mirror.

Ralston's rough green flannel shirt seemed an obvious attempt to make the man more rural than he was, and his neat whipcord trousers were too neat and tucked into a pair of comfortably worn L. L. Bean boots. Ralston's wearing them was the first bad thing Lewis ever knew about Bean boots. Lewis stuffed his balled-up fists into his pockets. What was coming over him? His knuckles were hardly scabbed from his last fight.

"Who's your pal?" Ralston asked. "Looks like you lost the argument." He noted Lewis's bruises.

"You should have seen the other guy," Lewis said, cheerfully, meaning it, every word.

"He a cop too?"

"He's the dog's owner. He'll come along to pick out his dog."

"Nothing in the law says I have to let anybody look except law officers. . . ."

"I could make you so much trouble," Nelson said, pleasantly enough.

Since Ralston seemed to be weighing just how much trouble Nelson could actually cause, Lewis said, "I'm Lewis Burkholder from White Post, Virginia, and I've come for my dog."

Ralston said, "You know, I think I will electrify that gate." He came out of his house and heeled the door shut.

272

Nelson kept right up with him though his feet were hitting the ground about twice as often as the bigger man's. "You buy many dogs?"

"We'll do between five and six thousand a year. I'm just a little guy, kind of a cottage industry."

"How much do you get for a dog?"

"Depends." They passed a row of trucks: big ones, little ones, all closed-bodied. They passed a rusty old corncrib, just a tin roof over wire mesh. The corncrib held twenty dogs. Most of them were alive.

A dog skull was half stuffed into the broken foundation. A single hole in the top of the skull, about the size of a twenty-two bullet. Ralston saw Nelson spot the skull. "Of course, I can't sell every dog I buy. Some months it hardly pays me to put my trucks on the road. I don't like to kill a dog, but the dogs I keep have to be just about perfect—intelligent, healthy, and I won't keep no vicious dog."

The dogs in the corncrib jumped at the mesh. Several did tricks that humans had taught them.

Ralston faced Lewis. He knew who his enemies were. "You see these dogs? These dogs'll bring me some bucks. Doberman skins look like sealskin and German Shepherd fur—you know those big expensive down parkas? Wolf fur to trim the hood." He pointed to the Setter. "Red Fox." He spread his hands to include all the dogs: "It's the newest thing—fun furs."

Nelson pushed right between the two smiling men. "We came for your dog. What was his name?"

"Nop. His name is Nop. He's a black-and-white Border Collie."

273

"That's what I thought you said," Ralston said. "I should have told you. I don't have no Border Collies, but," he added, lifting the heavy padlock out of the hasp, "you're welcome to look inside." With a flourish he skidded the double doors open.

Lewis looked in every pen. He narrowed his heart down to his single purpose and checked every cage and even prowled behind the heap of farm machinery.

Sergeant Nelson's day off was irretrievably spoiled. Though he stayed in the receiving pen, he couldn't help seeing some of the cages: hundreds of dogs; all the breeds he knew and some he didn't. He lit a cigarette. It smelled better than the smell in the barn.

Like a too amiable guide, Ralston accompanied Lewis on his excursion. "This pen here, young bitches. Most of them'll go to the puppy farms. Regular little puppy machines, they are. The puppies'll go to pet stores."

"You got papers for them?"

Mock surprise. "Why? Do you have some papers to sell?"

Lewis bit his lower lip and continued his inspection. He was looking for Nop so he couldn't see that bright-eyed German Shorthair and he refused to meet the eyes of those Beagles who looked so ill.

He ignored the pen of black Labs. Must have been twenty Labs, brown eyes set in deep black heads—older dogs—each, someone's boon companion.

"You'd be surprised who we do business with: all the big med schools, U. Mass., Harvard, U. Va., all those." Ralston waved airily. "That's top dollar. The smaller

pharmaceutical houses aren't so particular—but"—philo-
sophical shrug—"they don't pay so good either." He
poured dry dogfood into a trough and the dogs fought to
get at it.

"What's wrong with that one?" A Weimaraner had won
a place at the trough but was having great difficulty eating.

"I pulled his teeth." Ralston stooped to croon to the
dog, "You thought you were such a tough dog, didn't
you, sweet baby?"

Lewis wore a stone face. The chills ran up his arms and
into his cheekbones. He didn't trust himself to utter a
word. When they completed the circle back to the receiving pen, he jerked a nod of disappointment.

Nelson asked, patiently, "Where's the dog? Black-and-
white Border Collie with a bent ear?"

Ralston shrugged. "I've shown you all my dogs."

Nelson stepped on his cigarette butt. "I got a witness
places that stolen dog on your truck yesterday morning.
The state animal warden tells me you got to keep animals
you buy for twenty-four hours, federal law. If that dog
ain't here, you're in trouble."

Ralston laughed.

Stiff-legged, Lewis went outside. He didn't dare take
his hands from his pockets. Lewis looked at the horizon,
the brush in the gully bottoms.

"I don't want to pee on your parade, Sergeant, but
paperwork mistakes happen all the time." Ralston's laugh
was a rich, juicy chortle. "Dogs get misplaced. You think
a court's gonna get excited about that, then, you just go
ahead and take me to court."

"Uh-huh."

Lewis's gorge rose in his throat. It was painful swallowing it down.

The sergeant put his face in Ralston's and said, "You won't do any more business in my town. I drove all the way down here for a dog and, by Jesus, I'll go back with that dog. Otherwise, next time your truck parks in Cincinnati, gonna be a black-and-white parked right beside it. How many people gonna come around to sell you dogs if there's a couple officers watching every transaction? I'll ask a couple patrolmen who own dogs. Maybe the cops who train our German Shepherds. Those guys love their dogs more'n they love their wives. I'll have an answer out of you, Ralston, and I'll have that answer now."

Ralston licked his lips. "I think I remember a black-and-white dog going out to Detweiler Labs this morning. It must have been a paperwork mistake. I thought we picked up that dog three days ago. Honest mistake."

"Detweiler Labs, where?"

Ralston told him. He stepped deeper into his barn to cut the light switches. Swiftly, Sergeant Nelson moved outside, sliding the big doors shut and snapping the laminated chrome padlock.

"Hey! Hey! What the hell do you think you're doing? Open this door!"

When Ralston started hammering the door and kicking, the policeman moved a few steps away where it was quieter. He fired a cigarette and drew the smoke deep. "Don't take it to heart, Burkholder. People are scumbags.

You just got to get used to the fact." With his toe he nudged the dog skull under the foundation—out of sight. "How long you been foolin' with dogs?"

Lewis swallowed. "We always had dogs on the farm, but I've been running trials for eight years now."

"I never saw no stockdog trial. I never did have no special fondness for dogs." When he plucked the latch pin on the corncrib door, the metal door swung open of its own accord.

The dogs were suspicious of the opening.

"I can't help you no more," Nelson went on. "Law says I can inspect a dealer for stolen dogs, but I can't go into no research facility without a regular warrant. I got no pull in Kentucky."

A Shepherd slipped through. An Elkhound. A pair of Dobermans. None of them wasted a glance on the humans.

"I'll go by myself," Lewis said.

Nelson was rocking on his heels as the dogs streamed out of the cage. One of two looked back, wistfully, at the humans, but most of them were running flat out and the stragglers soon followed. A hunting dog bayed as they sped through the fields, running like a pack, dodging stubby cedars and brush piles.

The barn door shook. Ralston threatened to "have somebody's badge."

Nelson said, "Let me know when you get your dog back."

"Yes. Thank you."

"Look at that red dog run. Rate he's traveling, he'll be

in the next county by nightfall. Jesus! Look at the way he cleared that fence. He's got the pedal to the metal."

"Those Irish Setters can run. Fellow back home has a Setter, name of Rusty. Nice Setter. Runs right behind his pickup wherever he travels. Dog'll do twenty, twenty-five miles without breathing hard."

When Dogs Run Free

By nine o'clock, Detweiler Laboratory's executives were seeking their numbered parking spaces and car doors slammed and people exchanged how-de-dos and the building's machines started up (the air conditioner, lab machinery and computers). The smell of fresh coffee drifted out to the dogs on the loading dock and they could hear the lab techs gossiping and joking.

Nine-thirty, the forklift came for the cage. The driver scribbled the dog count on his clipboard. When the forklift's electric motor whirred and the cage shook under their feet, several dogs moved nervously, a couple growled.

The forklift rolled down a wide concrete passageway, pausing at labs J-1, L-3 and Chemo-16, dropping a few dogs here, a few there. The driver wore heavy elbow-length leather gauntlets, but the dogs were too apathetic to bite.

Nop lay in the farthest corner, very still. His brain was frantic but he was motionless as the Brittany bitch. Her eyes were wide open, but she wasn't seeing anything. Her breath was quick and shallow. She had given up on her puppies.

As the forklift purred toward the front of the building, the lab doors changed from plain metal to wood veneer.

Checked his clipboard: five for 312.

Six for 314. Dr. Barnhardt. Right.

Just two more dogs. Oops, Dr. Oblenz wanted six. Two's what we got. Two's what he'll get.

When the driver lifted the Brittany bitch into the lab cage, he knew she was dead or dying but that was none of his concern. Let Oblenz sort it out. He kept a good grip on Nop's collar and Nop knew this wasn't the time.

One wall of the lab was cages from floor to ceiling. Some of the cages still held food and water dishes from previous occupants but there were only two dogs: Nop and the Brit. Nop lay with his snout between his paws. The Brit was on her side, heaving and gasping.

Nop didn't watch. Death comes to us all.

An interior room, the lab was windowless, lit with fluorescents. Their soft steady hum was punctuated by the irregular *plink* of water dripping into the stainless lab sink. A laboratory table with shrouded instruments. An old office desk pushed against the wall. Opposite: the heavy doors of a walk-in cooler. The wall phone was beside a message board. The messages on the green composition board were standard industrial messages concerning safety and nondiscrimination and curled notes (and cartoons) from the last experiment.

Dr. Oblenz was a short, stocky man smoking a Balkan Sobranie cigarette in a dark amber holder. His eyes darted left and right. His hands were gripped behind his back.

He entered with the authority of a limousine. His assistant hurried behind. She was awry.

His gold hair was plump and slick and couldn't quite conceal his widow's peak. He rubbed his hands together. He opened desk drawers and dumped them: erasers, paper clips, a tin of aspirins. "You'll take care of this trash, Wendy, hmm?"

Too much eye shadow and her lipstick was too dark for her pale complexion. She was a little thing and her light brown hair was sun streaked. She brushed a wisp of hair from her eyes. "Yes, Dr. Oblenz."

They propped the hall door open while the stubby doctor emptied drawers and files and his assistant stacked them outside. He was, perhaps, fifty. She was half that. He wore his confidence like a tailored suit. She was always banging into sharp edges and handled lab glassware very, very carefully.

He paused to insert a new cigarette in his holder. With a slight flourish he laid a brightly colored folder on the desk. Oblenz was Middle European and flamboyant in small things. "We will be repeating Barnhardt's experiment," he said.

"Repeating it?"

"Ah, yes. Dr. Barnhardt's experiment indicated that our client's additive fed in great concentrations produced cancerous growth in the kidney and liver of test animals. Our client, naturally, was displeased by this result so we shall repeat the experiment using lower doses. Simple, yes?"

"Won't the FDA . . . ?"

A paternal chuckle. Oblenz beamed. "Wendy, I am sure

the client has anticipated that objection. In any case, it is not our concern. We shall replicate Barnhardt's work. It should not be too arduous."

Rubbing his hands, he turned to the cages. As chance had it, he saw the Brittany first. He bowed to look closer. He ran his right hand through his hair. "Dead," he announced. "This specimen is dead. It is quite filthy and it is dead. Who has brought me this specimen?"

Nop had one eye on the propped-open hall door. His nerves sang to the anger in the man's voice. When men get angry, they make mistakes.

Perhaps some ancestor had survived lying doggo, feigning unconsciousness under some prehistoric sky. Perhaps Nop had a genuine idea. Nop let his head slide off his paws and relaxed his jaw so his tongue hung down and lay on the cage floor. His eyes slid back so far in his sockets he couldn't see. Only the whites were visible. He shuddered. Shuddered again. "This too! Dying!"

Nop could smell the cigarette smoke. He shuddered, kicked one leg.

Rather sadly, Oblenz said, "I am a scientist. It is my work." Though he turned to Wendy, her ears were only representative of the many ears he wished to hear his complaint. "How am I to experiment with specimens like these? I have spoken to the director. To the director I have said, this supplier brings us filthy, unhealthy animals. We are not a veterinary clinic, yet we must clean and make healthy the specimens he brings us. I ask for six healthy specimens and here are two: one dead, one dying."

The smoke from his cigarette swirled around his head.

Nop didn't change his position but he didn't shudder either. Behind half-closed lids he was watching everything.

Oblenz went to the wall phone, dialed, paused to draw himself up before he punched the final number. His voice was smooth as fresh cream. "Jeannie? Dr. Oblenz. I wish to see the director on a matter of some urgency. I see. No. The assistant director most definitely will not do, as he is the one who awards suppliers with our contracts. So, when the director has concluded his long-distance call, perhaps he can do me the great honor . . . No!" He lifted his cigarette like an exclamation point. "I shall speak with the director, myself." Dr. Oblenz hung up. "Wendy, I want you to take the dogs from their cages and lay them on the big table. I shall bring the director here so he can see this outrage!"

Nop's heart sank when he closed the door.

The assistant parked herself on the corner of the desk and made a face. "Heavy," she said. She checked her makeup in her compact mirror and refreshed it. She hummed, "We all live in a yellow submarine," as she rolled on a pair of disposable surgical gloves. She slid a stainless-steel trolley under the Brittany's cage and wrinkled her nose and said, "Yeech," without breathing. The Brittany was skin and bones and swollen rock-hard dugs. When she arranged the Brittany on the lab table, she set it up on its paws so the dugs wouldn't show but the Brit's legs trembled and twitched and the corpse fell over. "Uck," she said, through her nose.

Though Nop hated to have anyone hold his forepaws,

he didn't tense when she hauled him out of the cage onto the smooth cold cart.

"Doggy," she said through her nose, "you stingk."

She grabbed at him when he moved but missed altogether. His claws found no purchase on the smooth steel but he caught himself on all fours once he hit the floor and went out immediately for his balance point.

"Oh," she said, hand to mouth. "Now I've done it."

Nop came around, facing her in his working stance. His crouch was low and precise. His tail flicked once to the side, catching her eye.

She hated that tail.

His jaw inches off the floor, his neck muscles tense, his shoulders slipping forward in the familiar stalking pattern.

She hated his eyes.

Wendy took a step back. "Hey," she said, "don't you do nothin' now. Don't you hurt me. Nice doggy. Nice doggy."

Nop's tail flicked. He forced her retreat. Her eyes shifted between him and that instrument on the wall. Nop didn't know why she wanted the instrument but he was determined she shouldn't do anything beyond his control.

She darted around the lab desk.

That instant Nop was on the lab tabletop, at the very edge, facing her.

Like a timber wolf. Just like a timber wolf!

Nop had herded five-hundred-pound calves driven wild by rodeo ropers. He had faced down heifers protecting their first calf. His eyes were hot and empty. He was so delicate, so extreme.

And Wendy's heart beat like it was going to burst.

If she had challenged him, he would have leapt into her face, just like he would have stopped an angry cow, but she did not dare and backed steadily into the farthest corner of the lab. She started to cry. He shifted gracefully to the left so he could hold her and still be near the door.

The hall door was bound to open again. Nop knew that much. Sooner or later, that hall door would open and he'd be through it.

The girl's tears were frightened and bitter. Her face ran. Nop was a free dog, strong and skilled. Pitiless. Without taking his eyes from her, he lay down and cleaned his forepaws where she had touched him.

Should he lock his car? Lewis Burkholder didn't know. He never locked in White Post. He always locked on the road; that was the general rule. On the farm or visiting a near neighbor, he never took his key out of the ignition. Who would want to steal the VW? He supposed it was possible. There was a sandlot baseball diamond right across the street from Detweiler Labs and half a dozen kids playing but none of them looked old enough to drive. He'd never had a vehicle stolen. There was always the first time. Lewis Burkholder was dithering. He took a deep breath and dropped the key into his shirt pocket. He cranked down the front windows and popped the rear windows open so Nop would have plenty of air. . . .

The little car was parked in a visitor space in front of Detweiler Labs. That's what the sign said on the metal standard with its ring of night floodlights clustered on the lawn.

Why would anyone want to be able to read Detweiler's sign at night? Maybe because they'd be unfamiliar with this little Kentucky town and had a truckload of dogs to deliver.

The laboratory was a long industrial shed. The front end was faced with brick beneath plate-glass windows. Though it was a pleasant morning, the building looked like it would be hot inside and the window blinds were drawn.

Through the glass door Lewis could see right into the reception room. The receptionist doubled as the switchboard operator. She wore one of those headphones and was pecking something out on the typewriter. The door was locked so Lewis rapped. Rapped again, harder. She looked up, annoyed. Mouthed words. Gestured. There was a button and metal speaker grille on the doorpost. Just like a drive-in hamburger place.

PLEASE PRESS BUTTON.
STATE YOUR NAME AND BUSINESS.
THANK YOU.

Behind the receptionist, a central corridor stretched the length of the building. Wide corridor.

"My name is Lewis Burkholder. I'm from White Post, Virginia. I'm here because you've got my dog. It wasn't your doing. It's a mistake."

The speaker sputtered. Bad static. "What mistake?" The woman put on glasses to peer at Lewis. The door was tempered glass. A man came out of the office right at the head of the corridor. The man had gold hair and wore a white lab coat. He was arguing with somebody inside the office.

"State your business, please." The intercom was still full of static.

Talking very slowly, Lewis specified, "You have my dog. I want my dog back."

The blond-haired man was all smiles now, nodding and bobbing to the person in the office. Once he had the door shut, Lewis could see he was terribly angry.

"We buy all our dogs from federally licensed dog dealers. That's the law. We can't buy from an individual."

She just wasn't hearing him. She'd got it backward. "You got it backward. I didn't bring you a dog. I come for a dog."

The blond man in the lab coat overheard and stepped right up to the glass door, not six inches away. He eyed Lewis for the longest time before he fitted a black cigarette in a stubby yellow holder.

When he turned to speak to the receptionist, Lewis heard every word. "Tell him we are closed to the general public. Tell him we don't have his dog. He may go to the dog pound which is just six blocks from here, if he has lost his dog."

Lewis shouted, "I know my dog's in there."

The speaker sputtered with the information that Detweiler Labs was closed to the general public. "Try the dog pound."

Lewis shook the door but it was too tightly fitted to

rattle. Inches away, already thinking about his own problems, the man in the lab coat looked right through Lewis. He scratched the side of his nose, thoughtfully, before going down the hall. Lewis pressed the button and put his mouth right up to the speaker and yelled that his dog was a black-and-white Border Collie named Nop and Nop'd come with the load from Elite Kennels in Ohio, but the receptionist turned to the switchboard where a light was blinking. Lewis told her that Sergeant Nelson of the Cincinnati Police . . . but she cut her speaker with an impatient flick of thumb and forefinger. Lewis found himself yelling at the glass door and the back of her head. Again he shook the door but it didn't wiggle.

So Lewis marched off, his heart beating very fast. The side of the building was smooth and the back door, beside the concrete loading platform, was guarded by an identical buzzer-and-speaker arrangement. No human on the platform to help him.

The far side of the building was blank, too, though Lewis walked all around it on new sod. He left big footprints in the soft soil. The clumps of dirt on his shoes made him feel awkward. He wondered if anyone inside could see him. He certainly couldn't see them.

He scraped his feet off on the front stoop. When he pressed the button again, the receptionist glowered and switched her speaker off again. She returned to the letter she was typing. Far down the corridor, the blond man had cornered another figure in a lab coat and was gesturing.

Lewis went back down the entrance walk, past his car and all the employees' cars. He kept on going down the sidewalk and when it quit at Detweiler's property line, he kept right on walking. Lewis wondered if the town was big enough to have a police station.

He walked by a little grocery store/gas station and it looked just like the grocery stores back home. He felt homesick. He wondered if dogs ever felt homesick.

The VFW had a hall here. It had been somebody's house once, but it was a VFW hall now. The grass needed cutting.

Eleven o'clock in the morning. What was he doing in Kentucky? He watched his feet proceed with apparent sureness down the sidewalks and when the sidewalks became dirt paths, his feet mastered those too. Probably five hundred, six hundred people lived in this town. More than White Post.

Far overhead an icy jet contrail slashed the sky. Higher than any bird could fly. Lewis found himself standing on the concrete apron of the Craigsville Volunteer Fire Department. The cornerstone in the building bore a date: 1948. Apparently, the volunteers were taking advantage of the weather to wash trucks. A couple soapy buckets and a garden hose, shut off now.

The tank truck was parked behind the International pumper. The pumper was painted yellow which was the color many departments were going to. Personally, Lewis preferred red.

Somewhere inside the firehouse a radio was playing. Crystal Gayle sang: "Don't it make my brown eyes blue."

The tanker was a homemade job with brushed aluminum gear bins underneath the tank. It had been an oil truck once, or maybe an army truck.

The yellow pumper had a rag lying on the front fender.

Careless. Lewis removed the rag and tossed it in the bucket. He supposed the volunteer had had to answer a call of nature or a phone call or . . . something.

Lewis raised his hands shoulder high, like a prisoner. He waggled his hands at the wrists like devil-may-care. The key was right there in the ignition, attached to a little chain so it couldn't be removed from the truck. Lewis wiped his sweaty hands on his knees and took time to examine the dash.

BRAKE LOCK. Flip that off. Lewis had driven fire trucks many a time but never noticed before how high they were off the ground.

CHOKE. All these engines that aren't run very often need a good choke to get them started.

Lewis Burkholder had a distinct thought. He thought, "I am committing a crime." He'd never thought he had it in him.

He fired her up, slipped the choke, popped her into high range/low gear. He kept one eye on the mirror but didn't see a soul, even as he rounded the corner that took him out of sight. It took a delicate touch on throttle and clutch to keep the cold motor smooth. From habit, Lewis reached for the box that housed light and siren controls, paused, and hit the lights but not the siren.

Past the VFW, the houses, the little grocery. Lewis was doing about fifteen miles an hour.

When he nosed into the curb at Detweiler, the kid baseball players came running to see.

He engaged the power takeoff, floored the brake and flipped BRAKE LOCK. There was a fireman's helmet on the floorboards so he picked it up. It had one of those flip-up clear plastic face shields and an emblem that read CHIEF. Since Lewis was a fire chief, he put it on.

Like most pumpers, the International carried three hoses. Lewis would have liked to use the two-inch hose but he didn't think he could handle that big hose alone so he unloaded the neat folds of the inch-and-a-half. The nozzle was a fog nozzle, set (like White Post's nozzle) to a forty-five-degree spray for the initial fire attack. Lewis unscrewed it and replaced it with the straight-stream nozzle. The straight stream was the old-fashioned power nozzle used when firemen couldn't get anywhere near a fire.

The baseball players were asking, "Where's the fire? Is the lab on fire? What's doin'?" One boy was jumping up and down in excitement and a couple new arrivals rolled in on bicycles.

Lewis hauled the limp hose out in a great arc. No kinks. Wouldn't want kinks. Carefully, he laid the nozzle on the stoop right beside the front door. He didn't ring the bell this time. He didn't even look inside.

The pumper's control panel was unfamiliar but the valves were labeled with punched plastic labels.

He revved the throttle and pressed the PRIME lever. Most of the newer trucks have quick prime pumps, but you never can tell; every fire truck's a little different.

TANK TO PUMP. He pulled that lever and the pressure needle bounced once, twice and started to climb. He'd want about a hundred seventy-five pounds. With the inch-and-a-half hose that was all the pressure one man could handle. The truck motor bellowed. Like White Post, these boys hadn't bothered to muffle their fire truck. Lewis would have bet fifty dollars they'd removed all the pollution-control devices too.

The water hissed around in the pump and the needle climbed steadily. The pressure needle swung past a hundred pounds, past a hundred fifty. At one seventy-five, Lewis throttled back. The RPM counter stood at just 2,500 rpm. One hose would be nothing to this truck and it looked to have a 750–1,000 gallon storage tank.

The kids surrounded him, many excited, puzzled faces. The oldest was perhaps ten years old.

"I need some help," Lewis said. "I'm by myself and I need a second man."

One of the kids, a towhead, said, "My dad's in the fire department and I don't know you."

Patiently, Lewis explained, "When I take the nozzle, I'll need someone to pull this valve open." He touched the big red valve labeled: 1½ PRECONNECT delicately, just a tap of his forefinger. "If I charge my hose myself, before I reach the nozzle, it'll be flopping all around and, there's no man who could catch and control it."

The towhead said, "Where's the fire? I don't see any smoke."

A few kids stepped back, taking themselves out of it, and the others were giving Lewis plenty of room.

"Anybody here got a dog?"

Three kids nodded. The towhead too. Kid wore a striped T-shirt and his baseball cap backward on his head in the dashing manner.

"If someone took your dog, what would you do?"

One of the kids said, "Tell the police."

"Look for it."

"Go out in the street and call."

"And what if somebody tried to kill your dog?"

One kid thought he'd "kill them." Another said he'd "punch him just like he punched that kid from Elizabeth City." Another suggested, again, that he'd call the police. The towhead didn't say a word. The other kids were playing with the exciting question and one boy was already dancing around demonstrating just how he'd punched the kid from Elizabeth City—*pow, pow*. The towhead looked thoughtful.

"My name is Burkholder. Lewis Burkholder. A man stole my dog, Nop. Nop's a real good dog and he means a lot to me. They've got Nop inside that building and unless I stop them, they're going to cut him up and kill him. I'm going to go get the nozzle. When you see me raise one hand in the air, I want you to jerk on that valve. It'll come easy. That's all you have to do. Pull the valve and get me water."

And Lewis went up to Detweiler Labs, not knowing whether he'd have the water or not, and picked up the nozzle and cracked it, just a bit so the initial rush wouldn't twist him around.

He raised his hand and got set.

It was a nice Kentucky morning. The fire engine roared.

The receptionist shrieked when the surge of water took the door right out of its frame.

Lewis shut down, stepped through the broken space he'd made. "Excuse me, ma'am," he said. "I didn't really want to do this. I've come for my dog."

She jerked the switchboard headphones right off her

head because she'd heard of people being electrocuted in their bathtubs and the water swirled around her feet.

That man. That man smiling the apologetic smile as he dragged his heavy hose past. The hose was stretched taut as a log, as a . . . the receptionist, a modest lady, blushed.

Lewis threw open the first office door. The man at the desk wore a blue suit, thinning hair and an expression that invited Lewis to explain the commotion. He had papers raised in his left hand, like he was signaling for attention.

"Excuse me," Lewis said, and shut the door.

"Excuse me." He shut the second door too. The laboratories were bound to be in this building somewhere. He'd just look until he found them.

The hose was very, very heavy. At a fire scene, there'd be plenty of willing hands to hump the hose behind the nozzle man but today Lewis had to go it alone.

"Excuse me, ma'am. You happen to see a black-and-white stockdog? A Border Collie? Sorry I bothered you."

Now here came trouble. A couple lab coats running toward him—one the gold-haired man from the front door. Lewis washed them, tumbled them back down the hall like bathtub toys.

There wasn't a soul in the next office, just mail cubicles and the company coffee urn. "Nop?" Lewis asked.

The corridor was awfully long. This building sure didn't look this long from outside.

The director opened his office door. Lewis closed it with ten seconds of straight stream at 175 pounds per square inch.

Heads popped out into the hall and Lewis bellowed at them, "I'm looking for my dog!" But they just ducked.

The water was ankle deep in the hall. At a fire scene he would have had boots and his feet would have been dry. He pushed into CHEMO LAB 3. No people. The cages were full of cats. Dead cat gutted on the lab table. The cat spread out like a fox had been at its innards.

The blond-haired man was coming down that slippery hall like a broadjumper, running head down, fists clenched and his broken cigarette holder jutting out of his mouth like a tusk. Twenty feet away, Lewis slapped him down. He rolled over and pushed through the nearest laboratory door.

And came right out of there like a jack-in-the-box. On top of the man—a dog blur: a black-and-white dog blur, skidding legs splayed like a moon lander. Hit the corridor wall pretty hard, pushed off, gathered itself and raced down the flooded corridor toward the loading-dock door where several timid souls were waiting, way down there out of hose range.

Tail down, front legs crossing the back legs and the water flew!

"Nop! That'll do!"

And the dog braked, slowed from dead run to trot to walk to stop. He turned his head and looked at the man. One ear was cocked and nervous.

"Nop, Nop. That'll do. Come here." Softly, between his teeth, Lewis Burkholder whistled the recall whistle.

And Nop came. Delicately placing each foot, like it was important how he set it down, Nop returned. As befitted a matter of importance, he came on very slowly and Lewis didn't try to hurry him.

When he came abreast of the gold-haired man, Nop fired off a single glance that pressed the man against the corridor wall.

Ten feet away, Nop stopped. One ear was broken, his hair had been jerked out, he was covered with excrement. He had a bad scar on his hind leg. Nop's eyes were full of question.

Lewis removed the fire helmet so Nop could see his face better. He gave the dog time before he snapped his fingers and said, "Come," and went back the way he'd come.

Without a single doubt, Nop followed Lewis, right at his heels.

The receptionist had fled.

Lewis Burkholder jammed the hose nozzle in between the broken doorframe and the wall, so the hose wouldn't start whipping around. Sodden letters and memoranda lay in puddles on the floor. When Lewis stepped into the outside air, his hands were trembling.

All the kids had run off. The fire truck was still roaring. The sun felt pretty good.

Nop just stood there, leaning against Lewis's leg.

Together, they waited for the police to come.

THIRTEEN

The Top Dogs

It was seven that evening when they turned Lewis Burkholder loose. For a while there it had looked like they weren't going to release him at all. The Kentucky sheriff had used terms like, "grand theft auto," and "assault." Not to be outdone, the county attorney added, "misappropriation of a public safety vehicle" and "breaking and entering."

Folks were pretty mad, none madder than the Craigsville Volunteer Fire Department. "What if there'd been a fire? What if some kid had been trapped in the flames?"

"I ain't making excuses," Lewis said. "I know I committed a crime."

Nop lay, quietly, at his feet right there in the sheriff's office in the County Courthouse.

The Kentucky sheriff phoned Sergeant Nelson. After he heard the Cincinnati part of the story, he phoned Sheriff Lohr to hear the Virginia part of it.

Lewis sat, hands in his lap, making polite response to all the questions they asked. He felt like all the sap had drained right out of him.

Sheriff Lohr had news of Grady and Lester Gumm. Seems that Lester missed a curve on Little Stony Mountain and hit a big spruce tree, wrecked the four-wheel drive and killed Grady outright. Sheriff Lohr got to Lester before Lester got straight and Lester answered all his questions. Lester confessed to crimes Lohr hadn't suspected were crimes. Lester said Doug Whitenaur had offered Grady three hundred dollars to steal Lewis's dog. Sheriff Lohr said (on the phone) that Lester felt awful bad about Grady's death and was trying to make a few things right again. Sheriff Lohr said he'd testify as a character witness for Lewis.

"What do you think about that, Chief?" The Kentucky sheriff had taken to calling Lewis by his official title. In his eyes, being a fire chief was Lewis's worst offense. If a couple joy-riding kids had snatched the truck, the sheriff wouldn't have minded near so much.

Lewis shrugged.

The county attorney looked at the big, quiet man and the dog lying beside him. He'd known farmers like Lewis all his life. "I'm setting your court date for July eighth, right here in this building at eight-thirty in the morning. Do I have to make you post bond?"

"I'll be here."

So Lewis got up and walked out into the evening. The grass was mighty green, greener than home, and a magnolia on the courthouse lawn was in bloom. Spooky white in the evening light, but sweet.

Mark's old VW was so dusty you had to guess at the original color. Still, it ran.

"You look hungry," Lewis said and Nop got in front.

A few miles down U.S. 150, Lewis spotted a Burger King with a Drive-Thru Window. He ordered two double cheeseburgers for himself and three hamburger patties, plain, hold everything, even the bun. "They're for my dog."

"That'll be six eighteen, sir."

Lewis broke Nop's burgers into small pieces because he didn't want Nop choking himself. Nop ate each piece and his eyes never left Lewis's face. He lapped water from a paper cup.

Lewis puttered north on I 75, doing about fifty, enjoying the faint twilight line above the green-black horizon.

Lewis felt the weight of Nop's head on his knee. When Lewis scratched behind Nop's ears, he touched scarred and broken tissue and wondered how many fights Nop had fought he'd never know about.

Nop climbed up on the seat and Lewis let him get away with it. As the VW puttered north, Nop scootched across the VW's emergency brake: his head—his chest, until Lewis had his dog entirely in his lap. When he looked down, he saw the steady glow of Nop's eyes.

Walnut Hall, where the Bluegrass Sheep Dog Trials are held, is one of the famous Kentucky horse farms. Years ago, a dispute between heirs divided the property. Half of it was sold to the state and now attracts thousands of tourists as the "Kentucky Horse Farm." Walnut Hall, still private, raises standardbred trotters and pacers.

There were lights in the stone gatekeeper's house but nobody came out to stop him. Lewis thought they probably let farm staff use the gatehouse. Probably they didn't even have a gatekeeper anymore.

The neat black single-lane asphalt road went on and on. To Lewis, whose farm lanes were all dirt, those asphalt lanes were the most impressive feature of Walnut Hall. The lane was bordered by gargantuan black walnuts. Grazing horses were protected from windfallen branches by neat enclosures around each tree.

White board fences. The moonlight lay on the bluegrass pasture, tidy as any putting green. No milkweed or Canada thistles anywhere. The farm office was locked up and quiet. During the day it was hectic with traders and breeders and oil sheiks and Texas men who loved fast horses.

A statue of the trotter Guy Axworthy dominated the horse cemetery. Guy Axworthy had been Walnut Hall's most famous sire.

Lewis wished Mark's radio worked. It must be after ten o'clock.

Signs pointed the way to the SHEEP DOG TRIALS down in the yearling pasture where they'd held these trials for the past twenty years.

The Bluegrass is the toughest and oldest stockdog trial in the country. Each year the farm buys eight hundred Texas sheep and brings them north, wild sheep who've never even seen a dog. After the trial, the sheep are sold. In '72 Lewis had taken a truckload home himself and they proved to be pretty good animals.

Handlers and their dogs flew in from Arizona and Texas and Washington state. Most years men came from Canada, but this year the Canadian National conflicted.

Big trees, open pasture. The handlers' camper park was

directly behind the trial ground and while the dogs ran, spectators could drag out lawn chairs and watch in real comfort. On hot days—and June could get hot in Lexington—any shade was welcome.

Lewis recognized many of the rigs from other trials. Some of the campers still had lights inside though most were dark. Somebody was walking dogs in the big pasture where the dogs had run today and would run again tomorrow. The dog walker wore a cowboy hat and walked stiffly and Lewis thought it might be Pope Robertson, who'd won here several years.

He switched off. The smell of hot oil. "Nop," he said, "you are awful darn heavy. Will you please climb off me?"

Nop bounded out and marked the VW's tire. He smelled grass, sheep, the starry night, dogs. His tail plumed.

Stink was chained to the back step of the Burkholder camper. Nop circled, sniffing, not quite daring to believe. He whined. He yipped. He yawned and pranced around. He pawed at her shoulder.

"Nop, is it thee? Oh, Nop." And she was whining too and smelling all his history.

Nop was too excited to say hello. He emitted tiny yaps.

In the square of the doorway, "Lewis? Oh, Lewis, you found Nop. Oh . . ." And Beverly started to cry.

She hugged Lewis and stared at Nop and cried harder when she saw how filthy he was and how thin. "Every rib shows," she said.

And Penny gave Lewis a careful hug, because she was pretty big now. "Oh, Daddy." She said she'd take Nop down to the cattle tank and clean him up. "You just sit and rest. Oh."

Beverly had gotten used to Penny in the modest camper, but Lewis and she excused each other around the little two-burner hot plate and the refrigerator until she said, "Lewis, you sit at the table and I'll serve you. I suppose it was Nop that got your good pants so dirty." With Lewis seated, things went smoother.

Beverly told Lewis that Mark had called. He'd had an uneventful trip home.

Lewis told Beverly what he'd heard about Grady Gumm's death.

Beverly said she was sorry and, coming from her, it was probably the truth. Beverly tried to be a good Christian.

Lewis warmed his hands with his cup of coffee and told about his search. He didn't describe Elite Kennels in detail because Beverly got real upset whenever animals suffered.

He took both her hands to tell about stealing the fire truck and breaking into Detweiler Labs. "I don't know what came over me, Beverly. I couldn't make them listen. It seemed . . ."

"You got Nop back, didn't you?" Her face was stern. Lewis had never known Beverly to break the law and he'd been worried what she might say, but she didn't think a thing of it. After all these years, Beverly could still surprise him. "Did Penny tell you? She made a real nice run with Stink this morning. Missed both drive panels but with these wild sheep they won't count that too much against her. Lewis, she may have qualified."

"Oh yeah?" Lewis laughed. "That's fine. There aren't many women who ever qualified here. Ada Karrasch was Reserve Champion a couple years back but Ada's exceptional. I'm real proud of Penny. How's she feeling?"

"Pretty good. She's uncomfortable, of course, carrying all that extra weight around, but she doesn't get the morning sickness anymore. Two weeks. She's a little impatient for the baby to come."

"They got a name picked out?"

"Well, they're partial to Lisa if it's a girl. If it's a boy, Mark will call him Scottie."

"What's wrong with 'Lewis' for a name?"

Beverly laughed like Lewis had been kidding though he'd been kidding only partly.

"That Whitenaur. He's here."

Lewis wasn't awfully surprised. "He qualify?"

"That little bitch of his, Bit O' Scot? Lewis, she's a beauty. They didn't announce qualifiers yet because they had eighty dogs to run and didn't get through all of them, but Bit O' Scot made the best run today. I don't know how such a nasty man can run such a fine dog."

"It happens that way sometimes."

By Bluegrass custom, the trial is open to anyone who will pay the thirty-dollar entry fee. On the first day and, sometimes, the morning of the second day, dogs are qualified. The top twenty dogs run in the finals.

Beverly stirred her coffee. "When I entered Nop and Stink, you said I should pull Nop, that it was a foolish waste of money."

Penny was just outside. "Don't you jump up on me, you wet thing. I don't care how happy you are."

303

"What are you telling me, Beverly?"

"There's eight dogs yet to qualify tomorrow morning. Nop is one of them."

Lewis shook his head. "He's not ready, Beverly, and neither am I. I don't remember when I've been so tired as I am. It's time for me to hit the hay."

But Lewis didn't get to sleep right away. Penny had to tell him about Stink's run. "Stink was so fine, Daddy. Her hips were hurting her real bad. Those are some *tough* sheep out there. She was worn out when she got them in the pen, but she put them in there."

And then, once they were in their beds, Nop set up a terrible howling outside, baying just like he was a wild dog and, of course, other dogs picked up on it, barking and carrying on, and Lewis figured they'd get no peace until he brought Nop right into the camper. Nop lay in the aisle all night, satisfied, so long as he could wake from time to time to touch Lewis's bare arm with the tip of his nose.

Sunday dawned bright and clear, and soon the air in the camper park smelled of bacon and coffee. Handlers exercised their dogs in the pastures. Most of the handlers knew each other. So, too, most of the dogs.

Before Lewis finished his breakfast, Ethel Harwood was banging on the camper door and, naturally, she wanted to know the whole story.

"What about Whitenaur?"

"With Grady dead, it'd be hard to prove anything against him. Of course, he likely doesn't know Grady's dead."

"He shouldn't be allowed to run dogs. There's rules in

the Sheep Dog Association. Lewis, you should get him banned."

"He's not his father's son."

She shook her head sadly.

"Thanks, Ethel. If it wasn't for you seein' Nop at that rodeo, I wouldn't have him today. You're a good friend."

Ethel blushed, lit a cigarette and smeared it with lipstick. Stubbed it out. She said this year's sheep were even worse than last year. She said (as she said every year) that the Bluegrass people should work their sheep a couple times before the show. "They're too wild and wooly," that's what she said.

And Lewis said (as he said every year), "It's just as tough for everybody."

They talked handlers and they talked dogs. Neither of them wanted to dwell on Lewis's long search. Running dogs and talking dogs—why else had they come to the Bluegrass?

After, Lewis wandered around the grounds greeting old friends. The stockdog world is small and many handlers knew Nop had been missing. They examined his scars and thin condition and sympathized. Lewis didn't talk about Doug Whitenaur. He didn't know quite what to say.

Workers setting up soft-drink stands and hotdog booths. One of the horse barns was filling with craftspeople, their trinkets and wares.

The barn behind the judge's stand was reserved for handlers and dogs. Some handlers kept their animals in these stalls until the very last minute so they wouldn't get overexcited by crowd noises and smells.

Nop trotted along at Lewis's heels, taking it all in.

Big Steve Brown, Walnut Hall's farm manager, shook Lewis's hand and said there'd been a couple real good runs yesterday, that Penny looked real good, real good, and they were going to start at eight on the dot so they could finish qualifications and get right on with the finals. "Good luck," he said.

The handlers who met behind the judge's stand were looking sharp: neatly blocked Stetsons, pearl-buttoned, wide-yoked western shirts, gabardine slacks. Most carried long Scottish shepherd's crooks. Some wore three-piece western suits and ties.

Doug Whitenaur looked terrible. His hands twitched, his eyes were muddy, he needed a shave. Perhaps his sport jacket was meant to be daring. It was merely shoddy. His hair was greased back, defying what had been a very good haircut. Doug Whitenaur didn't look like he belonged with honest men.

Lewis stared at him, angry and puzzled. But Whitenaur wouldn't meet Lewis's eyes.

One handler disputed a course rule with the judge. He argued that a sheep dog trial is meant to replicate real farmwork: gathering, fetching sheep, bringing them through the gates and, finally, penning them in the farmyard. To allow a handler to skip a gate and proceed directly to the pen would be unrealistic work.

The judge admitted the point but wouldn't change the rule. They'd always allowed handlers to proceed directly to the pen when time was short.

Whitenaur rubbed his raspy chin. He didn't speak loud.

"Yesterday was qualification day," he said. "All the dogs were supposed to be here. Right here." (He jabbed a finger at the earth.) "It isn't right for a dog to show up this morning and get the same chance to run as the dogs who showed up on time."

Mildly, the judge noted, "I didn't see you here yesterday, Lewis."

In his mind, Lewis listed a few of Whitenaur's sins. What effrontery! "I'm in the program, fourth from last. The final eight dogs are going to qualify today."

"Yes," the judge said. "But they were *supposed* to qualify yesterday. All the other dogs were here."

Lewis hadn't intended to run. He hadn't intended *not* to run, but he hadn't intended *to* run, either. Lewis tightened. The last time he lost his temper he nearly landed in jail. It would do him no harm remembering that. "My Nop dog was stolen from me," Lewis said, through his teeth, "and I recovered him yesterday. It's been a good many months since he saw a sheep and months since I worked any kind of dog, but we're here to win this trial."

The judge looked to the handlers.

"Let Lewis run," one grizzled handler growled.

"We're here to run dogs, not keep 'em from running."

"It's an open trial. Everybody who entered can run."

The judge bit at his upper lip. "Since Lewis's name hasn't been called, I don't see what harm it'd do."

"I just hope Lewis does as poor a job against those contrary sheep as I did," one Texas handler grumbled, which broke the tension and everybody laughed. Next time Lewis looked, Whitenaur was gone.

The first handler walked out with his dog to the handler's circle. Acres of clipped green pasture rising away from his feet. The dog sees the sheep and trembles. The course is fenced into a long diamond shape and three hundred yards away, at the far tip of the diamond, three sheep are released. The dog streaks out on his outrun, wide and true. When he comes around for the lift, he comes in too close.

The sheep bolt like rabbits, the dog in hot pursuit, and getting these sheep through those panels is like threading an embroidery needle at 70 mph. These sheep have never been a flock before so they break apart: a whiteface to the right, both blackfaces drifting downhill toward the drive panel.

A chill falls over the watching handlers.

"Last time those sheep saw a dog, it was a coyote eating their mama."

"Out west they got a way of handling sheep that like to break off like that. A rifle."

"I don't mind that those sheep don't know each other, but those sheep aren't even *speaking* to each other."

Three terrified range ewes, careening every which way. They are healthy yearlings, at the peak of their strength and, by God, they can outrun a dog in a dash.

At the pen one ewe crashes right over the dog. The dog doesn't bite.

The morning wore on, short-tempered and fleet. Even working fifty yards off the sheep, the dogs could scarcely control them. After a run, it took three or four men, dogs and sometimes a station wagon to clear the sheep off the course. Sixty yards behind the pen, spectators could hear the dogs panting. No dog had managed to pen those wild sheep this morning.

When his turn came, and he walked into the handler's circle, Nop looked poor. His skin was tight over his ribs and the bumps on his spine showed, every one. His coat was tattered, lusterless and rough.

He stood well on his feet. Yesterday he'd found Lewis and this morning he and Lewis had woolies to work. What more could any dog want?

His tail curled down against his buttocks. He locked on his sheep like guidance radar.

"Way to me, Nop!"

Ahhh. Nop whipped out in a pear-shaped outrun, going deeper, deeper: woolies, far away and high.

Two whitefaces, one black. They eyed the crowd near the pen and were afraid. None of the three had flocked before and none trusted the other. Very spooky.

Nop's heart hammered as he slipped around much deeper than his usual balance point because he sensed their nervousness, small movements, fear.

When he was directly behind, Lewis whistled him to a stop. Briefly, Nop was puzzled. He'd forgotten how to work with a man. When he'd worked the rodeo calves, he'd gone it alone.

A stylized step forward. Another. Freeze.

The sheep drift away downhill.

In the judge's booth, one judge murmured, "Full points for the lift. My God, that dog's got power!"

Another judge was diagramming Nop's fetch on a course map. "Remember Pope Robertson's Lash I? He had power like that."

Stiff-legged as maiden aunts, the sheep slipped down the hill with the dog coming steadily behind them. When they balked at the fetch panel, Nop froze. When they wished to dodge around the panel, he simply swayed his body without moving his feet and that delicate adjustment was enough to push his woolies through the opening.

Below, some handlers were holding their breath.

Nop's body was quivering. His breath was rapid. His legs felt very heavy, surprisingly heavy. He loved Lewis, but more, Nop loved his work.

The handler's circle was short clipped grass. Wild sheep have been known to balk at a chalk line drawn on the ground and every step these animals took brought them closer to the crowd they feared.

Lewis backed to the farthest edge of the circle, giving them room. "Steady, steady, Nop. Nop, Nop, ah Nop!"

The lead sheep stepped onto the grass and her mates followed, shoulder to shoulder. Nop had created a flock from three strangers and they worked now with one mind. Nop blinked and cleared his eyesight. He backed off and came around wide to urge them toward the first drive panel, only eighty yards uphill.

They didn't want to go through and maybe Nop had misjudged because one woolie broke bad and Nop had to pour on the steam to head her. He backed off to get to his balance point and stumbled. Cleared his vision again.

On the crossdrive he was working closer, too close really, but when the woolies got any distance away, they were just blurs. Lewis's whistles were urgent. All three sheep broke around the crossdrive panel. No points.

Nop raced full-tilt to head them before they got off course and managed to get out front, but his legs didn't do what they were supposed to do and he hit the dirt, rolled and twisted upright again, seeking control.

His legs went out from under him. Woolies escape. Shameful. No balance. No control. Lewis at the pen. Can't try. Tired.

And Lewis Burkholder screamed, *"No!"* He dropped his crook and ran onto the course, disqualifying himself and Nop.

Nop's breath was rattling gasps. He lay on his side and didn't see Lewis when he picked him up. With Nop cradled in his arms, Lewis ran for the nearest watering tank, feeling the sick feeling he was too late and wouldn't reach it in time.

Nop had gone into toxic shock. Unable to remove his own body wastes fast enough, he was poisoned.

One hand under his chin so he wouldn't drown, Lewis lowered the passive Nop into the cool water. His breathing chattered and choked. His eyes saw nothing on this earth.

Woolies. He did not work the woolies . . .

Lewis fluffed the cool water under Nop's fur, trying to lower his body temperature while his heart was still beating.

A vet knelt beside Lewis. "We could try decamethasone."

"Do it. I'm afraid he's dying."

This vet raised and trialed Border Collies. Lewis had seen him at many trials but never had really gotten to know him. "Oh God," Lewis said. The vet prepared his

311

syringe and gave the shot. Lewis said, "Crazy to run him. Crazy thing. Nop's starved for God's sake. No condition to run a trial on wild sheep. Nobody in his right mind . . . I wanted him to win. I had everything, absolutely everything, and I wanted him to win."

Though some handlers had joined Lewis at the cattle tank, others were clearing Nop's sheep off the course.

Lewis couldn't look at Nop but he felt his breathing under his hands. Automatically, Lewis sloshed water on his belly and testicles and under his forelegs, too. Nop's fur lifted and stirred in the water.

Nop stuck out his tongue and lapped. He lapped again, blinked, lapped, breathed, lapped.

The vet took Nop's temperature. "Lewis, I think he'll be all right. Generally, if you get a dog's temperature lowered, he'll come back. Don't let him get chilled, now."

"Yeah. Uh-huh. Thanks. Thank you."

Lewis kept Nop in that stock tank for fifteen minutes, cooling him, and when Beverly offered to help, he said, "No, no, I'll do it. Beverly, he would have died for me. He would have kept trying to bring those sheep until he died."

"Yes. It's awful, isn't it?"

The final qualifier made his run. The judges huddled over the results, using notes and maps to select the twenty finalists.

Lewis carried Nop back to his camper and laid him on his own jacket underneath the little dinette table. "I'm sorry, pal," he said. "I should have known better. It was that Whitenaur. If he'd kept quiet, I wouldn't have done a thing, but the minute he said I *shouldn't* run you, well, naturally, I thought I *should*. The man—he's not much—but he's got some awful power over me. I see him and I get hot and my brain goes haywire. I hate that man for what he brings out in me."

Nop thumped his tail.

"Never again, Nop. That's my promise. I'll never use you like that again."

Lewis closed the door on his exhausted dog. Right now Nop needed quiet more than love.

"Lewis! Penny qualified Stink!"

Lewis couldn't remember his daughter looking more beautiful. The color was high in her cheeks and she looked to him like his little darling girl. "Eighteenth, Daddy. Stink qualified. We'll run in the finals. We're eighteenth."

Lewis grinned like a fool.

"Lewis, don't you think you should change your pants? You're soaking."

"I don't want to disturb Nop. Let him rest."

Penny's face fell. "Nop? I was so excited I didn't . . ."

"Nop'll be fine."

"Oh, Daddy."

"It looks like you and Stink are gonna have to run for all of us."

That wasn't quite the right thing to say. The fear came into Penny's eyes, like a tremor. "Daddy, all those men. They're the best, Daddy. What can I do now?"

"You keep on doin' what you've been doin'. You're doin' something right."

Penny bit her lip. She thought she'd take Stink down

behind the craft barn. She wanted to be alone with her dog.

Her dog. Well, Lewis thought, she's earned it.

That afternoon, they ran twenty of the most brilliant dogs in America. Most of them were imported but a handful had been bred and trained in the States. Out in the big pasture, against those wild sheep, nothing mattered but how they worked.

The crowd got bigger and a couple of TV crews made an appearance. Next door, at the Kentucky Horse Farm, they were holding the National Saluki Show and the Arabian Horse Show was there too. Some of the people who'd come for the handsome horses and beautiful white dogs drifted over to Walnut Hall to watch the Sheep Dog Trials.

Wild sheep were brought to the release pen in bunches of five. One in each five was ribboned.

The twenty finalists had more time and an additional task. They had a full fifteen minutes but had to shed the ribboned sheep after the pen. No matter how quickly a handler finished the rest of the course, he'd have just three minutes for the shed.

The sun was hot and the handlers sweated and the dogs' tongues hung out a yard, but the sheep felt the heat too and slowed and most of the finalists penned.

Lewis saw some good runs that day: Ralph Pulfer, Bruce Fogt and Lewis Pence were very strong. When Bruce Fogt finished his shed at 14:59, he whooped and tossed his Stetson in the air.

A well-dressed young couple brought their saluki to the

trial and the dog started barking. Stockdogs rarely bark and never near stock and an official asked the young couple to take their dog somewhere else if they couldn't keep him quiet.

Near Lewis, a couple of Texans had a cooler full of beer in their truck.

Lewis said he'd take a beer, thanks.

Beverly said, "Oh, I wouldn't dare." She laughed. "Waistline," she explained.

Lewis and Beverly side by side. Twenty years of a lucky marriage.

Until Bit O' Scot, Bruce Fogt held high score with his bitch, Hope. Bit O' Scot was top qualifier yesterday, and today she was out to prove it had been no accident. Some were already calling Bit "the best little bitch this side of the water."

Perfect outrun, superb drive and crossdrive. She slammed her ewes into the pen about as sentimental as a jailer at Sing-Sing.

The crowd isn't supposed to make a sound until the run is concluded, but Bit got applause and yells for her penning.

Bit now had three full minutes for her shed. The sheep returned to the handler's circle and, as soon as the last sheep stepped on the short grass, the clock would start.

Doug Whitenaur on one side of the circle and Bit on the other, trying to shed that one ribboned sheep.

Whitenaur went left, went right, encouraging his little dog with whistles and cries. Constant attention. The ribboned sheep, a whiteface, hid in the center of the flock, presenting no opening for the dog to dart through.

In the three long minutes they worked, worked and failed, Lewis understood that some part of Doug Whitenaur was a fine stockdog handler, that Whitenaur *was* his father's son. Though he missed the shed, he had seventy-eight points and a strong round of applause. Bit was top dog.

Through the afternoon no dog equaled her. One after another they made their runs but none showed the style or control of Doug Whitenaur's expensive imported bitch. Some good handlers failed to pen. Many good handlers failed to shed.

The Texans worked deeper into their cooler and when their language started to get a little rough, they moved to the far side of their truck where they wouldn't offend Beverly.

When Lewis looked in on Nop, he was sleeping normally.

The announcer said, "In the Handler's Circle: Lewis Pence with Diamond. Diamond is out of Lewis Pulfer's Dell and litter mate to Bruce Fogt's Hope. Lewis has won this Bluegrass twice before, making him one of a handful of men to do so. On deck, the last finalist, Penny Hilyer with her dog, uh, Stink."

Some laughed at Stink's name.

Lewis didn't watch Lewis Pence's run because he was with the Texans, bumming another beer. He was afraid he wouldn't be able to stand the tension. He hoped Penny did okay. The top fifteen dogs got trophies or ribbons and Lewis hoped Penny got something.

When he returned, Beverly said, "Give me a sip. There

goes Penny now. Lewis, she's huge. Oh, my goodness. Lewis . . ."

Long shadows stole across the top of the meadow where Penny's sheep waited. Nobody was paying much attention. Whitenaur had won it. Handlers were talking about other trials, past trials, the trials down the road. The Midwest Classic Sheep Dog Trial was July 11 in Illinois and the Texas Futurity was the end of the month. Those who had miles to go before dark had already pulled out and there were others getting ready to leave. Gaps appeared in the camper parking.

Penny Hilyer wore green stretch maternity pants and a short flowered overblouse. Her Stetson was the same creamy Banker's Stetson Harry Truman had favored. The sun glinted on her polished shepherd's crook (when Lewis gave it to her, she'd been just fourteen) as she raised it in the air and her sheep were released.

When Stink started her outrun, Lewis winced. Stink ran with her right hindquarter lower than the other and a funny hitch in her step. She rolled from side to side like a sailor. She was favoring her pain.

But, by God, she got out there. Lewis got to his feet.

Penny whistled and Stink swerved to pick up her drifting sheep. The sheep got down into a low place on the top of the meadow and vanished, but Stink slipped down into that low spot like a spy and the next thing anyone saw of those sheep was five heads, coming on a straight shot to the fetch panel. The sheep didn't hesitate at the fetch panel either. They paused, briefly, before stepping into the handler's circle, and the sunlight glinted in the

Stink Dog's eyes as she dogged them through the drive panel and onto line for the crossdrive.

Penny's whistle chirping. Each time Stink's hip lifted, the flesh just seemed to slide off her back onto her downhill hip but she jerked across the grass after those sheep, in tune: concentrated.

One of the Texans climbed up onto the hood of the pickup. Another closed the beer cooler and stood on that. Nobody was talking as Stink forced those ewes through the crossdrive panel, dead center, and rolled around to start them toward Penny. Penny didn't watch her dog working behind her—she made her heavy way to the pen.

"Dog moves like a busted mower in tall grass," somebody said.

Another man cursed under his breath. Beauty strikes some men that way.

The sheep hated the pen. It looked like a trap—*was* a trap—the gate yawning open to receive them. They rolled around the mouth of the pen like an eddy.

Penny kept her crook hooked over her arm. Her voice was calm—she might have done this every single day in her life. "Get up, Stink. Stand. Way to me, back! Get back! Way. Walk up, walk up."

Still whirling, the sheep spun into the pen and Penny trudged the gate shut on them.

"Twelve thirty-eight. Penny Hilyer penned in twelve thirty-eight. She'll have two minutes, twenty-two seconds for the shed."

Lewis hadn't thought it had been twelve minutes. Seemed like forever to him. He took a breath. Beverly hugged his arm. "Wasn't she pretty, Lewis? Wasn't Penny pretty?"

The Texan leaned down from his truck cab. "Say, Lewis. How come you're not workin' that dog? You get tired of winning?"

Lewis said, "That Stink Dog saved my life."

"That's a good reason," the Texan lied.

Penny made her way to the far side of the shedding circle. For the first time, she unhooked her crook from her arm. "Stink. Bring 'em."

Though the Stink's hindquarters jigged like a mistimed engine, the sheep stalked into the circle, stiff-legged and bunched up.

Penny was half in sunlight, half in shade. She tilted backward to balance her swollen belly. The tip of her crook just touched the ground, way out in front, like some electric current was flowing from the earth through the crook into her body.

Five sheep.

Bitch on their left, woman on their right.

"Stink, come through!"

And she raised her crook to indicate the spot and the sheep separated at the crook, no more than six inches for a gap, but Stink hit that gap, filled it, whirled in her own body width, and the solo ribboned sheep and Stink were face to face. The other four sheep bolted behind Stink, unrequired.

The ribboned sheep bleated its terror. It had been singled out and every sheep gene was sounding the alarm.

The sheep hoofed the ground. Blustered.

Stink lifted her right paw, almost like a pointer.

The sheep lowered her head to force her way past.

Stink slunk low in the sheep's vision and glared.

The sheep took a hesitant step backward. Another.

"That's a shed, Penny," the judge said.

And Penny lowered her crook and pushed the point against the earth and rested on it. Her knees were shaking.

Lewis got to Penny's arm before anyone else did.

Somebody wanted to get her a lawn chair. Someone else offered lemonade.

Stink's hindquarters shook and she sank down. One of the Texans picked Stink up in his arms. "Lewis, I'll take this pretty girl to your camper. This girl dog don't ever have to walk so long as I'm around."

And that's how Penny Hilyer with her Stink Dog won the twenty-fifth annual Bluegrass Open Sheep Dog Trials. That's how Penny came to win the big sterling-silver tray and the check for five hundred dollars.

The Texan carried Stink gently and laid her gently down beside Nop. Nop licked her silky cheeks.

"Oh, I have worked woolies. I have worked them. Oh, I am a good dog."

"Thou art a good dog," Nop agreed.

Doug Whitenaur got the silver julep goblet for top qual- ifier and a two-hundred-fifty-dollar check for second place. Lewis caught up with him at his car.

Whitenaur dropped his car key in his pocket and put his silver trophy on the roof of his De Lorean. He faced Lewis, sullen, defiant.

"I wanted to congratulate you," Lewis said. "That was

a real fine run you made. If you'd had a chance, you might have made a real good dog handler—right up there with Ralph Pulfer or Jack Knox—up there with the best."

Furious spittle flew from Whitenaur's distorted lips. "You know who you're talking to? You know who?"

Very slowly, Lewis nodded. "I believe I do. Doug Whitenaur, you're not to ever run stockdogs again."

The two men locked eyes.

Lewis said, "You stole a good dog and tried to have him killed. You set thugs on me and my son-in-law. You hurt me and mine. I don't care if you run retrievers or bird dogs or put show dogs on the bench. No business of mine. But today was the last day you'll run a stockdog. Quit today and you quit a hero. Nobody knows what you done. Tyler Whitenaur, your daddy, was an upright man."

Whitenaur gnawed on his knuckle. "I don't care," he said. "I don't care." He was gnawing fierce enough to draw blood.

Lewis unlatched the door on Whitenaur's dog trailer and Bit came out right away. Her worried eyes questioned Lewis and Whitenaur, but she made no protest when Lewis fastened his lead to her collar.

"You quit and the police won't put you in jail for stealing Nop and the Sheep Dog Association will remember you as a fine man who was once Reserve Champion at the Bluegrass. I know plenty handlers who'd be pleased with that honor. I don't think you should keep a stockdog anymore." Lewis extracted his tattered wallet. "Since you won't be running in trials, you won't need a dog. This little bitch did real good for you and I expect she'll do good for me."

The bills Lewis handed him were mostly tens and twenties. "I paid . . . I paid ten thousand. . . ."

"I heard something about that." Lewis cocked his head. "But somebody else told me you thought three hundred dollars was an honest price for a good stockdog like my Nop. Three hundred dollars doesn't seem like very much to me, but it is your price."

Whitenaur's face was at war with itself. His mouth worked against squinched-up cheeks and his eyes wandered relentlessly. Lewis's money was clenched in his hand.

Since Lewis had done what he'd meant, he returned to his camper. Whitenaur did nothing to stop him and Bit walked quietly at his heels.

Because Penny was resting, Lewis and Beverly went up to the Walnut Hall office where they were serving beef stew, beer and ice tea to the handlers. Departing campers honked or waved. Whitenaur sped through without looking left or right.

Though he didn't have much appetite, Lewis took a little stew on a paper plate. He thanked Steve Brown for the good trial. He accepted some congratulations for Penny.

"That's two in a row for that dog, Lewis. How come you gave her up?"

Lewis just smiled.

A couple handlers were talking about Nop's outrun and lift.

"He's got the power," Lewis said. "Maybe I'll make a trial dog out of him yet."

Ethel Harwood said sure she'd keep quiet about Whitenaur. Was Lewis certain that's what he wanted?

Sure he was.

They got back to the farm before first light, next morning. Mark came out to kiss his wife's face and help her into her own bed. Lewis fed the stock.

Two weeks and four days later, Mrs. Mark Hilyer had a baby. Six pounds, five ounces. They named her Lisa.

Penny used her Bluegrass money for a downpayment on a used Ten-Wide and they set it down by the river, not so very far from where the old tenant house had been— but that wasn't until September.

July 8, Lewis drove back to Kentucky for his court date. Detweiler said they wouldn't press charges if he paid damages and didn't make any statement to the press. They were afraid (Detweiler said) that a lot of kooks would pester them looking for stray dogs.

The bill was eight hundred thirty dollars which Lewis thought excessive but paid. The fine for "misappropriation of a public safety vehicle" was two hundred dollars. The Craigsville Fire Department cooled off when they learned that Lewis had resigned as chief of the White Post Department. Mike Pearson, the assistant chief, moved up to take Lewis's place.

Court costs were seventy-five dollars.

The total came to eleven hundred and five dollars plus the cost of gas getting there. It could have been worse.

Once his ribs healed, Mark started doing custom livestock hauling. Lewis missed him on the farm, but the kids needed cash for payments on their mobile home.

Mrs. Hilyer ("Call me Bebe!") arrived for a week-long visit when baby Lisa was a month old. Though she and Beverly made an odd pair—Bebe's energy, Beverly's quietness—the two women got along fine. Mrs. Hilyer brought a trunkful of lotions and bath oils for the baby.

Gradually, Lewis worked Nop back into farm routines. Nop was strong on the cows: unwilling to concede an inch. Lewis worried he might be too rough on sheep, but he did fine, working them far, far back, letting distance diminish his power. Nop got uneasy whenever strangers came to the farm, and, if they got too near without a proper introduction, he'd show teeth. Nobody could work him except Lewis.

Since Penny was busy with her newborn, Lewis trialed Stink at some of the small Virginia trials. Bit was near her time so Lewis didn't work her. He didn't want to stress her or her unborn pups. Until those pups arrived, Stink ruled the dogs. Stink took her choice of the bones and reserved the warmest spot under the stove. The first morning Bit brought her pups out of the whelping box, Stink came trotting right up. Bit flew at her, seized her ruff and put her on the floor. Nop tucked his tail between his legs and made himself scarce while Stink made correct formal apologies to Bit. Lewis couldn't prove it, of course, but he thought he knew the pups' sire. Two pups had brown patches behind their ears.

Though it was a dry year, the drought the old-timers had predicted never materialized. Corn prices stayed low but the yields were good. Carl Obenschain had a small heart attack and went into the hospital. When he came out, he took a fresh interest in his granddaughter and great-granddaughter. To everybody's surprise, he paid for the trailer's septic field and electric hookup out of his own pocket.

The Hilyers wanted to get moved in by Thanksgiving. Penny wanted the Stink Dog to move in with them.

Nop won the Illinois Open and the Midwest Stockdog Association Trial.

The October issue of *The Southern Stockdog Journal* had a photo of Nop right on the cover.

Lewis heard Doug Whitenaur had got into some trouble. Apparently, a couple of his pals got arrested for loan sharking and Whitenaur had some of his money in the deal. His pals were sent away but Whitenaur got off light. Lewis never heard all the details. He thought Whitenaur was probably on the downhill slide.

When Lewis drove down to the East Tennessee Open, he brought the most promising pup as a gift for Ethel Harwood. Nop won that two-day trial handily. When breeders asked Lewis Nop's stud fee, Lewis said he hadn't made up his mind yet.

On the long ride home, Nop rode right up on the seat with his head in Lewis's lap. These days, they often rode that way when they were alone.

A Note to the Reader

If this has persuaded you to buy a Border Collie for a pet, I'd like to offer a caution. Border Collies are very bright, quick and more than a little weird. They are not suitable for most city apartments. Their working instincts are strong and their self-esteem comes from working well. A bored, mishandled Border Collie can get into awful trouble.

Acknowledgments

No real book is written without the courtesy, mid-wifery and simple forebearance of others. My thanks to those actual Border Collie people who let me mention them and their dogs here. No trial—not even a fictional one—would be complete without them.

Arthur Allen
John Bauserman
Steve Brown
Tom Conn
Bill Crowe
Bill Dillard
Bruce Fogt
Jock Gilchrist
Ada Karrasch
Richard Karrasch
Jack Knox
Lewis Pence
Lewis Pulfer
Ralph Pulfer
Pope Robertson

Mrs. Bryan Conrad, fine handler, incomparable organizer and great friend of the working dog.

Jack Knox, trainer and handler without peer. A kind, patient man, Jack taught me all I know about training stockdogs. Jack taught me how to *see* them.

Mrs. Mary Warner of Action-81 (Rte. 2, Box 151, Berryville, VA 22611). For years, Mrs. Warner's heart and help have gone out to those whose pets have been stolen.

The National Endowment for the Arts

Knox Burger

James O'Shea Wade

Jake Hagwood for letting me tell the story of him and his Stink Dog.

Grateful acknowledgment is made to:

—John Holmes, quoted from his book *The Farmer's Dog,* 8th ed., London, Popular Dogs, 1978.

—Tony Iley who quotes David McTeir in Iley's *Sheepdogs at Work,* 2nd ed., Clapham, North Yorkshire, Dalesman Publishing Co., 1979.

—Anne Marie Rousseau, whose *Shopping Bag Ladies,* New York, Pilgrim Press, 1981, first showed me the plight of America's homeless women.

Some descriptions of the Kentucky Bluegrass Open Sheep Dog Trials first appeared in my article "An Honest Dog," anthologized in *The Dog Book,* Jerrold Mundis, ed., New York, Arbor House, 1983.

And thanks to Pip and Silk: honest dogs.

F
McCaig

McCaig, Donald

Nop's Trials

DATE DUE
